TEN DEAD COMEDIANS

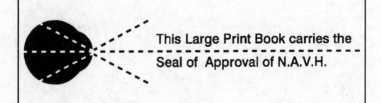

This Large Print Book carries the
Seal of Approval of N.A.V.H.

TEN DEAD COMEDIANS

FRED VAN LENTE

THORNDIKE PRESS
A part of Gale, a Cengage Company

Farmington Hills, Mich • San Francisco • New York • Waterville, Maine
Meriden, Conn • Mason, Ohio • Chicago

Copyright © 2017 by Fred Van Lente.
Thorndike Press, a part of Gale, a Cengage Company.

ALL RIGHTS RESERVED
This is a work of fiction. All names, places, and characters are products of the author's imagination or are used fictitiously. Any resemblance to real people, places, or events is entirely coincidental.
Thorndike Press® Large Print Mystery.
The text of this Large Print edition is unabridged.
Other aspects of the book may vary from the original edition.
Set in 16 pt. Plantin.

**LIBRARY OF CONGRESS CIP DATA ON FILE.
CATALOGUING IN PUBLICATION FOR THIS BOOK
IS AVAILABLE FROM THE LIBRARY OF CONGRESS**

978-1-4328-4324-3 (hardcover)
ISBN-10: 1-4328-4324-9 (hardcover)

Published in 2017 by arrangement with Quirk Productions, Inc.

Printed in the United States of America
1 2 3 4 5 6 7 21 20 19 18 17

For Mom

CHAPTER ONE

I

A bleep, a boop, a shudder, a swoosh, and there it was, on each of their phones:

> Hey there Funny Person.

Steve Gordon didn't see it at first.
He had a good excuse, though.
He was dying.
Steve had died before, of course. He knew how. At the Laugh Shack in Portland, Maine, in front of that bachelorette party. At that open mic in Des Moines, when he was first starting out. At his *SNL* audition, after his career was basically already over.
Dying on stage, in the middle of a set, was something every stand-up experienced. It was as inevitable and unavoidable as bad weather. The pros distinguished themselves

from the wannabes by not buckling under the weight of the dead room, of the surly crowd, of their own (hopefully temporary) suckitude.

But tonight felt different.

Tonight Steve felt like he was running out of lives.

"Hey, thanks, everybody, for that great welcome. Are you ready to be the best Finance Department we can be?"

Bifocals, bad ties, and pantsuits peered at him from the audience of the Chicago Improv Underground. The theater used to be a strip club and still retained the vague air of being somewhat ashamed of itself, with its low ceiling and bad lighting and support beams blocking sight lines from a third of the seats. Like every other performer, Steve had to memorize the location of the ancient lump of blue putty covering the hole in the floor where the stripper pole had been sawed off to avoid tripping or stubbing his toe on it.

The tumbledown surroundings were part of the act — they helped draw herds of accountants from the Whatever Co. out of the glass tomb of their conference room, down the concrete staircase beneath the Aldi supermarket, for this quarter's team-building seminar.

This ritualized descent into the underworld was all part of the initiation process. The staircase was flanked by black-and-white photos of the famous before they were famous, fresh-faced and poor, honing their skills on the Underground stage before their careers began to flourish on *Saturday Night Live, Mad TV,* and *The Daily Show.* By the time the audience arrived in the black box theater and took their broken-down seats, they understood they were ensconced in the loam of celebrity: the Improv Underground was the rich, dark soil from which impossible dreams were raised.

Or, in Steve's case, the pure earth to which he had returned.

In the stairwell's Before pictures, the audience had seen him twenty years younger. Now, as Steve faced them, one eye on the floor to avoid the ex-stripper-pole bump, they were looking at the After.

"All right, folks. For our first team-building exercise, I'm going to hunt you for sport, so if you could all line up against the far wall and get your panda costumes . . . What? No? C'mon, being hunted builds character! Man *is* the most dangerous game.

"No, you can tell I'm joshing. Tonight we're gonna have fun improvising sketches, just like we used to do on *What Just Hap-*

pened? Teddy, could you come up here on stage? Teddy is the manager of Improv Underground. He's a professional funnyman like me, which means he's also an amateur degenerate.

"So we'll make up a comedy scene right here in front of you. Now somebody give me a place. Any place. Doesn't matter where. No wrong answers here. The one word you can't use in improv is 'no.' "

"Auschwitz!" blurted out a middle-aged CPA in the back row.

Steve blinked.

"Oooo . . . okay? Auschwitz. Sure! Now can somebody give me a profession?"

"Rodeo clown!" yelled the Executive Senior Vice President of Something in the front.

Steve swallowed.

"No," he said.

"You said that was the one thing you couldn't say!" the ESVPoS exclaimed with a near-audible *harumph.*

"No, I said that was the one thing *you* couldn't say," Steve said. And looking at Teddy's face when he said it, and the face of the executive's assistant sitting next to him when he said it, he knew instantly he *shouldn't* have said it, because this guy hadn't been told no by anybody still with a job since 1998.

At that moment Steve thought maybe he really was dying. The spark that had animated his existence since he was a kid was sputtering out, that desire to make people laugh, to book that next gig, to not punch an audience member in the face. What was it all for, the bad food and canceled flights? He could go back to law school like his mother always wanted. At his age, it would be a sitcom waiting to happen. Or he could flip burgers.

Flipping burgers was sounding better and better by the second.

His phone vibrated again. Steve ignored Teddy's look, a look that said "Oh no you will not check your damn phone while you're in the middle of a gig, you pitiful sketch-show has-been" and turned his back on the audience.

"Just a second," Steve said. "I'll be right back."

He pulled out the phone out and read:

II

You don't know who I am, but you MIGHT know who I work for.

"Do you need to take that?" the middle-aged reporter from the *Christian Science Monitor* asked Zoe Schwartz when her phone made another sad trombone *wah-wah* sound.

"Nah," Zoe said, ignoring the notification. "What was the question again?"

The reporter checked her pad and said:

"Will you ever stop making jokes about your vagina?"

Without missing a beat, Zoe said, "Why would I want to stop making jokes about my vagina? It's literally my funniest body part." She stood and reached down to hike up her skirt. "You wanna see?"

"No, uh, that's all right —"

"No, seriously, it's a scream." She pulled the hem almost but not quite to her panty line. "You want to get your camera ready? I'm a blonde, and let me tell you, the curtains *do* match the drapes."

"No! Thank you, Zoe! I think I've got all we need!"

The reporter leapt up and fled from the

ballroom press junket in the Brooklyn Bridge Marriott. Zoe had spent close to six hours sitting in a canvas director's chair in front of a large cardboard standee of herself as a parade of reporters, bloggers, and TV crews filed in to ask the same five questions about her upcoming Netflix special over and over again while a bored publicist giggled at her phone in the corner. Zoe was cranky and bored. Judging from the chipper beats of '80s pop throbbing from the wall behind her, it seemed pretty obvious that everyone at the wedding reception in the ballroom next door was having a way better time than she was.

Her next victims were a camera crew from Spectrum News NY1. Zoe's bedraggled, salt-and-pepper terrier mix, who had laid dutifully at her feet throughout the whole junket, barked protectively at the sound guy as he clipped a lavalier mic to the shoulder strap of her dress.

"Quiet, Asshole," she said to the tiny mutt. She smiled at NY1's painfully handsome entertainment reporter, what's-his-name, Square-Jaw. "Not you. Him."

"I know, I watched the early screener of your special. He used to be named Bandit . . ."

". . . then I got to know him better, yeah."

"Are we ready? Great. Zoe, can you start? Even greater. So, we're here with funny lady Zoe Schwartz. Zoe, it's great to see you. Your second Netflix special is called *Laughs Like a Girl.* Do you have a theory as to why some people don't think girls are funny?"

Zoe struggled to maintain her smile. By her count this was the seventh time she had been asked that question in one day. Often while riding the Carousel of Interviews she was tempted to give the exact same answers to the same questions to see if anyone would notice, but professional pride kept her in check. A lot of people had sunk money and work into her Netflix special, and she was terrified of letting them down. This mixture of duty and fear cleaved through her exhaustion and hunger and cleared the way for an original response to the what's-your-theory-girls-no-funny question:

"Is stupidity a theory? Because usually it's the right one."

"Do you want to hear my theory?" Before she had a chance to respond, Square-Jaw said, "You know how so many of the metaphors of comedy are about violence? If you do really well in a set, you *killed.* You *slaughtered* the audience. If you do really badly on stage, you *bombed.* So much of it is wrapped up in this macho B.S. I can see

14

how women would feel shut out."

"I don't know, it's been my experience that a pretty girl cracking dirty jokes is a turn-on for most guys."

"It seems to work for you."

"You think I'm pretty? Aww."

Apparently, Square-Jaw had predetermined his hard-hitting line of questioning, and now he refused to deviate from the script: "But you've never felt excluded around male comedians, backstage or anywhere else?"

Zoe barely repressed a sigh. Did Chris Rock or Louis C.K. or, God help us, TJ Martinez ever have to answer questions like, What is it like to be a Boy Comedian? Why are there no Men-in-Stand-Up roundtable interviews and think pieces like "Penises: What's Their Deal, Really?"

She thought of bringing up one particular incident, in one network dressing room not so long ago, but she also knew that if she did, it would become all this interview was about, all the next three hundred interviews of her life would be about.

Her stomach growled loudly in the silence. Asshole looked up, startled, to see if there was another dog around. Zoe hadn't eaten since the early morning, when she grabbed a chocolate croissant from the continental breakfast as she ran out of the hotel lobby.

The stuttering beats of the A-ha classic "Take On Me" pulsated from the adjacent wall, reminding her that there was still joy to be found in this world.

Her phone made the *wah-wah* noise, indicating another text had arrived, and the little mutt jumped up to all fours and started barking. Zoe rolled her eyes apologetically. "Uh-oh, I'm afraid *someone* needs to do his dirty doggie business."

Square-Jaw furrowed his neatly plucked brow. "Oh — I mean, we're almost done. Maybe we could ask the publicist —"

"This will only take a second, I'm sorry. I can't let Asshole out of my sight. He's a support dog. Whenever I have the urge to drunk-dial my ex, he bites me."

She took Asshole's leash and let him lead her out to the hallway. They crossed into the next ballroom, where many lumpy humans in tuxedoes and gowns were doing the Electric Slide. Head held high, Zoe Schwartz marched across the dance floor to the row of steam trays for the Bernstein–Kaufman wedding and helped herself to some rice pilaf, broccolini, and black cod.

When the father of the bride looked cockeyed at her, she lied, "I'm the comedian, I'm on after cake."

16

Zoe was having so much fun picking up Asshole and dancing to "You Spin Me Round (Like a Record)" with the eight-year-old flower girls, she forgot to look at her new texts until the song ended:

III

Ha ha, jk. You know exactly who I work for: Dustin Walker.

Dante Dupree propped himself up on his elbows on his hotel bed and squinted at his phone. A large tribal drummer had taken up residence inside his skull and was pounding out the infectious jungle rhythms one usually associated with sacrifices to Kong. Between these throbbing beats, what remained of his mind parsed the meaning of the name "Dustin Walker," right after the meaning of "jk," "exactly," "work," and "ha."

Dustin Walker. *Dustin Walker* is texting me? *The* Dustin Walker?

He's still alive?

Had he even *met* Dustin Walker? Dante felt certain he would have remembered that. But on the other hand, he couldn't remember a lot of things. That must have been quite a night at the club. The *club* club, that

17

is, where he went with the honeys who hung around after his set at the tiny comedy club in Rochester, New York, named, in a stunning burst of creativity, the Comedy Club.

He sort of remembered that he had tied one on not three days ago, so he swore he was going to take it easy on the tasty beverages for the foreseeable future.

Tell that to his eyes, which were now so stinging and shrunken as to tumble out of their sockets. Or his mouth, which tasted like he had sucked off a glue gun.

He tried to swallow, found that he was unable to, and looked around in the pre-dawn gloom. The usual anonymous limbo of a hotel room sharpened into focus: door, latch, peephole, laminated evacuation instructions, flat-screen, bureau, table, lamp, armchair.

He had a bad case of "the fuzzies," as the grandmother who had raised him used to call them. You spent your whole life trying to tame the fuzzies by clarifying them. So you were a fool if you went out of your way to make things fuzzier than they already were.

Something else in the bed moved along with him, bringing the fuzzies into, immediate clarity.

He held his breath and pulled back the

18

bedspread. Lying by his side was a woman — wait, no, *women,* one black-haired and white, the other blonde-haired and black. They were not the women he had gone to the club with.

Goddamn. What was the point of doing all this awesome freaky shit if you could never remember it well enough to get a good story out of it? Or at least work it into a tight five minutes on *Conan* or *2nite*?

A shouted conversation blundered into his memory:

"Do you screw as fast as you talk?"

"Girl, my mouth don't stop moving for an hour and a half. Just like my act."

But did that actually happen at the club last night, or was it just a bit he made up in his head? With guys like him, you never could be sure what was real and what was a fuzzy.

Dante looked around the hotel room again, which, after a few minutes of careful study, he realized was not his own.

He got up, naked, and walked over to the window, inspired to investigate something he had noticed before but had subconsciously tried to ignore: a Tim Hortons sign blazed on a donut place across the highway. Atop the flagpole in the parking lot flapped a red maple leaf on a white field.

"Am I in Canada?" he asked.

The white girl turned away from him and muttered, "Shut the hell up, eh?"

IV

> Dustin asked me to contact you about doing a project with him.

The headset-wearing stage manager had to cue Oliver Rees again because he was looking right through her. Goosebumps covered his entire nearly naked hairless body.

A PA snatched the phone out of his hand and replaced it with an oversized mallet before he could stop her. He looked again at his lock screen and made sure he hadn't imagined what he'd just read.

Just beyond the wings, his warm-up man, Kenny Kinny, was onstage gearing up for his closer, the one about getting his car stuck at the airport, thereby combining two great comedy subjects into one perfect joke. It was so hard to find an opening act that wasn't blue, *eff this* and *g-d that* and *I want to ess in your mouth.*

Kenny would ess when he heard this. Dustin Effing Walker's mounting a comeback? An HBO special? A streaming web series?

Whatever it is, he wants *my* help?

After all these years, after all the sold-out tours, the Emmy-winning specials, his Grammy, the IMAX documentary, packing the same theater in the Bellagio for months straight, tickets going for four figures on StubHub, none of it mattered to Oliver's peers. They still wouldn't let him play their reindeer games. They made fun of him at roasts that weren't even about him.

Yeah, I get it, you hate prop comedy. How original. Have you seen my house on Painted Feather Way? Would you like to count the bathrooms?

No, seriously, would you please count them, I forgot how many there are, *that's how many there are.*

Boom! Kenny dropped his closer, and the two thousand strong in the former Cirque du Soleil theater erupted with laughter.

The stage manager and Ollie exchanged thumbs-up. He reached out with his free hand and another PA put another rubber mallet in it. He made sure his shoulders were straight and his spine was relaxed and his chi was flowing properly down through his legs and out his toes.

Ollie was one of the most successful performers of his generation, but Dustin

21

Walker could bring him the only thing he lacked:

Dignity.

Kenny yelled:

"Give it up, fellow seekers of the Radical Yes! It's time for a play-date with . . . *Orange Baby Man!*"

Ollie somersaulted onto the stage with wide staring eyes and a manic grin. He was the exact color of a traffic cone. He even had a bright white stripe in the form of a diaper around his nether regions.

Giant multicolored whoopee cushions rose from the floor to meet Orange Baby Man. He beat out "My Heart Will Go On" on them in fart noises with his mallets.

The crowd rose to its feet as one.

V

He would like to extend to you an invitation to join him, me, and a select group of collaborators of equal stature for a long weekend of creation

When she read that, Janet Kahn screamed:

"Elena! Elena, goddamn it! Elena, get in here!"

"Ms. Kahn, please . . . ," murmured her

22

plastic surgeon, Dr. Shamdasani, and not for the first time. For the past twenty minutes he had been trying to get her to set down her phone so that his anesthesiologist could step in, but the insult comic still known as the Shotgun remained a raging dynamo of invective even while lying in an operating room at Cedars-Sinai.

"Look at your creepy serial-killer smile, Dr. S. It never wavers. You dipping into your own stash? Sticking your lips with the Botox? You auditioning for the villain in the next Batman movie? *Elena!*"

"Right here, Ms. Kahn," her personal assistant said. She had been standing just inside the door the whole time.

"Jesus Christ! Don't do that! You already made it across the border, you can stop sneaking around. Wear high heels once in a while so I can hear you coming. I'll hold off Immigration long enough so you can stomp away."

Elena had been born to second-generation Brazilian Americans in Framingham, Massachusetts, twenty-two years ago. She was the fourth personal assistant to work for the Real Queen of Mean that year. The placement agency swore to Elena that the real Real Queen of Mean was nothing like her insult comedy act.

It took two hours on the job for Elena to realize that was quite true.

The real Janet Kahn was much worse.

"How did whoever this is get my private number? Did you give it to her? If it was you, I'm gonna strangle you with your own fallopian tubes."

"Who . . . ?"

Lady Put-Down shoved the phone in Elena's face. She took it and scrolled through the text messages thus far.

Elena frowned:

"Who's Dustin Walker?"

"Christ on a crutch, are you serious? What are they teaching in public schools these days? Your generation can rank every member of One Direction by penis size but you don't know Dustin Walker? He's one of the few legends in this business who hasn't been carried out in a double-ply Hefty bag. Yet. That's why I'm in this chair, right, Dr. S? You're gonna make sure I live forever?"

"I shall do my very best, Ms. Kahn."

"Look at you, grinning and nodding, grinning and nodding. They should give you out on bobblehead day at Dodger Stadium."

Elena turned to leave. "I will find out whoever's calling and make sure they do not contact you again —"

"What? No! That's not what I said. The

short bus just drop you off? Listen! Find out who gave them my number. Then I'll know if the offer is on the up and up. Which I hope it is. Because the idea of it doesn't entirely, you know, suck."

Elena left the room trembling in awe at the nicest thing she had ever heard Janet Kahn say about anybody. She instantly looked up Dustin Walker on IMDb as soon as she got to the waiting area.

"Besides, Dusty's spread will be a grand place to recuperate from you using my face as a hibachi grill, ain't that right, Doc?"

"Perhaps, Ms. Kahn, if you ever give me your kind permission to perform the rhytidectomy . . . ?"

"Oh, you *can* get pissed, Doc. I can hear it in your voice. Real human emotion. I like this side of you. Yeah, okay, do your worst. I don't expect you to make me a 10, but I am tired of throwing up on my bathroom mirror every morning."

for a long weekend of creation at the house he's got on a small island off Saint Martin. Yes, that's the Caribbean. Sand, sun, and jokes. What's not to love?

TJ Martinez put down his big-ass Desert Eagle handgun and picked up his phone to make sure he had read that right.

Saint Martin? That was one of those island countries with no extradition treaties, right? Where the brothers had a revolution and kicked out the white man and made sure he'd never come back except by paying through the nose at high-end luxury hotels? That sounded nice. Particularly now. Things were getting way too heavy on the home front for his liking. He could hear punks stumbling about in the bushes outside his big-ass mansion right now.

TJ had been playing *Call of Duty* in his silk bathrobe and Michael Kors boxer shorts with the sound jacked all the way up on his headphones. The walls of his man-pit were reinforced by framed platinum records and photos of the guests he had on during his twenty years hosting *2nite.* There were five presidents, forty-two Grammys, thirty-eight Oscars, and eight Nobel Prizes among them.

He threw off his headset when shadows passed across the shutters on the big bay window. There were definitely creepers creeping around in his shit. Somebody jiggled the bulletproof panels from the outside.

He hadn't always bunkered down like a wounded animal. But after he retired from *2nite,* after two decades of the daily grind of a nightly variety show, after all the articles on his significance, after Miley Cyrus jumped out of his farewell cake in pasties on the last show, he woke up the next morning feeling like Rip Goddamn Winkle.

What *was* this new world, with everyone at DEFCON 5 24/7, losing their minds at every little thing. He used That Word in a tweet once — once! — and that's all it took for planet Earth to start screaming for his blood. All his awards, all those how-will-we-live-without-him think pieces, all forgotten in an instant.

Does TJ Martinez need that nonsense? Hell no. I got nothing left to prove. Not since I was seventeen years old, back when they stopped kicking my ass for my mouth and started giving me cash money for it instead.

TJ turned off the TV and padded over to the front door with the Desert Eagle. He could hear voices arguing in whispers on the other side. He quietly undid each of the six dead bolts so he could catch the mofos with their drawers around their ankles. He didn't have any security cameras in his big-ass mansion, because Anonymous or WikiLeaks could hack into those and he didn't want anyone posting videos of him jerking off onto MySpace or whatever. That ain't right. He didn't have an alarm system, either. That just begged *la policia* to show up unannounced claiming that the system gave them a false signal and do you mind if we have a look around your property since we're here anyway oh look at all this heroin we found for some reason. No, thank you.

Before *2nite* TJ had starred with that crazy white boy Dusty Walker on *What Just Happened?* They had been thick as thieves back in the day, scoring coke together and destroying any pussy that had the bad sense to blunder into the orbit of their insanity.

He hadn't talked to Dusty for years and years, since they did that movie together, the one about the guy who married a cat. It was a piece of garbage but it paid for Dusty's sweet crib in the islands. Might be good to see him.

Might be even better to lie low for a while. Because he was about to straight-up murder some fools.

He grabbed the knob and threw open the door.

VII

> The only potential sticky wicket is that the dates are kind of already locked in — Aug. 8–11 — so hopefully that'll work with your schedule.

Once Ruby Ng read this, she stifled a cry. By this point she had spent a solid twenty minutes creeping around TJ Martinez's bushes trying to find a window to look through that wasn't covered with bulletproof shutters.

Ever since the ex-*2nite* host had tweeted That Word, then deleted it eighteen thousand retweets too late, then set a land-speed record for deleting every single one of his online accounts, Ruby burned with the desire to get him on her podcast, *Comedy Ambush*, ranked #44 overall on iTunes, #2 in interview/humor (watch your ass, Marc Maron). But it looked like Martinez had gone full-on Colonel Kurtz. His mansion was locked down to survive a zombie attack, bunker-buster bomb, and/or the Rapture.

Lucky for her, he had left his front gate open.

Normally, Ruby would have turned off her phone notifications to avoid interfering with its microphone attachment and Bluetooth connection to the small video camera mounted on her Kaiser Wilhelm bicycle helmet. But any remaining thoughts of leaping out of the bushes and strafing TJ Martinez with an impromptu interview about his privilege flew out her ears as soon as she looked at her phone and the text hit her between the eyes.

ZOMG Dustin Walker THE Dustin Walker wants to work with me.

Ruby popped out of Martinez's bushes and walked across his front lawn, dialing rapidly. Where did he see my stand-up? YouTube? Must have been YouTube, since none of the phallocentric gatekeepers of Hollywood had the cojones to put her on the air.

When her fiancée, Yvette, answered, Ruby blurted out, "I've got great news," and read the Walker message back verbatim.

Yvette screamed:

"Oh my God, honey! That's wonderful!

That's amazing! I'm so happy for you. Except . . . you know. For that last part."

"What? Why?"

"You . . . you *do* have plans that weekend."

"Not anymore I don't!"

She could feel the bubbling hot magma of Yvette's unleashed fury surging through the phone. "What — what are you talking about?"

"What are *you* talking about?"

"*Dammit Ruby, our wedding is that weekend!*"

Ruby blinked.

"Oh."

She blinked again.

"Oh yeah."

She blinked a third time.

"Well."

After an awkward pause:

"Guess we'll have to reschedule, then."

"No — no, we are not rescheduling our wedding! We'll lose our deposit at the aquarium!"

"I'll make it up to you, baby."

"Make it up to me? How can you make it up to me? How can you pay me back? You haven't had a positive net income since we started dating!" An estate tax lawyer, Yvette was definitely the sugar mommy in the relationship. "When will Yogi Gomes find another time to leave his ashram? That's the best ten-date window for a wedding between Tauruses! *Do you have any idea how hard it is to rent doves, for Christ's sake?*"

"I swear, I'll figure out a way. 'Vette! This job is a slam-dunk game-changer!"

Yvette burst into tears.

"The most special day of our lives together is a slam-dunk game-changer! What about that?"

The veins in Ruby's neck started popping out. "I don't think you understand what an opportunity this is, not just for my career personally, but to increase the non-accommodationist queer presence in mainstream American comedy! I thought you believed in the revolution of representation! *What about the revolution, Yvette?*"

At that moment, TJ Martinez burst out of his front door, waving a handgun at Ruby as big as her head, screaming, "I'LL SHOW YOU A REVOLUTION!"

"Gottagotalklaterloveyahon!" Ruby Ng sprinted through the gate and toward her recumbent bike chained to a lamppost down the block as fast as her unshaved legs could carry her.

Anyway, drop me a ring or a text back if you're interested — Dustin would absolutely loooooove to work with you.

Fascinating, William Griffith thought when he read the series of texts. He had never met Dustin Walker, or heard anything but a track or two of his most famous album (*Can't Help Himself*), but that was not unusual. William was not familiar with most of his fellow practitioners in the art of observational monologuing.

"Mr. Griffith, if you'll allow me, I'd like to show you this piece. M. Vallier suspected you might find it right, as they say, up your alley."

"Yes, of course, Dominique. Lead on."

Dominique led William across the high-rise gallery offering spectacular floor-to-ceiling vistas of the Arc de Triomphe and Champs-Élysées. Normally the gallery was closed on Monday, at least to all collectors not named William Griffith. He had to red-eye back to JFK to tape Fallon on Tuesday, so arrangements had been made.

William looked at the mixed-media work for some time, then asked:

33

"Whose vagina is that?"

Dominique said:

"The artist's mother's."

William nodded:

"Ah, yes. Of course. They make the most exquisite sound when they brush against one another."

"The colored-glass vaginas are hand blown, ironically enough, *by* the artist's mother. This is why M. Vallier has called it *The Birth Call.* Instead of —"

"*The Birth* Caul, of course. Droll. A pun. Very daring in the art world."

Dominique shot him a hungry, expectant look:

"So, do you think you might be interested —"

Just then William's phone tinkled again, the sound of a fork tapping a champagne flute. When he read the text, he felt a pang of disappointment. It was from his manager, Jessica, and not another flattering message from the Dustin Walker people:

> Hey Billy sorry but the Phoenix guys are really on my ass about the promos can you just call in that number and give them 1 or 2 takes real quick thx xoxoxoxoxoxox

"Pardon me, darling, I need to make a call. May I . . . ?"

"Please, use my office. Over there."

William entered the small side room and closed the door. He dialed the number in Jessica's text, and when the recorder beeped on the other end, he let out a rebel yell:

"Hey there, this is Billy the Contractor and you're listening to KTEA, Kay-Tee, Phoenix's real place for real talk for real Americans! Remember to hold your fire till you see the whites of their panties! Fix 'er uuuuuuuup!"

He waited a beat.

Then he said:

"You know what criminals call gun-free zones? *Target practice!* You know that, KTEA knows that, and Billy the Contractor knows it, too! You can't see I'm open-carrying on the radio, but you straight-up know I am! Fix 'er uuuuuuuup!"

Beat.

"How many liberals does it take to screw in a light bulb? Who knows, none of 'em have worked a day in their lives! This is Billy the Contractor tellin' Real America to set their dial to KTEA, Phoenix's radio home of Hannity and Limbaugh! Fix 'er uuuuuuuup!"

Dominique's face was blank with shock when he stepped back out of the office. She must have heard every word.

And she must have been more familiar with his bank account than with his act.

That was true of most of his fellow travelers. He decided he was going to take the Dustin Walker people up on their offer. He had been paddling around by himself in his own little pond for far too long.

William handed the stunned Dominique his black Amex and said:

"M. Vallier knows me far too well. This piece would look exquisite next to the pool at my guesthouse. I'll take it."

IX

Hope to see you there!
Best,
Meredith Ladipo
Assistant to Dustin Walker &
Funny-Person-in-Training

"You're fired, Steve!"

Teddy's words were drowned out by the metal stage door crashing shut in the alley behind Improv Underground, where illegal immigrants in white aprons pitched giant garbage bags of rotting produce from Aldi into blue plastic Dumpsters. Steve Gordon had dashed out as soon as he read the last part of the message, leaving his accountant students slack-jawed in amazement.

As soon as Dusty's name appeared on his lock screen, he had to grab the stage-right curtain to keep from falling over. He hadn't heard from Dusty in years. Years. He assumed Dusty still hated his guts because of . . . well, you know. But now, after all his pitch meetings to stone-faced producers, after all the pilots not picked up, after the sink into the dreary sameness of improv classes and infomercial hosting . . . Dusty wanted to see him again? This was destiny calling, wasn't it?

This was salvation.

Steve wasn't halfway to the alley before he pulled up Meredith Ladipo's contact details from her message and dialed her number: 310 area code. Los Angeles.

By the fifth ring his panic mounted, but then a woman answered:

"Hey there, Funny Person." A young voice

with a British accent, brimming with the confidence of the extremely good-looking.

"Yeah, hi, this is Steve Gordon —"

"I know."

"And this is Meredith?"

"I hope so, I'm wearing her underwear."

"Ha. *Real Genius,* nice. So, hey, Meredith —"

"Hey."

"I've only got one question, which is —"

"No."

"No what?"

"No, it's not a joke. It's a genuine offer."

"Oh, thank God!" Steve blurted out, and Meredith laughed:

"It's all right, most of the others have had the same reaction."

The others?

"Well, sure, sounds like fun. Send the details, I'll look them over, and we'll go from there."

"You still with ICM?"

"I . . . think so?" Steve chuckled. "It's been a while since I've spoken to anyone over there. My agent may have died from lack of interest. I just, uh — I was wondering . . ."

"Yes?"

"Is Dusty around? Can you put him on? It's been so long since I've spoken to him."

"Dust—? Oh. That's brilliant you call him that. No, I'm in L.A., crossing t's and dotting i's. Dustin's already at the island. The cell reception there's rubbish; we communicate through Skype mostly. I'll let him know you want to touch base, maybe he'll find the time to raise the port before you arrive on the island."

Steve took a deep breath, exhaled:

"I . . . this is . . . wow. I don't know what to say."

"Say yes," Meredith Ladipo said.

X

And he did.

In the end, they all did.

When God almighty walks down on a beam of light and asks for your help, what the hell else are you going to say?

And that was just what their host was counting on.

Dustin Walker

Filmography

Actor (55 credits)

Writer (15 credits)

Producer (19 credits)

Director (1 credit)

Known For

Can't Help Myself
(1988)
As Himself

Filmed concert version of Walker's multiplatinum Grammy-winning comedy album.

What Just Happened?
(TV series, 1990–1994)
As Various

Funnymen Dustin Walker, TJ Martinez, Steve "Gordo" Gordon, and surprise guest stars improvise comedy sketches based on suggestions from the audience and inspired by current events.

Help! I Married a Cat
(1995)
As Jerry Russell

Shallow ladies' man learns the true meaning of love when his eccentric aunt's will stipulates that in order to inherit her fortune, he has to wed her ill-tempered calico, Miss Puffytail.

Help! I Married a Cat 2
(1998)
As Jerry Russell

Jerry and Miss Puffytail must contend with a bigoted senator (Christopher Walken) fighting to pass a constitutional amendment banning interspecies marriage and a gold-digging neighbor (Fran Drescher) in this sequel to the box-office smash.

Help! I Married a Cat 3: The Claws Come Out
(2000)
As Jerry Russell

Miss Puffytail schemes to ruin a growing relationship between Jerry and her pretty new vet (Jennifer Aniston).

Help! I Married a Cat 4: Divorce, Feline-Style
(2003)
As Jerry Russell

A jive-talking tomcat (voice: Martin Lawrence) seeks to sabotage the marriage of Jerry and Miss Puffytail so he can collect her millions.

King Lear
(2004)
As the Fool

Kenneth Branagh's attempt to relocate Shakespeare's classic tragedy about a misguided ruler (Derek Jacobi) and his three daughters to 1920s gangsterland Chicago was an ambitious critical and commercial failure.

The Adventures of Cosmic Carson
(2005)
As Cosmic Carson

A roguish space trucker and his sentient fart sidekick (voice: Gilbert Gottfried) must protect a nymphomaniac princess (Chyna) from intergalactic loan sharks. One of the most expensive box office bombs of all time.

Dandy Waller, Your Destiny Awaits You
(2008)
As Dandy Waller

Dustin Walker's semiautobiographical directorial debut about a suicidal stand-up reviewing his life before leaping from the Golden Gate Bridge was described by the *New York Times* as "less a feature-length film than a cry for help from a comedian who was briefly one of Hollywood's most bankable stars."

Help! I Married a Cat: The New Litter
(2009)
As Jerry Russell

Jerry's son (Zac Efron) has to marry one of Sir Toms-A-Lot and Miss Puffytail's kittens for financial reward in this failed attempt to reboot the blockbuster franchise.

— IMDb.com

43

CHAPTER TWO

I

Steve thought that Meredith Ladipo, Dustin Walker's personal assistant, was as good-looking in person as she sounded over the phone, if not more so. She was on the petite side, about five foot and a half, with dark skin and a bright smile and natural hair tied up in a halo bun. She was standing ramrod stiff when she first ascended into his field of vision. He was descending the escalator to baggage claim at Saint Martin's Princess Juliana International Airport.

She held up an iPad with WEAVER PARTY on the screen in big letters. That was the agreed-to code name to throw paparazzi off their scent. Nevertheless, the locals and opportunistic tourists knew of their arrival thanks to whatever collective sewer of celebrity intel the TMZs of the world swilled from. Autograph seekers swarmed the baggage claim and mobbed TJ Martinez as soon as he appeared, a Marlins cap and sunglasses insufficiently Clark Kenting his identity. Without expression, and without complaint, he dutifully signed every notebook, ticket, and boob presented to his Sharpie.

Fans then swarmed each successive Weaver party member who came down the escalator by descending order of how recently they had been on TV. Janet Kahn was nearly unrecognizable in dark glasses, and a kerchief covering her hair, her recently revised face held together with a plastic muzzle, neck brace, and crisscrossing bandages. But to the autograph seekers, her identity was as transparent as Martinez's.

The crowds for Zoe Schwartz, Oliver Rees, and Dante Dupree shrank in size and intensity, in that order.

But theirs were bigger than the crowd for Steve, which numbered zero. Not that he expected anyone to ask for his autograph. He'd been in his early twenties when he appeared on a weekly network TV show, and now he sported a neatly trimmed English lit prof beard and wire frames to match. His secret identity was perfectly concealed, involuntarily, to all but one.

"Mr. Gordon? Welcome to Saint Martin.

I'm Meredith Ladipo, we spoke on the phone? How was your flight?"

She offered her hand and he shook it. "Uneventful, the way I like it."

"Brilliant. So, if you checked bags —"

"One, yeah."

"Well, we're not in a huge rush because a couple of your colleagues' flights were delayed, and as we only have the one charter boat to get over to the island, we'll have to wait for them to arrive. If you could just point out your luggage as it comes off the spinner bin, the porter will make sure it gets into the limo and make its way to the charter . . ."

Steve frowned. "I'm sorry, spinner bin? You mean — the baggage thing?"

"Yes, that's what I said."

"Oh, uh . . . okay?"

Ruby Ng staggered away from the spinner bin bearing her bags and wearing an Oberlin sweatshirt and Elton John sunglasses.

When she emerged from the baggage-claim doors and Dante Dupree saw her from inside the stretch limo by the curb, he groaned in despair.

"What the hell? I mean, who in his right mind would invite her? What was Walker thinking?"

Zoe Schwartz, sitting next to him, peered

over his shoulder to look through the window at the newcomer. The two had met at the Montreal Comedy Expo three years back, and then just six months ago they had both done the Comedy Central Roast of Alec Baldwin and lived to tell the tale. Though they hadn't spoken since, they had the easy camaraderie of foxhole buddies, picking up effortlessly where they last left off. Once they'd signed their autographs, they retreated to the relative safety of the limo, with its purple floor lighting, and talked shit about their colleagues as they arrived.

Dante said, "You know, I was actually looking forward to this weekend. Kicking back with some amazing comics, cutting loose, coming up with a bunch of funny shit. Then I see her and my dick goes soft."

Zoe said, "You been *Comedy Ambush* ed too, huh?"

"She called me a racist."

"She calls everybody a racist. That's kind of her thing."

"She said my face belonged on a box of rice."

"She said I was the worst thing to happen to women since the chastity belt."

"Grandma heard that nonsense. She didn't eat right for weeks."

47

"Grandma listens to Ruby Ng's podcast? Is she a lesbian? Or a twenty-eight-year-old artisanal bartender from Brooklyn?"

"Grandma is an avid consumer of all things Dante Dupree."

"Aw, that's adorable."

Dante watched Ruby Ng directing the porters and threw up his hands. "Now I can't say a damn thing this weekend without worrying about whether or not the whole world will hear about it on her stupid podcast. Because you know everything out of our mouths *will* wind up there. Hell, she'll make half the stuff up herself."

"I love people like Ruby. The world has to be full of dragons for her to slay. It's the only way she can maintain the illusion she's a good person."

"Hey guys," Ruby said as she popped open the limo door and climbed inside.

"Hey!" Zoe beamed.

" 'Sup girl," Dante said.

II

The island began as a tiny lump on the horizon, a slight discoloration almost indistinguishable from the ocean itself. As the charter boat approached, it metastasized, expanding in height and girth until it com-

48

manded the surroundings, its tall looming cliffs crowned in green.

Oliver Rees stood at the narrowing of the bow, giggling with each swell the boat humped over. The wind was threatening to lift his boonie hat; he shoved it down on his blindingly white, hairless bowling ball of a head.

He turned back and yelled "I hope there's shuffleboard!" to anyone who would listen, which was nobody.

Ruby Ng was equally popular. She sat on the aftmost bench with legs drawn up to her chest and vaped quietly, staring at the Caribbean through opaque sunglasses.

Zoe Schwartz leaned on the railing and watched the island approach. By her feet lay a cloth case she had carried off the plane and hadn't let out of her sight.

She glanced to the other side of the boat and saw TJ Martinez talking to Dustin Walker's English maid, or whatever the hell she was supposed to be, his arm on the back of a portside bench, leaning into her, just as skeevy as Zoe had remembered.

Steve Gordon walked over and said with a smile:

"Hey, TJ, I thought that was you! Long time no see! You look great! Dusty's getting the whole band back together again, huh?"

49

TJ turned his black lenses Steve's way. "Sorry, friend, I know you?"

"Yeah . . . TJ . . . It's me, Steve?"

"Who?"

"Steve Gordon. You know, Gordo? We were on *What Just Happened?*"

"We were?"

"Yeah. Together. With Dusty?"

"Huh. If you say so."

"For four seasons?"

TJ looked at him for what seemed like a long time and shrugged. "Doesn't ring a bell. Sorry, bro."

He turned back to Meredith Ladipo with definitive finality. She had a strained, awkward, confused smile on her face. She looked at Steve with an uncomprehending glance, a very British *I don't know what is happening but I would be most appreciative if it would just go away.*

Steve had no choice but to quit the field with a pointless, face-saving nod. He went to the starboard bench and sat down to look out over the horizon and wait for the burning in his cheeks to subside.

Zoe Schwartz watched the whole incident from the side railing with a deep frown, but didn't say a thing.

III

"Fascinating, simply fascinating," William Griffith said as he stepped outside the bridge door. Not long after launch, apropos of nothing, he had invited himself into the crew area and had a long boisterous conversation with the captain, an islander with a face like cracked bomber-jacket leather, in French.

To Janet Kahn, the only passenger who had retreated under the overhang shade of the foremost bench, William said:

"Do you know Saint Martin is split down the middle by France and the Netherlands? Our captain had quite the childhood, caught between two worlds, two cultures. It's a shame such a beautiful place is home to such ugliness. Drugs, gangs. Poverty."

It took Janet a second to realize he was talking to her. She squinted up at him.

"Forgive me, darling, but . . . who are you? I thought maybe you were Dusty's lawyer, but your nose is too small."

"That's quite all right, few people recognize me out of character. And I rather prefer it that way."

He switched to a drawl so distinctive that his business manager had trademarked it:

"You know that dating website, Farmers

51

Only? They had to change the focus once they realized livestock can't use the internet. Then it was called Kissin' Cousins for a spell, but that name'd already been taken by a very specialized escort service in Alabama."

"Right, okay, you're that patron saint of shit kickers and meth heads . . . Buddy the Contractor?"

Remaining in character, William said, "Billy. Pleased to make your acquaintance, ma'am. You are quite the legend."

"Yes, I am. You call me ma'am again and I'll kick your balls into your nostrils."

"Just being polite. Madam? Miss?"

"Try Janet on for size, you might like it. But I don't get the joke. There's a website called Farmers Only?"

William smiled and reverted to his real voice. "You need to get outside the coasts, Janet."

"I have performed in every state in the Union, honey, even the Canadian ones. I know they call it flyover country, but I'd vote to amend that to 'bombing practice.'"

He couldn't help but stare at the bandages on her face.

"That looks horribly painful, Janet, if you don't mind me saying so."

"You should see the other guy."

"Really?"

"Yeah, I'm putting his kids through college."

"Were you in a car accident or . . . ?"

"I'm a big believer in self-improvement, doll. And defrauding Medicare. And when I get to do both at the same time, so much the better."

IV

No shore or beach surrounded the island. Instead, tall brown cliffs festooned with flowering vines rose higher and higher as the charter ferry approached, until they were all that the passengers could see.

A gray pier jutted from one side of the island, facing the boat. At the opposite end of the dock, a staircase crawled up the side of the cliff. The color and age of its wood varied from level to level, since steps and landings had been replaced after continuous lashing from hurricanes and the elements.

The boat's three-man crew worked quickly but without urgency, the way people who labor at repetitive daily tasks do, hopping onto the dock and, as the boat was brought around, securing it with heavy ropes. They then removed the passengers' luggage from the lower deck and stacked the bags on the pier. It took all three crew plus the captain to grunt and curse Janet Kahn's trunk out of the hold. It was big enough to fit most of the other passengers' bags inside it.

"Good Lord, woman, did you leave any clothes at home?" William Griffith said.

"What, I'm supposed to travel with a bindle over my shoulder, like a hobo?" Janet tried to wrinkle her nose in disgust, then winced in pain.

The captain disembarked and handed Meredith Ladipo a piece of paper on a clipboard, which she signed.

"You'll be by with supplies at the usual time tomorrow, then?"

The captain nodded and gestured for the crew to reboard and shove off. William Griffith waved good-bye.

The captain looked at him, grinned, and tipped his hand to the bill of his cap in a barely perceptible salute.

William couldn't tell if he was being mocked.

Meredith Ladipo talked sideways into her cell phone like it was a walkie-talkie. "Right, Dave, we've arrived, so c'mon down." When nothing but silence responded, she said, "Dave? You read me? We're all here. Chop-chop."

Not waiting for the response that never came, Meredith walked over to the other end of the dock. Carved out of the cliffside beside the stairs was a small alcove that contained little more than several life jackets hanging on a plaster wall and the doors to an elevator.

It wasn't until she was a few strides from the alcove that she saw the OUT OF ORDER sign, handwritten in marker on a flap ripped off a cardboard box, stuck to the front of the elevator with a strip of duct tape. She punched the call button several times anyway, but nothing happened.

Meredith Ladipo drew her chin up high, a model of British resilience, and marched back to her guests, who stood in a clump on the dock eyeing her with suspicion.

"Right," she said. "It appears we have stepped in some sticky pomade. I'm having trouble raising the staff, and the lift is knockered."

"What?" Ruby Ng said. "Did you say knockered?" She looked to the others. "Did she say knockered?"

Janet pointed at the towering stairs, which induced vertigo even from ground level. "How the hell am I supposed to get my trunk up that?" She looked to the top. "How the hell am *I* supposed to get up that?"

Meredith Ladipo raised her palms in defense. "I would advise you to leave the bags down here. We'll send someone to get them later. Don't worry, they'll be as safe as bugs in rugs. As for the stairs, I know they look a bit daunting but really, as long as you pace yourself, they're not bad at all. I run up and down them every day as part of my morning jog."

The group took this news in stride with minimal grumbling. Zoe shouldered the cloth case she had kept with her since the airport. When William Griffith asked, "May I help you with that?" she hugged it close and said:

"No, that's all right, I've got it."

Most of the others took a carry-on or a purse with them and tromped in a winding queue up the stairs.

Midway along the side of the cliff, breathing heavily and brow slick with sweat, William Griffith turned to look back for his captain friend. He saw that the boat was already nearing the vanishing point where sea met sky and soon would disappear over the horizon.

Most of them were short of breath by the time they reached the top of the stairs. TJ Martinez had to lean a hand against the railing and catch his breath. "You make me do that again, screw Dusty, I'm going home."

"How? Does Uber have a navy now, too?" Dante Dupree said.

Once William Griffith, bringing up the rear, staggered to the landing, Meredith said, "We all here? Everyone still alive? Splendid. This way."

The great house was set back at the end of an allée of towering coconut palms. It was built during this century but in later French-colonial island style, the turquoise hurricane shutters open against bright ocher walls. The structure had two terra-cotta tile roofs, one over the gallery on the ground floor and another on the second-story belvedere. It sat on a slight hill at the edge of the cliff, with its gallery doors open at opposite ends to catch the prevailing trade winds. As the group approached, flanked by the tall trees, they could see all the way through the central hallway to the rear of the mansion, where a pool shimmered. A large fountain rose up before the entrance, shaped like a giant concrete lily pad. Concentric rings of robin's-egg blue mosaic tiles radiated from its gurgling center.

Looking off to one side, Ollie cried, "Is that a bouncy castle? No way!"

A grand pink inflated castle stood between the main house and a more modest cabana guesthouse set into a steeper slope. Flapping atop a turret was one of those elongated inflatable men alerting motorists to car washes and auto lots. It wore a red track suit and glasses and had thinning hair with an obvious comb-over.

"Is that . . . is that supposed to be Dusty?" Steve said.

"Isn't it swish?" Meredith said.

"Are you his assistant or his enabler?" Janet said.

Meredith Ladipo led the group into the partially enclosed front gallery, part living room, part reception area. It had large louvered windows and earth-tone tiles that matched the mahogany furniture.

"I could get used to this," Zoe said. "I could absolutely get used to this."

"Dustin? Mr. Walker? We're here!" Meredith Ladipo called out as they entered. Her voice rang off the blindingly white plaster walls. "Dave? Dave, can you hear me?"

No answer.

"I feel so very wanted," William Griffith said.

Meredith Ladipo did her best to conceal a nervous smile, and failed. "I guess I should go see where everyone is. While I'm doing that, please feel free to freshen up and settle into your rooms. Here, I took the liberty of printing a layout of the grounds for you all." She handed out maps, each individualized with the location of the recipient's bedroom. "It's . . . three o'clock now? Let's meet at five in the writers' room — marked clearly on your maps. Dustin can explain exactly what this project is all about in his own inimitable way, over cocktails."

"Where *is* Dusty?" TJ said.

"I am going to find out," she said, and walked out of the gallery through an archway leading deeper into the house.

"Great," TJ sighed, "we just got here and the show is already a total mess. Might as well be a network production."

"Typical Dusty," Steve said.

"How'd you know?" TJ shot back.

Steve opened his mouth to say something but Janet Kahn suddenly whipped off her sunglasses and cried out, "Oh my God, will you look at that?"

She stepped toward the gallery's east wall, which was covered with letter-sized black-

and-white photos framed in black. The images were arranged in three neat rows of three. Each of them was represented, in action onstage in a club or theater, mic in hand.

They all gathered around for a look.

"Looks just like the back wall at the Comedy Store," Dante said.

He pointed at a photo of Meredith Ladipo on stage gripping a mic stand in front of a black backdrop:

"Hey, look, the African Queen of England is a stand-up, too."

William Griffith smiled at the shot of him packing the Grand Ole Opry in full-on Billy the Contractor drag: Bud Light tallboy in hand, Farm King cap turned backward on his head, the sleeves of his plaid shirt ripped off so everyone could see the copious flame tattoos shooting out of his biceps. "That was a good night," he murmured.

"Will you look at that," Janet whispered.

She reached out and touched her photo. It showed her several decades and a few facelifts ago, sporting a beehive hairdo and striped lamé dress, standing on the floor of a taste-free Vegas lounge. Her joker-card smile inveighed humorous abuse on a tuxedo-clad and evening-gown-wearing audience. Every man and woman in the photograph had faces frozen in laughter.

"The Shotgun, mid-salvo," Steve said.

"You were out there breaking barriers before any of us," Ruby said.

"Not just the greatest, but the greatest of all time," Dante said.

"Hell yeah," Zoe said, and touched Janet's back. "Though you do have shoulder blades like a man."

"Thank you, dear. You can drop dead, too."

Janet's eyes shimmered. She yanked a half-used Kleenex out of her sleeve. "Sometimes you wish life was like this, you know? You could just stop some moments in time forever."

"Not everybody," Dante said. "Jesus, Ollie, look at you here."

"What? I'm up there? Let me see?" Ollie was considerably shorter than the others and got stuck behind when the scrum rushed to the photo wall. He elbowed his way to the front and his cheeks flushed crimson at what he saw.

"Whoa, look at the size of that Jew-fro, Ollie," Janet said with a cackle. "The Anti-Defamation League is calling, telling you to cut it out, you're making the rest of us look bad."

TJ said, "Aw, c'mon, give him a break.

61

That's cool, Ollie. I didn't know you tried to do real comedy."

"What?" Ollie blinked. "What do you mean?"

"You know," TJ said, "as opposed to that horrible hacky prop crap you do for tourists."

"Yeah, like, it basically belongs at five-year-olds' birthday parties instead of on-stage," Zoe said.

"Or old folks homes," Ruby deadpanned.

"Oh," Ollie said. "That."

VI

Ollie didn't cry when he left the gallery.

He didn't cry as he walked up the stairs winding through the center of the house.

He didn't cry as he walked around the upstairs gallery to his room.

He didn't cry at all, in fact.

But as soon as he shut his door, he grabbed a pillow and screamed into it all the curses he would never say out loud, way worse than *eff your mother* and *ess on your dad.*

It all came back to him downstairs. He had forgotten how much those words could hurt and how casually cruel other comics could be, backstage before and after he went on, no matter how well his set went — or, more often, how badly.

The photo on the wall had come from one of his earliest attempts at stand-up, at an open mic at Carolines, in Times Square, where he bombed worse than scientists had previously believed possible. His thick corrective lenses, his overbite, and the dark Chia Pet curls covering his head stirred the audience's predatory instincts as soon as he stepped onstage. He had spent three long January nights freezing his ass off handing out fliers to tourists taking pictures with a giant Elmo wearing a fanny pack, chirping "Do you like comedy?" over and over just to qualify for the privilege of being nearly assaulted by a roomful of mooks from Nassau County.

The whole experience brought back stress memories of the schoolyard before first bell, that horrible purgatory of kids milling about on the basketball court waiting to go in, how he was the target of any kid not born with curly hair, squat legs, bad eyesight, and Jewish roots. He wasn't as quick as the others downstairs, the ones who were able to fight insults with even better comebacks.

Ollie never learned how to parry, dodge, and counterattack. Then as now, when mocked, his brain just buzzed with a white noise of panic. He was like a superhero who had the same origin, but got different powers.

It was Dustin Walker's album *Can't Help Myself,* the *Thriller* of comedy, that originally inspired him. He played the cassette over and over until the tape snapped, but fortunately by then he could do all the routines by heart in front of his bedroom mirror, using his mother's hairbrush as a microphone. He could do all the characters, all the voices, on command — he just struggled to find his own.

After the Carolines fiasco, he decided to give up traditional stand-up altogether. He had worked the Orange Baby Man persona into his act for the first time on the night depicted in the gallery photo, inspired by a *Can't Help Myself* track called "Born Yesterday." Using his background in magic and clowning, he developed a persona so bright and innocent and vulnerable, no one in the audience would dare heckle him.

And from there, he'd built an empire.

When he looked up from smothering his screams in the pillow he saw a bright-orange square on the bedside table. He immediately recognized it and simultaneously doubted what it was. As he approached, however, he saw that he was right:

An Orange Baby Man regional-franchise handbook binder lay beside his bed. The trades had yet to receive the press release, but he was well under way to opening Orange Baby Man Theaters around the globe, from New York to Macao, London to Rio, each with its own local OBM performing Ollie's routines. The binder contained rules and regulations and a mission statement, which he had dictated to his assistant during breaks between rehearsals. They were meant to inspire in all "a childlike sense of spectacle" while promoting the values of "peace and play." It was his gift to the world.

And Dustin Walker had the binder in his house! Amazing. Did he want to be an investor? Did he want to open an OBM theater in Saint Martin? (That might conflict with the regional exclusivity deal he had cut at the Sandals resort in Saint Thomas, but, whatever. When a star of Walker's magnitude got involved, all things became negotiable.)

The corners of his mouth turned upward. Those stuck-up jerks looked down on prop comedy, huh? Well, wait till they saw this. He'd show them.

He'd show them all.

Ruby Ng sighed when she saw her room. White rug on brown hardwood floors. White cushions on beige wicker chairs. White sheets over a dark mahogany bed frame, tastefully bunched white mosquito netting garlanding the four posts. Nice colonialist decor, she thought.

Still, it was hard not to admire the view: when she opened the hurricane shutters she was greeted by a spectacular showing of the endless blue Caribbean beyond the coconut-lined cliffs. She snapped a few vacation-porn shots to text to Yvette as a "hey, I've arrived alive" notice. But a red exclamation point in her Messages app reminded her of the unbearably cute Meredith Ladipo's warning about the cell reception, or lack thereof. She opened the Settings menu to join the island's Wi-Fi network.

Meredith had included the network pass-word on their maps. It was a meaningless jumble of letters and numbers. The first time Ruby typed the sequence into her phone it buzzed irritably. And the second time, and the third time.

"Well, shit," Ruby said.

As she gave up, putting away her phone, she noticed a small, old-timey, gunmetal-gray flip phone on the end table. Presumably it had been left by the room's previous guest.

Thinking she'd hand it off to Ladipo to dispose of later, she picked it up and popped it in her pocket as she headed out to explore the rest of the building.

VIII

A black square box of Winchester shotgun shells lay on the end table in Janet Kahn's room. An exploding clay skeet discus was drawn on the front ("X-Tra Lite Target Load").

The comic known as the Shotgun picked up the box and opened the lid: all but two of the shells appeared to be in place.

She put the box back on the table with a tight smile.

IX

On Dante's end table he found a brown bottle of Lagavulin 12-year-old. You knew it was the good stuff because on the label they spelled it "Scotch Whisky." Extra e's were for filthy commoners, apparently. Yet the English loved sticking extra u's into everything. British people just made this shit up as they went along, of this Dante was convinced. He didn't understand half the crap out of Meredith Ladipo's mouth, as nice as she was on the eyes. They just had to have a different word for everything.

Dante picked up the bottle to admire it and frowned. It wasn't glass, but plastic. Not so fancy for him, apparently.

He thought about opening it and having a quick taste, though he had promised himself he would take it easy this weekend. The drinking got even worse when he wasn't touring.

He thought about it some more. Maybe he should show some self-control.

An old saying of Grandma's tickled the back of his mind:

"Watch out for white people bearing gifts. They're always trying to buy your ass on the installment plan."

He set the bottle back down, unopened.

X

Steve Gordon saw it as soon as he walked into the room: something square and cardboard on the bamboo end table. He picked it up.

And his breath caught in his throat.

It was *Can't Help Myself,* Dusty's first

stand-up album, the one that catapulted him to Instant Legend status. "The *Thriller* of comedy" was how it was most commonly described — every home had a copy, and at one time it was as ubiquitous as the Rubik's Cube and Big Mouth Billy Bass combined. On the dust jacket, an early twentysomething Dustin Walker looked cross-eyed at the camera wearing a straitjacket while having his mug shot taken.

Or he usually did. Someone had taped a photo of Steve's face over Walker's on this particular album cover.

I guess he's still carrying a wee bit of a grudge, Steve thought.

THE RADICAL YES

To All Aspiring OBMs:

The most important thing to remember about Orange Baby Man®, and the main reason he is loved by audiences of all ages all over the world, is that he was LITERALLY BORN YESTERDAY.

• He does not have our baggage and hang-ups.
• He does not have our fear, hatred, and prejudice.
• He knows nothing of our world or any human society.
• He is too young to have learned how to talk. He speaks in a rudimentary but semantically rich form of prelanguage called BABY RAP® that all regional and touring OBMs will have to learn. Written and oral exams will be required.
• He is an alien, except he was born here on Earth and is completely human (like Superman).
• His is a journey of EXPLORATION and DISCOVERY that he invites the audience to accompany him on.

All sketches revolve around Orange Baby

Man® encountering and interacting with unique aspects of his world, all of which are, at first, completely alien and baffling to him:

- A giant smartphone
- Brightly colored squirty paint tubes
- PVC-pipe musical instruments
- Watermelons
- Exercise equipment

And so on! Unlike us, Orange Baby Man® does not approach the unknown with trepidation or hesitancy. Instead, he embraces the unknown enthusiastically with what Mr. Rees likes to call THE RADICAL YES.

The RADICAL part of the Radical Yes is what activates the humor in our sketches. Orange Baby Man®'s enthusiastic and often rambunctious embrace of the props he finds onstage put him in amusing and outrageous situations. He acts before he thinks, and like so many of us he often finds himself in over his head.

When this happens, it triggers what we like to call the Pivot™, and the rest of the sketch becomes about him trying to escape an awkward situation. (Example: the sketch in which OBM gets on the treadmill without realizing he has a paint tube squirting out of the bottom of his diaper. Boy, he makes quite a mess, doesn't he?)

And this is where the YES part of the Radical Yes comes in. Every sketch, no matter where it begins, or what happens during it, must — and we can't stress this enough — resolve in a life-affirming place, a positive place making us understand that if we did have worries about how things were going to turn out, those worries were proven to be completely unfounded at sketch's end.

Sometimes Orange Baby Man® causes damage (see "The Mallet," below) and sometimes his environment damages him, but it is always in a spirit of play and learning. It is never malicious or intentional.

Sometimes Orange Baby Man® finds himself in strange or uncomfortable situations, but never in ways that may be offensive to other ethnic groups or nationalities.

Orange Baby Man® is a presexual being with no knowledge of or experience with coitus. OBM sketches must never reference dating, romance, marriage, pregnancy, rape, fisting, etc.

Mr. Rees has often said that the main reason he dropped out of Ringling Bros. and Barnum & Bailey Clown College to create Orange Baby Man® was to empower his audiences to leave his theaters with a smile on their faces and a little piece of OBM inside each of them.

Through the joy and laughter of comedy we want the audience to learn how to embrace the Radical Yes in their own lives.

The primary way the audience can do this is by purchasing OBM-branded merchandise at the Orange Baby Man®'s Bassinet & Blanket Shoppe in the lobby of the theater. According to our best projections, merchandise plus intermission alcohol sales will comprise 50% to 70% of the average franchise's net profit, so you are advised to direct the audience toward the bar and merch kiosk early and often.

The Mallet

The only prop that remains with Orange Baby Man® throughout the entire show, and is used in more than one (but not necessarily all) of the sketches, is his oversized mallet. The mallet can be used as many things — cane or crutch, air guitar or assault rifle — but in the logic of the mythology of OBM's world, we understand that the mallet is the one toy from his oversized crib Orange Baby Man® took with him on his journey toward the Radical Yes. For OBM the mallet is his best friend, security blanket, and conscience all wrapped into one — indeed, sometimes he interacts with it as one normally would with another person.

But, of course, the mallet's most important purpose is to smash fruit and water balloons at critical junctures of the show. Ticket holders in the first five rows of any OBM theater are in the Splash Zone™ and have paid a 150%-above-average ticket price to be splattered with something.

And satisfying our audience isn't just our duty — it's our pleasure!

(IMPORTANT NOTE: AT NO POINT ARE ANY OBM EMPLOYEES OR SUBCONTRAC-TORS ALLOWED TO REFER TO THE OBM MALLET AS A "SLEDGEHAMMER." DUE TO THE SETTLEMENT OF RECENT LITIGA-TION, ANY ACCIDENTAL OR INTENTIONAL REFERENCE TO THE OBM MALLET AS A SLEDGEHAMMER WILL RESULT IN THE OFFENDER'S IMMEDIATE TERMINATION.)

The Diaper

It is highly recommended that regional and lo-cal OBMs not attempt to carry objects such as wallet, keys, cell phone, inhaler, pocket-knife, or small props inside their diapers while performing, as the risk of injury is prohibitively high.

The Bib

The bib is an essential visual element of Orange Baby Man®'s unique trademark as registered with the United States Patent and Trademark Office and for that reason must never be removed and must remain at least partially visible during all OBM performances.

Orange Baby Women

Due to the embrace of OBM by people of all genders, we have understandably had many requests for female performers to take over the role of Orange Baby Man®. Unfortunately, the minimalist nature of the costume (diaper + bib) precludes its deployment by members of that biological sex so as to comply with local decency and obscenity laws.

A packet on how to evade equal opportunity hiring laws in your locality is available from the home office on request.

— Orange Baby Man Theatre Regional Franchise Manager's Handbook (excerpt)

CHAPTER THREE

I

After carefully unpacking his carry-on and hanging his shirts, William Griffith reached into a side pocket and removed a small rectangular cloth cooler containing smoke-aged gouda, red wine salami, and octagonal rosemary-infused crackers in a Ziploc baggie semi-refrigerated by a cold pack. He hadn't eaten anything since the Delta Club in the Miami airport and he was absolutely famished.

Heading downstairs to find a knife to slice his cheese and sausage, he tried the first door he came to and found himself in the floor-to-ceiling library. William glanced at the titles on the spines and read words like BOOK, TOME, and VOLUME. When he tipped the books toward him, he found nothing but Styrofoam blocks inside the covers.

He tried a door and nearly bumped his

nose stepping through it, meeting a brick wall with a cartoonlike black outline of a running figure cut out of it.

Hilarious, he thought.

He remembered Meredith Ladipo's incredibly anal printout (a lovely young woman after his own heart) and fished it out of his blazer pocket. He found the other set of real doors in the room and stepped into what was marked on the map as a lounge.

It was a large room with low divans and a wave-curved wet bar decorated in velour candy-stripe wallpaper and clown paintings. There were hobo clowns, sombrero-wearing clowns, clowns in chef hats, cello-playing clowns, lady clowns, clowns in bathtubs, clowns in glasses, clowns with balloons, clowns *in* balloons of the hot air variety. One portrait showed the artist, comedian Red Skelton, sitting in front of a mirror, Norman Rockwell–style, carefully painting on the canvas his own mundane reflection as that of a scarf-wearing clown.

Skelton had been a huge radio and vaudeville comic who hosted a variety show bearing his name that ran on CBS throughout the 1950s and '60s.When he went off the air, he retired his act to concentrate on painting, mostly clowns, presumably inspired by his most famous character, Freddie the Freeloader, a tramp with a five o'clock greasepaint shadow. Griffith could sort of appreciate the pieces, intellectually, as outsider art, even if the imagery made his eyes bleed. He didn't doubt the paintings were worth more than a million dollars and that Walker must own the biggest collection of Skeltons in the world. Maybe it wasn't something to boast about, but he couldn't completely dismiss the accomplishment just the same.

Following the map, he at last discovered the kitchen, well-appointed with a refrigerator the size of a small room and a marble countertop brimming with smaller appliances like mixers and such. He located a wood knife block beside a pasta press, but it was empty. So was the chrome dishwasher.

He pulled open every drawer and found nothing with which he could cut red-wine salami or smoke-aged gouda, only aluminum sporks.

Every single blade had been removed from the kitchen.

William sighed loudly:

"Do they expect us to starve?"

II

"There's no Wi-Fi," William said to Meredith when she walked into the writers' room. He was the first one there, seated at the conference table.

"What?" she said, distracted. The room was basically a solarium, with floor-to-ceiling windows commanding wide views of the robin's-egg blue Caribbean. The French doors at the far end of the table listed open against the sea wind, which had blown seven or eight stray palm fronds and brown balls of dead Spanish moss into the far corners of the room. The breeze had scattered pens and yellow legal pads across the long table.

"There's no Wi-Fi. Or, at the very least, the password you gave us isn't working. There are no knives in this entire house, either, though I have to presume that fact is unrelated."

"Chizzum," Meredith said under her breath. "Was this room in this gammy state when you came in here?"

William looked around a bit. "Yes, but then I assumed we were supposed to be" — he made finger quotes — "roughing it."

"No, we are most certainly not supposed to be roughing it," Meredith said as she used her feet to push as much of the detritus as possible onto the balcony beyond the French doors. "Dustin despises roughing it, and Dave knows it. How could he let this place go so utterly butters?"

"And who is this Dave?"

"The caretaker of the estate. He's the only person who lives here year-round."

"And would he know the Wi-Fi password?"

"The what?"

"Wi-Fi doesn't work," Ruby said as she walked into the room. Meredith finished getting most of the debris off the floor and closed the French doors.

"Use the password I gave you," she said.

"I stand corrected," Ruby said, taking a seat and putting up her feet on the long table. "The Wi-Fi seems to be working fine; it's your password that doesn't work."

"No, this is the one," Meredith said, and from memory she scrawled fifteen characters' worth of nonsense onto the nearest legal pad.

"That the Wi-Fi password?" Zoe snatched the pad from Meredith as she walked into the room and sat down, pulling out an Android phone bigger than her head.

"It does not work," William said, slowly and distinctly.

"You're sure?" Meredith said. "I mean,

you tried it more than once?"

"I —"

Ollie walked into the room with a bright-orange binder in the crook of his arm and pulled her aside. "Miss . . ."

"Ladipo. But you can call me —"

"I was wondering if you could help me out with something?"

"Of course, Mr. Rees, how can I be of assistance?"

"I was wondering if you could get me access to the Wi-Fi network. I need to check my emails as I had a number of in-process business dealings involving the world-famous Sandals resort company right before I left the U.S. that I need to check the status of —"

"Of course, Mr. Rees. If you would please just use the password I gave you."

"You gave us a password?"

"Damn password doesn't work!" Zoe cried, throwing up her hands.

"I know, I tried that shit like seven times already," Dante said as he entered the room and dropped into a chair.

"Tried what?" Janet asked as she followed him in.

"Wi-Fi password," Ruby said. "We're living like animals here."

Meredith emitted a despairing little sigh.

"The password really doesn't work? Maybe Dave changed it . . . though I don't know he would have access."

"Dave Letterman?" Ollie cried out, rapidly clapping his hands. "He's going to be here?"

"No, different Dave."

"He is the caretaker," William said.

"Yes," Meredith said.

"Well, where is he?" Janet said.

"I'm not sure," Meredith said. "I can't find him anywhere."

"Dusty! What up, my brother! How's it hang —" TJ walked into the room with his arms spread wide.

But looking around and not seeing his friend anywhere, he turned to walk back out. "Screw this, I thought I was late. I'm always the last one to the writers' meeting."

"No, no, no, please, Mr. Martinez, we really should get started." Meredith Ladipo managed to steer a grumbling TJ around the table and toward a chair. Instinctively he took the one at the head of the table on the far end, beneath a large wall-mounted plasma screen.

"Sorry I'm late, everybody," Steve said when he walked into the room and took the last seat on the other end, beneath a gold-framed mirror as big as the TV on the opposite wall.

"Hey, can I ask a question?" Steve said. "Does anyone have the Wi-Fi password?"

"No," came the in-unison reply.

Steve blinked.

"Well, all righty then," he said.

III

Meredith Ladipo took a remote in hand and walked to the head of the room, on one side of the plasma screen.

"I'm not sure what's delaying Mr. Walker, but I have no doubt he will be joining us shortly. He left instructions that I was supposed to play this video regardless. It should give you all the background you require on this particular project."

She pointed the remote at the screen and pressed a button, and soon they were looking at an empty chair and a table.

After a second or two Dustin Walker walked into the frame and sat down. He wore a red track suit with luminescent white piping, the same outfit worn by his inflatable doppelgänger over the bouncy house outside. His hair remained in its iconic widow's peak, though it was thinning and grayer than they had last seen it on television. His eyes were still wide, the lenses of his glasses still Coke-bottle thick, his demeanor still the nervous slouch of a middle-class accountant lost in the bad part of town.

"What the hell is that on his head?" Janet said.

Strapped to Walker's forehead was a small square camera, its unblinking eye pointing directly at them.

"It's a GoPro," Ruby said.

"*Ssh!*" Ollie put a finger to his lips.

"Eat me, Props Boy," she said.

On the screen, Walker gazed around the room, eliciting chuckles simply for his wide-eyed expression. Walker was one of those rare lucky people who just *looked* funny; that was part of his brilliance. The anticipation of the joke was as funny as, if not funnier than, the joke itself, once it arrived. Everyone felt the corners of their mouths turning upward through no conscious effort of their own. The quiet moment, that was what Dustin Walker excelled at: he was wiping the chalkboard clean before scrawling whatever he wanted across its virgin surface. An impression, maybe? His impressions were the best. As a mimic, at not breaking character, at never breaking character, he was legendary, like an anti–*Carol Burnett Show*. What made it all the more astounding was that he was able to convincingly impersonate Cher, Nelson Mandela, or Darth Vader without ever removing his trademark magnifying-glass spectacles. The performance just made you forget the glasses were there — or, more accurately, he made you think the people he mimicked wore those glasses all the time.

"He really is the best," Zoe said.

"*Sssssshhh!*" Ollie put a finger to his lips.

"I swear to God, you shush anybody one more time and I will come over there and beat you red-assed with your own sledge-hammer."

"It's a mallet!" Ollie said, jutting his nose into the air.

"If we could, um, just sit and . . . listen to this prerecorded message, I am sure it would be, uh, important and useful to our work," Meredith murmured from her post by the door.

Suddenly Walker started slightly in his chair, a wide grin spread across his face as he appeared to notice the camera for the first time.

"Why, hello there," Walker said.

He waited.

"I said, *hello there*," he repeated, leaning forward.

"Hello there," the live audience said in unison, chuckling.

Walker cocked his head and in a sooth-ingly paternal PBS-kids-show-host lilt said, "It's so special that many mostly rich and mostly famous people came all the way out here just on my say-so. You are such good neighbors. And the fact that, as many of you have said to me personally and in public, I was such a huge influence on you is very flattering. Also, completely horrifying."

Slight, nervous laughter, except from TJ, who just sat frowning in puzzled silence.

"I bet all of you funny people started out in this business just like me — in school, right? Making a class full of kids laugh with a fake fart in the armpit or a funny drawing of the teacher or mimicking the principal's voice — remember the classic fart in the armpit? Adorable. Look, I modified it just a bit."

Walker lifted his left arm, revealing a hole cut in the armpit of his red track suit that exposed his hairy underarm. He stuck his right hand into the crook of his arm and rapidly pumped his bicep, roiling out juicy fart noises that made the entire room, including TJ, explode with laughter.

Next, Walker used only his voice and his arms to transform into a Southern tent-revival preacher, throwing out his hands and calling to heaven:

"Yes! Yes, Lord! That's when you felt it! The laughter! Do you remember the first time you heard that and knew it came from you? It was in the second grade for me, Lord, long before I knew the demon temptations of women, booze, and money. This was the rush! The most powerful thing in the world! I held the attention of an *audience*. I felt for the first time the power and the glory of the Church of Comedy! The spirit moved me, Jesus, and I was reborn in the gospel of the Chasing of the Holy Laugh. No other worldly pleasures mattered to me."

Then he became a taciturn Midwestern farmer, clutching imaginary overalls straps:

"Yessir, I chased that laugh, and I did pretty well for myself. Yessir, yes I did. Cut a few albums. People bought 'em. Did a TV show. Did a few movies, and some of 'em I was actually proud of. I made a lot of money for a lot of folks and made a lot of folks happy." He turned and spit invisibly at the earth.

"Does anyone know when dinner will be?" William Griffith said, and now everyone else *sssh*ed him.

Out of Walker's mouth came the Teutonic monotone of Werner Herzog:

"But somewhere along the way, I became

lost. As a child I had childish fantasies of being Lenny Bruce, or Richard Pryor, or George Carlin, telling truth to power. But the dreary cowardice of show business ground out the daring parts of my soul. Telling people what they don't want to hear and making them laugh while doing it did not perpetuate the lavish lifestyle to which my early successes had made me accustomed. So I stuck with safe, banal subjects. Driving. Airplane food. Relationships. Then, in cinema, I stuck with the dick jokes and the jokes about farts. It's just so much easier to get the quick laugh, the easy insult, the obvious comparison. Give them what they want instead of what they need. Before you know it, you're back in that childhood classroom. But the wonder at inspiring laughter is gone. Instead, you fear the void opening before you. You fear that today will be the day the laughter stops, and you'll have no memory of how to get it back."

"No, really, Ms. Ladipo, when is dinner?" William looked to Meredith but she was staring transfixed by the Jack Nicholson twinkle on the screen:

"This comedy thing we've got — it's a beautiful, delicate canvas. And we just keep dropping trou and squeezing out a Cleveland Steamer right on its chest, you know what I'm saying?

"Yeah, I said 'we.'

"Those of you gathered here — you're as bad as me. Those of you that aren't worse."

No one made a sound. Walker rose out of his chair, and the camera tracked him. He pointed a finger at each of them from behind the screen, speaking in the stentorian tones of a syndicated daytime TV judge:

"I accuse each and every one of you of crimes against comedy. I am qualified to pass this judgment because I inspired, by your own admission, and in my own way, each one of you. I consider you all to be my children. Except you, Janet."

"Thanks, darling," Janet said, and blew a kiss at the screen.

"Is this a bit?" Zoe asked no one in particular. "This whole thing, it's got to be a bit, right?"

Walker picked up something off the table in front of him and began widening it with both hands.

Dante Dupree squinted at the room on the screen, then turned and looked at the mirror on the opposite wall.

"He shot it in here," he said. "He shot this in this room."

Dustin broke character then and started talking in what they presumed to be his regular voice. "When you're as rich and forgotten as I am and spend a lot of time sitting around waiting for a phone to ring that never does, you have a lot of time to think. And to . . . arrange things."

He blinked, and they could see a sort of glistening in the eyes beneath the thick glasses. "I've decided that because I created you, I am going to un-create you. I am striking the cosmic gong. I am wielding the vaudeville hook of destiny and pulling you off stage. There's going to be a new dawn in Funnyland, thanks to me. I am delivering my closer. For your acts as well as mine.

"Am I rambling? I feel like maybe I'm rambling."

He put the noose he had been holding around his neck.

And pulled it tight.

He said nothing for a second or two.

He breathed in deeply. Exhaled:

"Can you blame me for wanting to stay onstage a little longer?"

"This has got to be a bit," Zoe whispered.

"I am sorry for bringing you here under false pretenses," Walker said, "but I can't be sorry that none of you are leaving this island alive.

"Including me."

The camera angle shifted abruptly, moving off his reflection in the mirror so that they were no longer looking at him but through his eyes, to the right side of the writers' room.

Together Walker and his audience ran through the French doors, bursting them open.

Meredith Ladipo started screaming.

And onscreen the camera plunged over the railing of the balcony outside and for one endless moment, they were hurtling downward to the rocks and white surf below, and now everyone was screaming.

But then the drop stopped with a blurry jolt and the camera cocked to one side, swaying with horrific gentleness.

"Oh my God," William Griffith said. "Oh my God oh my God oh my God."

"Look!" Meredith Ladipo yelled. "Outside!"

Both Steve Gordon and Dante Dupree had gotten up and crept toward the French doors. At first they couldn't see what she was pointing at.

Through tears Meredith said, "The doors were open when I came in, and the wind had scattered the pens and pads everywhere. I didn't see before but — look! Look!"

"Holy shit," Steve said, "she's right."

When he pointed, Dante saw through the

French doors, on the post of the banister near the base:

A length of black rope was tied there, the same rope as in the video.

Dante and Steve stepped forward, each looking at the other, each taking one door and opening it.

The two men stepped onto the balcony and looked down over the railing:

Sea winds batted the thinning white hair on top of a head attached to the other end of the rope.

In unison Dante and Steve crouched down and dug their fingers into the loop around the banister but failed to loosen it.

So Dante laid on his stomach and grabbed the dangling rope with one hand, then the other, and tried hauling the body up. Eventually there was enough slack that Steve could help as best he could, grabbing a different coil.

They managed to pull the body high enough that they could see the vivid sunburn atop Dustin Walker's bare, desiccated scalp, the GoPro still strapped to his forehead. The dull miasma of rot hung close now, making the two men instinctually avert their eyes and nostrils.

The jostling must have been too much for the state of the neck because the head abruptly tumbled off the noose. Dustin Walker's head and Dustin Walker's body dropped separately into the foaming surf below, without a sound.

"Shit!" Dante cried, releasing the rope. Steve did the same.

When they looked over the railing, there was no sign of the body, just waves battering cliffs.

They walked back inside the writers' room, where everyone sat stunned. Meredith sniffled and desperately kept her tears at bay with a fraying Kleenex.

Zoe said, "Is it —"

Dante cut her off:

"It's not a bit."

IV

TJ Martinez threw up his hands.

"Of course it's a bit!" he said. "It's such a bit! That was the bittiest bit in the history of bits! If you could only see your faces . . . I guarantee you, Dusty's got cameras all over this place and he is laughing his ass off at each and every one of you right now."

Zoe said, "If that was a bit, Walker owes me a new pair of panties. Jesus."

"Oh, please, like you ever wear underwear."

Zoe gave him the finger. "You will spend the rest of your life never finding out."

"How can you be sure it's a bit?" Ollie said. He was even paler than when he arrived, which didn't seem biologically possible.

"Because, Cantaloupe Head, he would pull this crap all the time on set. The man was obsessed with pranks and pranking and keeping the act going on and on and never breaking. I mean, *never* breaking. One time he took the place of a lot janitor for a week to get back at this one director. Like, planting kiddie porn in the guy's office, just the most vicious stuff. Dusty gets his rocks off messing with people."

Meredith Ladipo sat in a chair against the wall, shoulders heaving in desperate gasps. TJ went over and patted her back. "There, there, kid, we're supposed to believe you're not in on it, huh?"

Meredith shook her head vigorously. "I'm not! I'm not in on it! I don't even know what it is! And even if I did know it, I would most definitely *not* want to be either in or on it!"

"Okay, okay, it's all right. So the joke's on you, too. But all of you, calm down, because there is absolutely, positively no doubt in my mind: this *is* a joke."

"TJ's right — well, about this one thing," Steve said. He had dropped down in a chair after coming back in from the balcony and was breathing heavily. "Dusty loved these elaborate put-ons. One week the writers really pissed him off, so he had Kinko's print out, like, thousands of copies of this script he hated and paid PAs under the table to come in to the office over the weekend and ball up each page individually and throw them into the writers' room. By Monday you couldn't even open the door because the room was full of these balled-up scripts. I mean, he had that place filled to the ceiling. The producers threatened to fire his ass, and they did fire the PAs, but he thought it was the funniest thing he'd ever seen."

TJ scowled. "How would you know, man? I didn't see you there."

Steve rolled his eyes. "C'mon, TJ, it's not funny. It wasn't funny before, and it sure isn't funny now."

"What?"

"You know exactly who I am!"

TJ tapped his chin. "But then how do you explain this feeling like I don't?"

"I don't know. Because you're a titanic asshole?"

TJ shook his head. "That's just a lucky guess."

Dante paced the room. "I don't care what you say. And I don't care what he says. That thing smelled like a dead body. That thing looked like a dead body. That was no god-damn bit."

TJ sighed at Dante's naïveté and looked to Ruby. "There's no way he could have uploaded that thing after he was dead, is there?"

Ruby did a double take. "What, you think just because I'm under the age of thirty I'm your IT department?"

"No. Because you're Asian."

"Oh, that's so much less offensive."

"What is it with you people being all sensitive all the time?"

"You people? Asians?"

"No, people under thirty."

She just looked at him. "I am going to stop talking to you now, because you make me sad." She turned away to Meredith Ladipo and reached for the remote. "Mind?"

Meredith, still glassy-eyed from shock, shook her head. Ruby took the remote off the table and pointed it at the screen, which still bobbed with the hanged man's view of the surf lashing the rocks at the bottom of the cliff.

She exited out of playback and went to the desktop of whatever computer controlled the screen, which displayed a single icon.

"I knew you could do it," TJ said.

"It's still racist to assume I could," Ruby said.

She pointed at the icon.

"Okay, so . . ." She sighed. "Looks like the whole hard drive has been wiped except for this GoPro file. If he saved it to the computer as a new document before he started, the camera would have kept filming to that file until its charge ran out. Then it would be the only file on here for Meredith to play back. So it is actually quite possible that an actual live person was not needed to upload the file — it was always here to begin with."

TJ barked a laugh. "See? Classic Dusty prank planning!"

William Griffith said, "You just said it was proof it was a prank if it *couldn't* be uploaded by a dead person."

"True," TJ said, pointing at him, "but keep in mind I don't have any idea what I'm talking about."

"Wait! Wait! Wait!" Ollie stood up, waving his arms.

When everyone was looking at him he

blurted out:

"Are we *not* doing Dusty's comedy special? Is he not coming? What were we all brought here for, then? We all have lives! Important lives! More important than regular people's!"

Everyone looked away from him without responding.

On the screen, Ruby called up the statistics window for the GoPro file. "This thing says it was taped a week ago today."

"A week?" William Griffith said. He asked Meredith, "A *week*? When's the last time you spoke to Mr. Walker? Directly?"

"It's . . . it's been longer than a week," Meredith said. "I told you, I've been spending most of my time in L.A."

"You came here without having spoken to anyone here for over a week? What's wrong with you, woman?"

"I've been talking to Dave every day."

"Fuck's Dave?" Dante said.

"Dave, the caretaker. He lives here year-round. But he's not here now."

"Are you sure?" Janet asked.

"I searched this place top to bottom," Meredith said through clenched teeth. "We nine are the only people on the island."

"Are you *sure*?" Zoe said.

"Dave's not here, man!" Meredith yelled,

98

hands balling into fists.

There was silence, briefly, after her outburst.

"Now *that's* a bit," TJ said.

V

Dante Dupree knew when he had reached the limits of his sobriety, which was as solid as the layer of sugar atop crème brûlée.

"I need a drink," he said.

Janet said, "That's the smartest thing anyone's said all day."

They went across the hall to the Red Skelton Memorial Clown Lounge, which, while creepy, had the advantage of being fully stocked with booze.

William Griffith filled a highball with Jameson and began talking with his arms:

"This is nonsense, isn't it? Complete utter nonsense! Some of us rearranged tour dates for this. Shooting schedules. You can't just shift those things around like you're parking cars."

He turned to Meredith, who was slumped in one of the leatherbacked bar chairs like all the bones had been removed from her body, and stuck a finger in her face:

"If I have lost a dime of income, and I mean a single dime, as a result of this idiot stunt, I am going to sue your employer, his production company, and probably you, too."

Meredith sat up. "Me? Why me?"

"When you sue, you sue everybody. That's the first rule of suing."

Dante said, "Jesus, leave her alone, Billy. She don't know shit."

"According to who? According to her?" Griffith downed the highball, then grabbed the bottle for a second pour. "And you believe her? After all this? I don't trust anyone responsible for this cockamamie operation."

He turned back to Meredith. "I want a boat back to the mainland. Or the main island, whatever you call it. I want you to call it in immediately."

"I can't," Meredith said wearily. "I have no way of calling if I can't get on to the network, and as you all so graciously keep reminding me, the password I have doesn't work. Captain Harry usually comes out with the day's supplies every morning by ten. That's the best I can offer you, I'm sorry."

"There's no landline?" Zoe said.

"Not that I'm aware of, no."

"Thank you very much, twenty-first century," Janet said to no one in particular.

"He said we all committed crimes against

comedy." Ollie shook his head in disbelief. "Us. Criminals! What kind of criminals? All I ever wanted to do was make people laugh."

Ruby said, "Yeah? When are you gonna get around to doing that?"

Ollie stuck his tongue out at her.

TJ Martinez said, "You guys all need to chill. Dusty's gonna pop out of a palmetto bush or whatever as soon as he gets bored watching us."

"You . . . think he's watching us?" Ollie paled.

"Don't you get it? This is it. This is the special he invited us here to work on. This is his big comeback."

"Another reason to sue!" William cried.

"Nobody's suing anybody, Billy the Contractor," TJ said. "*She* made us sign those nondisclosure agreements, and they all had the usual indemnity clause."

"My God, you're right!" William slammed down his glass. "I wonder if I can swim back?"

"Oh, please, try," Ruby deadpanned. "I beg of you."

"We should just stay put," TJ said. "I'm sure he's doing this to get back in my good graces."

Zoe laughed, hard and loud, making TJ look at her. "Why exactly would he want to do that, TJ? Maybe you forgot: you don't have a TV show anymore. You've been sent out to sea on the show business equivalent of an ice floe."

TJ chuckled. "You keep thinking that all you want, sweetheart. My word has a lot of pull with the network."

Steve said, "Really? Is that why your ratings fell below that infomercial for Abs Blaster?"

"And why they hustled your ass out the door faster than a Jehovah's Witness with a serious case of gas?" Dante said.

TJ barked out a laugh. "Room full of comics turns into a shark tank with one sniff of blood in the water. Sad. Sad and predictable. Believe me, I'd rather have one week of my career than all of yours combined."

"You can have your career, Tomás Javier," William said, enunciating each syllable of Martinez's name and listing in his bar chair. While no one had been paying him any mind he had poured his third and fourth highball. "Do you know that this man never had a live studio audience? Never, not one, in over a decade. Every single reaction you heard was from a laugh track. A laugh track! Can you imagine? Can you imagine how insecure you have to be to need finely adjusted canned laughter for every lame monologue joke, every piece of celebrity puffery, every —"

"I'm not going to apologize to you or anyone else for being a perfectionist." TJ jutted out his jaw.

"Please, it was the worst kept secret in comedy," Ruby said. "Since no one watching your show would know real comedy if it slithered out of their buttholes and bit their dicks off, I doubt it mattered all that much."

"Mr. Walker may be an unforgivable garbage person for trapping us here under false pretenses," William slurred, "but he got one thing right: you are a disgrace to our profession, Tomás Javier."

"Fake-ass cracker, please!" Dante said.

William blinked his watery eyes in Dante's direction. "I am sorry, were you referring to me?"

"You can't talk shit about shit," Dante said. "You're all NASCAR, pork rinds, and homophobia onstage, but once the camera goes off you're *Downton* fucking *Abbey.*"

William blinked again, looking genuinely confused. "And?"

"And if Dustin called us all fakers, you are, without a doubt, the fakest faker in the room," Zoe said.

"That is categorically unfair," William said. "For one thing, despite your use of the epithet 'cracker,' Mr. Dupree, and all your thuggish street affect, your diction is as good as Mr. Livian's, whose class I took at Juilliard."

"Oh, so now I'm not black enough, is that it, Billy? C'mon, you're gonna have to do better than that. I've been hearing that shit since I was eight years old."

"Billy the Contractor is no more or less a put-on than any of your acts. I adopted his persona as a larf for a reunion of the Purple Crayon of Yale; a video of my performance made the rounds among attendees on Facebook. It went viral, much to my very pleasant surprise, among the very" — he made air quotes — "folk I was mimicking. There's nothing wrong with that. Nothing wrong at all. Often the lines blur between satire and its subject —"

"Man, you're gonna make me throw up," Dante said. "You're making fun of those people, and making them pay you for it!"

"No! No, that's not true. I have learned to embrace them as they have embraced me. The more time I spend with them, the more I have learned to adopt — no, love — their ways."

Steve rolled his eyes. "Jesus Christ, Griffith, they're trailer park rednecks, not a lost tribe of the Amazon."

"True, but they have similar bathing habits," William said.

"Well, look what I have here," Janet said with a grin, producing a Bud Light tallboy from the minifridge behind the bar. It was stamped with an image of Griffith in full Billy the Contractor drag, giving would-be binge drinkers a thumbs-up and a FIX 'ER UP. "I'm sure you wouldn't mind setting aside that fancy brown to partake of a drink of the people, would you?"

William beckoned her to him. "Please, I'd be honored. Give it here." Janet popped open the tab with a fizz and a hiss and handed him the can.

"To the great American white working class," he said as he raised the tallboy high. "May their Percocet be plentiful and relatively uncut."

William drank it in a mostly single gulp, pausing halfway through to grimace. When he was done, he gave a satisfied gasp and threw the can into the nearby fireplace pit, which it bounced out of instantly.

"Well?" Zoe said.

"It tastes like pisswater," William said, "by which I mean it tastes like what one pisses out after real beer is drunk — an IPA or a true Belgian ale — but I can see why a certain class of drinkers nnggllk gllllrk gaaaaaaaa."

Blood gurgled between his lips as he spoke. He spit it all over Zoe, the nearest person, and she started screaming.

William staggered toward her, reaching out as if she was a buoy, but Zoe instinctually shoved him backward, into Dante Dupree. He managed to turn Griffith around just as red spray exploded out of his mouth, cascading down his shirt and soaking his blazer. Dante yelled and quickly pushed William away.

The once and forevermore Billy the Contractor tripped on the edge of the carpet and crashed face-first to the floor.

He did not get up again.

VI

No one moved, or breathed, for ten full seconds.

Steve bent down and took William's pulse at the neck.

Steve stood again.

"He's just sleeping," he said.

"Really?" Ollie said.

"No, he's clearly dead, fuckwit!"

Ollie pouted. "No need for names."

TJ pointed at Janet. "You gave him the beer!"

She held up her hands. "And you saw me open it in front of him! You all did! I couldn't do anything to it!" She pointed at the highball sitting on the marble bar. "How do you know the whiskey wasn't poisoned?"

Dante, who had been holding a highball of his own, dropped the glass on the floor with a curse.

Out of nowhere, Zoe looked at Meredith and started screaming.

Meredith started screaming, too, and tried to run away, but Zoe tackled her and both of them crashed to the floor.

"You bitch you fucking bitch if you have anything to do with this I will claw your fucking eyes out!" Zoe grabbed the other woman's head and screamed in her face while Meredith tried to slap her hands away.

Dante managed to pull Zoe off Meredith. "Whoa, whoa, that's enough now, girl. That ain't helping nothing!"

Meredith, on her ass, scootched over to lean against the nearest wall, breathing in huge gulps of air:

"I swear, *I swear,* on my mother, I am in the jammy doxy as much as any of you. I've only had this job a couple of months! Dustin said — Dustin said he'd help me become a standup!" She burst into tears.

"Yeah, and I'm sure he helped you become

107

a lie-down too," Zoe said, back on her feet and putting her hair back in order. "There's something not right about this chick! I mean, jammy doxy? Who says that? I did a semester abroad in London and I'm pretty sure that's not a thing."

"Yeah?" Meredith sniffled. "You spend a lot of time in council estates with your sorority sisters?"

"What's that supposed to mean? Are you saying a white person can't fully appreciate the black experience?"

"Well — yeah!"

"Okay, that's probably true!" Zoe pushed her bra strap back under her blouse.

"Hey! People!" Janet pointed at William's body. "Dead guy here! Focus, huh? What do we want to do with him?"

TJ had just bent down to take William's pulse for himself. He rose to his full height and fell quiet.

"I . . . I don't have any experience with this," Steve said.

"Don't worry, the rest of us are undertakers in our day jobs," Ruby deadpanned.

Dante said, "Maybe we should, I don't know, roll him up in the carpet? He's ruined it anyway. And we'll put him in the writers' room. C'mon, who's going to give me a hand?"

"I can help," Steve said.

"Me, too," TJ said.

Together, the three men rolled the carpet around the body and lifted it out of the room.

VII

"Can we be sure it was *really* murder?" Ollie said when the men were gone.

Zoe's eyes nearly popped out of her head. "As opposed to what, man? Maybe it was a kumquat?"

"No, I mean — just hear me out — what if nobody poisoned anything, and Mr. Griffith was really sick, like he was going to die anyway? And he agreed with Mr. Walker to help him out with this mean trick he's playing on us, his big hidden-camera comeback special, and so he poisoned his drink himself? I mean, so he wouldn't go through a long decline and all the pain and suffering he'd put his family through. So he killed himself."

Ruby said, "That's no more insane than this big-shot bringing us here to kill us because he thought our acts sucked."

"No," Janet said, "it's just 98.2 percent as insane."

Zoe turned toward Meredith. "What

109

about a boat? Is there a boat?"

Meredith turned away. "I'm not talking to you."

"You'd hope if there was a boat Meredith would've mentioned it by now," Ruby said.

"We have to tell the police," Ollie said.

"With what, smoke signals?" Janet said. "Semaphore? Flashing mirrors?"

"We have to do *something,*" Ollie said. "At least I'm *trying* to think of a solution!"

They all froze when someone cried out down the hall. Before they could look at one another they heard:

"Everyone! Come here! Now!"

VIII

It was Steve Gordon's voice. They walked quickly to the front gallery, where he stood, hands on hips, in front of the wall of head-shots.

"Now, this is exactly the kind of thing we just can't do," Steve said.

"What?" Meredith said.

"Whoever did it, own up right now, and we can forgive it. As long as it doesn't happen again."

"What are you babbling about, Nobody?" TJ asked.

"Look," Steve said, pointing at the photo

wall. "A picture's missing. William's picture is gone."

They all looked: so it was.

"One of you took it," Steve said. "Fess up, now!"

"How do we know you didn't take it?" Ollie said.

"I *know* I didn't take it. TJ and Dante and I were in the writers' room laying him — William — down and I just noticed it was gone when I stepped out here for a smoke. That means it was one of you."

"Or there's someone else on the island," TJ said.

"There *isn't,*" Meredith insisted.

"You really want us to believe that," Zoe said.

"Because it's bloody well true."

Steve said, "So . . . no one's admitting it, huh?"

"I can't confess to something I didn't do," Ollie said. "That would be unethical."

"I didn't take it, either," Ruby said.

Janet said, "We were all in the same room together, staring at each other. There's no way any of *us* could have taken it. It must have been one of you three."

"But Steve got here before TJ or me," Dante said.

"Besides, why would I want his stupid

photo?" TJ said. "Why would anyone?"

"Then we need to search the island," Steve said, "and make absolutely sure we're the only ones here. If we are . . ."

"If we are what?"

"One of us must be helping Dusty try to kill us all," he said.

IX

Everyone returned to the clown lounge.

"We should split up and search the place as quickly as we can," Steve said. "No one should go alone, but we should have as many groups as possible, so if there *is* someone hiding on the island, he can't get away from one group of searchers without running into another."

Ruby raised her hand:

"Point of order: why are we taking orders from the one guy here I've never heard of?"

TJ pointed at her but looked at Steve:

"See? It's not just me."

Ruby continued, "I mean, granted, you're white and male and no gay man would be caught dead in that beard, but still, that doesn't automatically make you our cis Caucasian overseer, okay?"

Steve sighed. "I'm just making a sugges-tion."

112

"A highly privileged suggestion," Ruby said.

"If anyone thinks they have a better plan, for Christ's sake don't keep it to yourself."

"The plan is fine," Dante said with no small irritation.

Ruby made a scoffing little laugh under her breath. "Of course you'd say that."

Dante's voice rose several octaves. "Bitch, you call me an Uncle Tom to my face and I swear to God you're gonna find out the primary difference between real life and the internet is my foot up your ass."

Ruby backed up six feet. "I refuse to be on the same team as this aggro bro."

"And I do not want to be on Social Justice Warrior Woman's team," Dante said. "That's for damn sure."

"Maybe we can draw straws for teams?" Ollie said.

"Absolutely not," Ruby said. "Relying on chance robs individuals of freedom of choice."

"I'll go with Dupree," TJ said without prompting.

Dante looked at him, surprised.

TJ added, "If that's cool."

Dante shrugged. "Sure, it's cool, man. It's cool."

"I'll go with Steve," Zoe said, and Steve

was equally surprised.

"Okay," he said. "Sounds good."

Janet motioned for Ruby to come over. "Why don't you go with me, honey. I don't understand any of your buzzwords so you won't be able to piss me off."

"Actually, Janet, I'd be honored," Ruby deadpanned.

"You don't sound like you'd be honored."

"That's just my voice. Think of it as a speech impediment."

That left Meredith and Oliver. They looked at each other.

"I, uh, don't want to be paired up with her," Ollie said. "She scares me."

Before Meredith could say anything, Ruby said, "Don't worry about it. Meredith, you can come with us."

Meredith walked over, and Ruby took her by the hands, looked into her eyes, and said, "You are clearly the biggest single victim in all of this. I can tell. So I will believe whatever you say."

Meredith blinked. "I'm sorry . . . what?"

Ollie looked around and screeched like a cartoon housewife surprised by a mouse. "But now I'm by myself!" He couldn't believe it. The choice was between him and a probable murder accomplice but he was *still* picked last. This was why he wanted to draw straws in the first place.

"You can come with me and Zoe," Steve said. "Three search parties should be fine. It's not that big of an island."

"You just have to promise not to say anything," Zoe said.

Ollie sealed his lips with his fingers and threw away the imaginary key.

"Or mime," Zoe said.

X

Thinking it might not be wise to explore the island unarmed, Dante Dupree went into the kitchen to find some weapons.

He discovered an empty knife block on the marble counter. He found a couple Billy the Contractor–branded tallboy cans in the fridge but no bottles. The silverware drawer was filled with cheap aluminum sporks. Nothing with a blade on it.

When he returned to the lounge and reported this, Steve said, "Yeah, all the bottles behind the bar are plastic, too. Not to mention barely full. And Griffith finished off the Jameson. We won't be able to throw much of a party."

Dante threw up his hands. "C'mon, there aren't even any golf clubs? What rich old white guy doesn't have at least one bag of clubs?"

"One who plans to kill us all from beyond the grave and doesn't want to leave behind anything we could use to defend ourselves with?" Ruby said. "There's not even a poker in the fireplace. He's stacked everything in his favor before the word *go*. In that sense, he's the oldest, whitest old white man who ever lived."

"What's that funny thing in your hands?" Ollie said.

Ruby lifted what looked to be some kind of misshapen bronze trophy. "Funny is the word. I thought maybe I could swing this thing, but it's just too heavy and awkward."

"Is that . . . a smiling brain?" Zoe said.

"Yeah." Ruby read the plaque at the bottom: "With gratitude from the Dorothy Walker Clear-Mind Clinic. Five healing years, 2011–2016."

"Yeah, he's proven himself to be a real humanitarian," Janet said.

Ruby placed the trophy on the bar top. "I'm just as likely to pull a muscle swinging this thing as hurting anybody else. It'd be like trying to kill somebody with a bowling ball. I'm leaving it behind."

"Great," Dante said. "If we find anyone we'll have to really lay into their self-esteem."

"Super-nasty snaps," TJ said. "About his mom."

"Colorful language that would be bleeped out on basic cable," Zoe said.

"Cutting insights into human nature," Ruby deadpanned.

"I have some very, *very* naughty limericks memorized," Steve said.

"They Died with Their Jokes On," Janet said.

Meredith Ladipo didn't say anything. She just looked at the floor like she was going to be sick.

MONDAY IS SLAIN

(Cheers, applause)

How we doing how we doing *how we doing?*

Man, look at my audience. Look at my audience. What did I ever do to deserve such a beautiful audience? I love ya. I love ya. I really do. Mmm-wah.

Boy, you seem happy tonight! You're rarin' to go! I think I know why you're so excited. Yeah, I think I do.

Monday is over, it's done, you slew it, it's slain. You know that statistically speaking, right now is the longest it will be all week before it's Monday again?

(Laughter, cheers, applause)

I'm not making that up. Yeah. That's science.

Some stuff happened today and over the weekend you might not know about. Any tennis fans here? Show of hands so I can see your cute little wristbands? Yeah, there you are, I see you. You catch the U.S. Open on Saturday? Yeah. Yeah! History was made. Venus Williams defeated her sister Serena to win the U.S. Open. Yeah. It made history two ways. For one thing, it was the first Grand Slam title match ever pitting one sister against another. Uh-huh. I mean ever.

(Applause, cheers)

Yeah. For another, it's gonna lead to the worst Williams family Thanksgiving ever.

"Serena, can you pass the mashed potatoes please?"

"Can I pass what? Can I pass? I'll show you a pass, Venus! I'm serving a yam to your end of the table with a drumstick! Watch me! See if I don't! Rematch! Right now!"

(Laughter)

I want to be anywhere else but the Williams house for Turkey Day, you know what I'm saying?

What else, what else?

Unemployment's ticked up to 4.9 percent: 4.9 percent, that's not good, people, no, it's the opposite of good. The Bush administration swears we are not in a recession, no, no. Definitely not. Nope. The fact that Laura put the Lincoln Bedroom set up on eBay, no, that's just a coincidence:

"Slightly used. Previous owner was known to share with intern and cigar, dry-clean thoroughly after purchase."

(Laughter)

Things have gotten so rough, I read that in Bisbee, North Dakota — have you seen this? Jobs are so scarce in Bisbee, the *mayor* is moving out of town. They've lost all their doctors, all their lawyers, all their plumbers, the priest got recalled by the diocese, and — get this — they closed their police station. Yeah.

In unrelated news, O.J. says he's moving there to find the real killers. Yeah.

(Wild laughter, applause)

Representative Gary Condit says he hasn't decided whether or not he's going to run for reelection here in California, but he is seriously looking at relocating to Bisbee. Yeah. That's his kind of constituency:

Missing.

(Laughter, groans)

What? Check your watches. I waited a whole minute into the monologue before making a Gary Condit joke. C'mon. That's personal growth, people. That's self-restraint.

This week in what my writers like to call "TJ's Condit Obsession," we had a couple interesting developments. Did you see his daughter, Candee, on *Larry King*? Candee said this whole Chandra Levy scandal has been really tough on her dad. Yeah.

She said, "I don't know if he'll ever get the twinkle in his eye back."

To which all the interns in Washington, D.C., said, *"Whew!"*

(Laughter)

Yeah, I also saw that Buy-Costumes.com, yes, Buy-Costumes.com, they reported that their most popular Halloween costume request so far this year has been for Representative Condit.

(Laughter)

No, it's true! They're rushing those right into production. So if he ever wants to flee the country, you know, now he's got the perfect date. October 31. Halloween. No one will be able to tell one vacantly grinning blond guy from another that day. Yeah. I mean, he kind of looks like he's wearing a mask of himself anyway, right?

(Laughter)

Buy-Costumes also said they got a lot of requests for Chandra Levy costumes, too, but —

(Groans)

I know, right, some people? No class. No class at all for Halloween. But good for Buy-Costumes.com, they stood firm. They said, no, we are not going to produce those Chandra Levy outfits. No sir. No way. Uh-uh.

The makers of sexy nun and slutty grandma costumes have our dignity to think of! Yes, sir!

(Wild laughter, applause)

You know who's not worried about unemployment? My old pal, funnyman Dustin Walker.

(Cheers, applause)

Yeah, he's great. And I read in the trades, out

here in La-La Land, that he just inked a deal with Miramax to write and direct a movie about his life. Yeah, it's autobiographical. A real serious flick about how hard it is to be a rich, famous comedian, doing all those *Help! I Married a Cat* movies, I guess, because that's mostly what he's been up to these days.

But I've got some free advice for Dusty — Dusty, if you're watching? Dusty's had a real tough time breaking free of those cat movies, you know. His other flicks haven't been so successful.

So I'm just going to suggest a title for Dusty's autobiographical movie:

Pussywhipped.

(Deafening applause, thunderous laughter)

You like that? You like that?

Well we've got a real 100 percent USDA-approved Grade-A show for you tonight. Larry David is here! Yes, Larry David, here to talk about the new season of *Curb Your Enthusiasm.* Uh-huh. Funny guy.

Our musical guests are a great up-and-coming band from Detroit, a husband-and-wife duo, the White Stripes, they're terrific. The White Stripes, everybody!

And if we're lucky, something will happen soon so I can retire all these Gary Condit jokes! Help me! Help me! I have a problem!

(Laughter, applause, fade out)

— 2nite with TJ Martinez
Taped in Burbank, CA
Monday, September 10, 2001

CHAPTER FOUR

I

Ruby Ng and Janet Kahn volunteered to explore the main house, with Meredith Ladipo leading the way so she could steer them clear of doors that opened to face walls and staircases that rose up, turned a corner, and abruptly stopped, along with all the other allegedly hilarious architectural elements added by Dustin Walker when he had the mansion built.

They started with the ground floor. Each of the three women took turns opening side closets and pantries solo while the other two stood facing the doorway. They made almost no sound, and so everywhere they went they could hear the caw of a thrush in the banana tree just outside. It kept crying out in a rhythmic bleat for a companion to come or for enemies to stay away. No one knew which.

"We're not going to find anyone," Meredith said as they closed the door to the walk-in pantry in the kitchen. "I am quite certain no one has been here in a week. You saw the state of the writers' room. The grass is too tall. It's just . . ." She sighed and wiped her eyes. "I don't know why Dustin would do this. He seemed perfectly happy the last time I saw him. I can't imagine where any of this is coming from."

"I'm sure Dusty had his demons, like we all do," Janet said. "Happy, contented people don't get into this business."

"Oh, I don't know," Meredith said. "I consider myself to be a pretty happy, contented person." They were walking out of the kitchen and into the central hallway with the grand mahogany staircase leading up to the belvedere level. "I've wanted to be a comedian since I was a kid. I used to memorize my dad's Cosby CDs."

"Interesting choice of role models," Ruby said.

"I mean, obviously when I was a kid, I didn't know anything about that . . . other stuff."

"Some of us did," Janet said. "Going back to the seventies."

"Really?" Ruby said. "Did he ever . . ."

"Me? No. He knew my reputation. I

would've bitten off his Jell-O pop at the stick." Janet shrugged. "Of course, if he had doped up my Sanka, how would I know?"

Ruby scowled at her. "And you never said anything? Perpetuate rape culture much?"

"Put down the hot irons, Torquemada. It's not like I'm proud of it or anything. And if I had known it was *that* many broads he gave extra-extra-extra-decaffeinated to, I'd like to think I wouldn't have kept my mouth shut. But he was a big deal. Not somebody smart to cross."

"That's *why* you cross him," Ruby said.

"Hey! Internet activist! Or, for short, in-activist! I didn't have a keyboard to hide behind in the seventies and eighties! And you know, showbiz people didn't talk about other showbiz people's dirty business in those days. It was us against the press and the gossip columnists. Or, in your case, pod-casters."

"This is why what I do is important. You can't leave this bad behavior alone, that's where it thrives. I mean, you should hear the shit I've heard about TJ Martinez."

"I'd rather just leave it alone, if it's all the same to you, honey. I'm not from the social media generation. I don't need to know everything about everybody. If it weren't for repression, none of us would have jobs."

"Truth *is* the job. Dustin Walker may be a douchebag but he was right about that one thing."

"You're exhausting to talk to, anyone ever tell you that?"

"More or less constantly."

Janet turned away from Ruby and walked into the fully enclosed rear gallery facing the pool, which had been converted into a long arcade or playroom, filled with obscure '80s video games, air hockey, a bank of skee-ball lanes covering an entire section of wall, and, of all things, a ball pit as big as a medium-sized backyard pool.

Ruby turned earnestly to Meredith Ladipo as they entered the room and took her by the hands.

"Dustin's gone," she said into Meredith's eyes. "He can't hurt you anymore."

Meredith frowned. "I don't get your meaning."

"You can tell us whatever you want. This is a safe space."

"Are you daft? There might be a murderer on the loose!"

"Well . . . okay, technically — you're right — this is not a safe space *literally*. But wherever Janet and I are is a safe space psychologically, spiritually, for anything you want to say. We won't judge. We just want you to share your truth."

"I'm sorry, Ms. Ng, I'm just not following. I'm British. We don't talk like this. Or feel like this. Or talk about our feelings."

"I am very sex-positive. No shaming. You can tell us if . . ." Ruby's voice dropped to a whisper. "Dustin tried something. That you were not . . . into."

Meredith pulled her hands away. "No! No. Definitely not. Dustin was always a perfect gentleman."

"So your boning was consensual," Janet said.

"No! There was no boning! Do you find that so hard to believe?"

"Yes," Ruby said.

"I'm gonna have to go with yes," Janet said.

"Why, because you don't believe a man like Dustin Walker could, out of the goodness of his heart, take in a protégée and give her tips and pointers, in exchange for honest employment as a personal assistant without, you know, wanting to get down her knickers?"

"No, I do not."

"Me neither," Ruby said.

"Well, that's the way it was. So sorry to disappoint."

"Geez, no wonder he killed himself," Janet

muttered, and Meredith gasped.

Ruby looked at her, shocked. "Blame the victim much?"

"Say much, much?" Janet shot back. "Answer: Yes. Much."

Ruby turned back to Meredith. "What were the kind of things he advised you on?"

"Oh, all sorts of things. Like joke construction, how to read a crowd, how to develop a closer, how to shut down a heckler . . ."

"Give us an example," Janet said.

"Okay, well, pretend I'm on stage, and you're a drunk nibber in the audience."

Ruby made a show of adjusting the phantom penis inside her sweatpants. She put her hands to her mouth:

"Take your top off, beeyotch!"

Meredith jumped into her face, pointed and screamed, *"Shut your fucking cunt hole you dumb motherfucking piece of fucking shit!"*

Then she giggled a bit.

Janet and Ruby looked at her.

"You sure you two weren't boning?" Janet said.

II

"I'm sorry TJ Martinez is such an incredible asshole," Zoe Schwartz said out of

130

nowhere as she, Steve, and Ollie made their way to the cabana on the other side of the grounds.

"Me, too. I just wish *he* was sorrier," Steve said.

"I bet he will be. Sooner rather than later," Zoe said. "But I don't know what his problem is. I saw what he said to you on the boat on the way over. That was some straight-up nonsense. *I* remember you from *What Just Happened?* They'd run two episodes back-to-back every day when I got home from school. You were amazingly funny. You used to be huge!"

"I am huge; the pictures just got not-huge," Steve said.

"Like, really not-huge in your case. Postage stamp size. No offense."

"None taken. They're more like electron microscope size."

"What happened? If you don't mind me asking."

"I don't mind." Fleetingly, very fleetingly, it occurred to him to tell her the truth, even just for the hell of it, but he'd been avoiding that for so long it was an easy impulse to ignore.

He turned back to the large pink bouncy house they had discovered on the grounds. The minute they approached it, Ollie had emitted a screech not unlike an anime schoolgirl and ran inside. Through its mesh walls Steve could see the prop comic's egg-shaped bulk bouncing in a blur with a series of squeals and yelps.

"Who inflates a bouncy house at a murder scene?" Steve asked.

"The same sort of person who'd murder a bunch of comics for being hacks, I guess," Zoe said.

"Come on, you're no hack. I saw your Comedy Central thirty. Pretty hilarious stuff. You've got great chops."

"Thanks, Gordo. That means a lot coming from you."

"And didn't I read you got a show on FX, with Apatow producing? That's amazing."

"Yeah." Zoe chuckled. "It's literally unbelievable. Especially to me. You still read the trades, huh?"

"Technically, I am still in the industry. If only in a professorial capacity."

"Improv teacher — what's that like?"

"It's better than working for a living. I tried that, too, didn't like it. It's not the same as stand-up, though. I mean, improv people . . . They're not like us. They're so . . ."

"Normal."

"Ugh, right? Well-adjusted."

132

"They work together well in groups."

"No sabotage or competition bullshit."

She mimed a two-handed burrito. "Whoa, this burrito is weird." Next she rotated an imaginary steering wheel. "Hey look, I'm driving!"

"Yeah, it's just not my scene. I could do it on TV because I was young and hey, it was TV, but man . . . I'd give it all up to get back on stage with a mic in my hand."

"So why don't you?"

Time to change the subject, Steve thought. "Should you be worrying about this right now, considering where you are and what's happening to you?"

Zoe took a deep breath. "You don't think I wouldn't mind thinking about something else? And by 'else,' I mean my career. I know I look like a strong female protagonist on the outside, but on the inside I'm a churning jumbled washing machine of insecurities, constantly in spin."

"You want to make sure you don't get any of my loser juice on you?"

"I don't want . . . any of your juice . . . anywhere near me."

"Sorry. Bad analogy."

"Indeed. But please continue."

Steve watched Ollie bounce up and down, up and down for a bit.

Then he said:

"The question every noob asks, all my students ask is, how do I break in? How do I get my shot? When you're just starting out, you don't know why you were put on this Earth and it must be because you're special. That all of history is leading up to your birth, you just need to go out there and prove it. And so you spend all your energy and all your brainpower trying to break in, and they never tell you . . . that's the easy part."

"What's the hard part?"

"*Staying* in." Steve looked at her. "That's so much harder. It's like breaking in times a million."

Zoe nodded, mulling over his words. He felt good for telling her *a* truth, even if it wasn't *his* truth; it wasn't like he was actually lying or anything. Hopefully, she wouldn't ask him to elaborate.

"You're really not easing my general anxiety level," Zoe said.

"Want a yes-man? Get a dog."

She watched Ollie bounce, then turned to Steve and said, "I can't believe I'm going to say this to somebody who didn't come out of my own womb." Then she marched toward the bouncy castle yelling, "Ollie! I think you've had enough! Don't make me come in there and get you!"

Ollie bounded toward the exit flap and half stepped, half fell out of the castle, waving his cell phone. "I was seeing if I could get a signal higher up!" he gasped. "I thought I maybe got a signal for a second but I think maybe I just jostled the phone enough to get a false reading!"

He weaved toward them the same way a dragonfly flies, not taking anything resembling a linear route, but then stopped, legs swaying.

"I think . . . I think I need to sit down for a minute you guys! You go on ahead!"

He staggered back toward the main house.

III

Dante Dupree and TJ Martinez walked to the stairs leading down to the dock.

"Hey," TJ said, looking around. "Hey, man."

Dante stopped. "Dude, I'm right here. Say what you got to say."

TJ waited until Zoe, Steve, and Ollie disappeared behind a row of palms toward the pink bouncy house and said, "I'm thinking you and me, we should form an alliance."

"An alliance?"

"Yeah, an alliance."

"Man, you've seen too much *Survivor*." Dante started walking again.

TJ grabbed him by the arm. "Wait, wait, just hear me through. We're not like these other fools."

"Who *we* — you and me *we*?"

"Yeah, man, we're both from the streets. We need to watch each other's backs so we make it out of here alive while the rest of them get picked off like fluffy deer, man. Like a big, fat, dumb, rich, petting-zoo deer who gets released back into the wild and gets his throat ripped out by a squirrel."

"But not us, because we're from the hood."

"Yeah, man, exactly, I'm from the Pork and Beans projects down in M-I-A, and I saw your act, I know you're, what, from the Gowanus Towers in Brooklyn, am I right about that?"

"You seen my act?"

"Yeah, man, it was funny shit."

Dante crossed his arms. "When'd you see my act?"

TJ blinked. "I mean, who hasn't seen your act, man? You're known as the hardest-working road comic for a reason. When I had you on my show —"

"You never had me on your show."

"I didn't?"

136

"No. You didn't."

"You sure? Because I kind of feel like I did . . ."

"Yeah, I'm sure. My manager sent you a reel every year, and every year you passed. For twelve years straight."

"Well, you see, that's where I saw your act, then. Your sizzle reel."

"No, I went drinking with your booker, and she said you never watched comics' reels. You just had your producers pitch jokes from them and then you said yea or nay."

"Which booker is this?"

"Cassandra."

"Cassandra?"

"The one who sued you for sexual harassment?"

"Which one?"

"Cassandra!"

TJ waved his hands. "Look, you lost me. You can't listen to a chick like that anyway. Any girl who can't handle a boob grab or two clearly doesn't have a sense of humor. And, ergo, should not be booking goddamn comics."

Dante groaned. "She said you said my act was 'too urban' for your show. You know, too from the street? Too from the hood? Too *black*? Wouldn't play to the key fat, white,

137

petting-zoo demographic?"

TJ shook his head. "I would never say that. No way."

"That's what Cassandra said."

"Then Cassandra not only has no sense of humor, she is also a lying bitch."

Dante spread his hands. " 'Fraid I got to go with Cassandra on this one, TJ. I'll pass on the alliance, thanks."

He continued walking to the dock stairs.

IV

Ruby and Meredith and Janet agreed to go check the secret room next, the result of an exchange that went something like:

MEREDITH: Should we go down and check the secret room next?

RUBY AND JANET: Secret room?!? What secret room?!?

Meredith tried to explain that they should calm down; the secret room was just a panic room concealed in the wine cellar — and no, there couldn't be anyone hiding in there because she'd checked the secret room when she searched the house right after their arrival. ("Just like I checked *all* the rooms when we first arrived and I found *no one*," she reminded them for the umpteenth time.) The access log in the panic room's built-in tablet computer showed that no one had accessed the keypad lock for a month. Even if she didn't have the log, the visible layer of dust on every surface spoke for itself. The cleaning staff hadn't been allowed inside since the day a maid had accidentally locked herself in and drank all the Courvoisier.

Meredith tried to explain this to Ruby and Janet in the calmest, most rational tone possible, but they made her walk down the stairs in the central hallway to the dark cellar first, anyway.

The dodgy auras of the women on the stairs behind her scared Meredith even more than the darkness she was descending into. For a single, irrational second she was afraid they might lock her in the basement, just like her older brothers used to lock her in the dry, low-ceilinged, tiny concrete laundry room underneath their building when she was a little girl. That room scared the coriander out of her. It was like a subterranean mausoleum, its air dully sultry from dryer exhaust.

But she made it to the cellar floor and found the light switch without incident. The fluorescent panels set into the ceiling buzzed to life. Facing the stairs along several walls and several central panels were stem after stem of wine bottles arranged in an alcoholic's honeycomb, rows upon rows of sleepers waiting to be summoned awake.

"Geez, baby loves his bottle," Janet said when she reached the bottom of the stairs.

"Dustin is . . . was . . . twelve years sober," Meredith said with as much pride as if it had been her own accomplishment. "The wine collection is for guests only."

Ruby walked to the nearest honeycomb case and discovered that a clear Plexiglas door was covering it. She pulled on the edge to no avail: locked. "You got a key?"

"Not my department, really," Meredith said. "I do know the combination to the panic room, though."

"What is it?" Janet asked.

Meredith looked at her.

"C'mon, sister, have a heart. What if you get dirt-napped, too? Any one of us should be able to get into any corner of this dump. Our lives might depend on it."

Meredith weighed this assertion, then said, "It's 03-12-88. The day his album *Can't Help Myself* dropped."

"Somebody's living in the past," Ruby said.

"At least he *has* a past," Meredith said in a way she must have thought was cutting. Ruby just rolled her eyes.

140

Meredith flipped open a small panel on the side of a wine case jutting from the far wall, revealing a ten-button numeric keypad. She punched in the six-digit combination.

A small red light in one corner of the panel flashed at her but nothing else happened.

Meredith frowned. "I must have keyed it in wrong."

She tried the combination again, more deliberately this time, but with the same result.

"*Brexit,*" she said under her breath. "It worked just fine not four hours ago."

"Are you sure you're putting it in right?" Janet said. "You know Americans, we do the month, then the day, not the weird mixed-up way you do across the pond. Like how you people drive on the wrong side of the street."

"Yes, I am aware of that," Meredith said through clenched teeth. "You do realize we think it's *you* people who do it the mixed-up way, and *you* who drive on the wrong side of the street, yes?"

"Aw, do you? That's cute. Here, sweetie, let me give it a try."

Their back-and-forth had lulled Ruby into a half-conscious state of nearly intolerable boredom, so it took her a few moments to realize her left buttock was vibrating.

While Janet and Meredith bickered over the panic room entrance code with their backs to her, Ruby stepped behind the nearest monolith of wine and removed the phone from her jeans pocket. It wasn't her phone, but the drab flip phone she had discovered inside her guest room. A gray text bubble appeared on its tiny pixelated screen:

> We need to talk

Ruby peered back at the other two women and made sure they were looking at the keypad and not at her. The third rail of her existence had gained power, and she trembled with the knowledge: she was connected to the internet.

"Unknown caller" was who the phone said was talking to her. She typed back, the plastic keys of the flip phone making tiny kissing noises under her thumb:

> Who is this?

A few seconds later, the response appeared:

```
Meet me
Library
```

She quickly thumbed:

```
Not unless you tell me who you are.
```

The response was so quick, her correspondent couldn't possibly have been reacting to her text; he (or she) must've already been typing:

```
5min library
Youll wanna here this
Dont tell others
Comedy Ambush Xclusive
```

Ruby debated the wisdom of this.

But wisdom had never been her strong suit.

"Guys, we're just spinning our wheels here," she said to the backs of Ruby and

Janet as they still bickered over the door. "I'm gonna case the ground floor a little bit, the rooms we haven't been in yet."

"Give us five seconds and we'll come with you," Meredith said.

"I'm sure it's fine," Ruby said, "I'll yell if I find anything."

Then she scampered up the stairs before either of them could object.

V

TJ followed Dante to the dock stairs, yelling:

"C'mon, man! You're making a mistake! You should set aside all that outside shit, man! We're in a tight spot, and the only way we're going to get through it is if we stick together!"

At the top of the stairs Dante spun to face him again. "But here's the thing: I don't trust you, TJ."

"Why not? What did I ever do to you?"

"It's what you *didn't* do to me. Do you know what a five-minute spot on *2nite* would've done to my career? Do you how many overnight car trips on no sleep and ten Red Bulls I've had to go on to get from one tiny club to the next? How many times I didn't draw enough because there was a

144

basketball game that night or it rained a little, so I actually lost money on the gig? You think it's fun being 'the hardest-working road comic in the business'? The key word in that phrase is 'work.' You actually remember what it's like to *work* at stand-up instead of just sitting on your throne giving thumbs-up or thumbs-down to the poor bastards being paraded in front of you? Five minutes on your show, on one night, for so many comics, like Zoe, or Billy the God-damn Contractor, may he rest in peace, that bumped them up from a middle or an opener to a headliner. How many shows in twelve years you do? How many thousands? And you never gave me a shot, you stingy bastard. One shot, that's all I needed. And you wouldn't give it to me."

TJ's face became flat and placid while Dante ranted. When the other comic was done, he said, "You, what, you could've been a contender? Yeah, I heard that speech a few times. You know what speech I never hear, though? 'I went on TJ's show, and nothing happened. I killed, I did a great set, but it just didn't happen for me. I don't know why. The comedy gods didn't smile on me, there was a bigger guest on some-body else's show on another network. I got my shot, I nailed it, but I still didn't make a mark. It happens. It's nobody's fault. Show-biz is just a tough row to hoe.'

"I never hear *that* speech, man, because there's no villain, there's no puppet master to blame. Maybe that chick Cassandra was right once in her life; maybe I didn't think you were right for our show. But so what if I did? I wasn't put on this Earth to discover you. I'm not Broadway Danny Rose. I'm not *Star Search.*

"I book you on my show, I book anyone on my show, for one reason and one reason only. So *you* can make *me* look good. So you make people want to tune in again to me. I got hundreds of people working for me, with families, and problems of their own, whose jobs depend on me. I can't be looking out for you, man. I'm too busy looking out for me, because no one else will. I got puppet masters of my own up my ass."

Dante gave him the slow golf clap.

"Thank you. Thank you for making my point for me, TJ. Of this whole crew, you are the one most likely to stab a brother in the back because you're just looking out for number one. And wasn't it you who kept going on and on about how you're best friends with crazy-ass Dustin Walker? For all I know you're working with him. So, with that in mind . . ."

Dante stepped to the side of the stairs and invited TJ to proceed ahead of him.

"After you."

TJ shook his head. "Hell, no. I'm not going anywhere with you."

"Aw, did I hurt your feelings?"

"After that speech? You got a lot of pent-up hostilities against me! You got murder motive!"

"I got murder motive?"

"Yeah, you got murder motive, son."

"Murder motive. Okay. Sure." Dante rubbed his face with his hand. "You're probably right, now that you mention it. You stay here, I'll check out down there."

"Don't tell me what to do, *puto.*"

"Whatever, man," Dante said, and started to descend. "Do me a favor, though, and if you hear me getting murdered, go get help, okay?"

"No promises!" TJ called after him.

VI

"Didn't Meredith say this was supposed to be where Dave's-Not-Here the caretaker lived?" Steve Gordon said as he and Zoe Schwartz stepped inside the cabana, up the hill from the main house. The eave over the front portico had a golden sunburst set in

147

the center like a Mayan calendar.

Just inside the curtained glass entry doors was a large room with dark tile floors. Several small circular tables and chairs faced a stage with a brick backdrop and a microphone on a metal stand. Steve couldn't help but think it looked like a hostile droid gazing with one baleful eye over the hapless audience it had vaporized.

Zoe said, "Wow, yet another thing Intern McJailbait said that didn't pan out. What a shock."

"Boy, you're a big fan of hers, huh?"

"Well, she's sleeping her way to the top and I'm trying to do it with, you know, talent. And hard work. Like a schmuck. So there is a natural hostility there."

"Like cartoon cats and mice."

"Also, there's something she's not telling us, trust me. No one is as clueless as she acts."

"What about Orange Baby Man?"

Zoe thought about it. "Okay, I stand corrected."

Tucked away out of the sight line of the doorway was a bar, stacked with booze.

Steve walked behind the bar, picked up a Bacardi bottle by the stem, and hurled it to the ground as hard as he could. Four-fifths empty, it bounced up and down several times before rolling to a stop beneath a table.

"Plastic?" Zoe asked.

"Plastic."

Faux votive candles on each table glowed with the only illumination in the faux club. Zoe squinted at the wall tiles and blue dots and purple triangles, each color rendered in gradients to produce an unconvincing 3-D effect. "Jesus. You know the saying, such-and-such raped my childhood? I feel like my childhood raped this room."

"Yeah, the early nineties really threw up all over this place."

Beside the bar Steve found a doorway and a short flight of steps ascending into darkness. He felt for the light switch along the black wall and flicked it on, then headed up.

Zoe climbed onstage and grabbed the mic. "Helloooooo, Murder Island! Who's ready to laugh tonight?"

She looked out over the empty, silent club.

"Yeah, I know how you feel," she said.

Next she turned her attention to the brick backdrop. Rapping a knuckle on it, she discovered that, as she suspected, it was plastic. Seeing one corner not entirely attached, she pulled it back a bit and found a spongy foam beneath.

"Hey, Steve?" she called. "I think this room may be soundproofed."

"Yeah," came a voice booming from the ceiling. Zoe jumped halfway out of her skin.

"Jesus! Don't do that!"

"Sorry. Look over the bar."

She did and saw the black window of a sound booth on the wall above it.

"He's got a sound board, a mixing board, a MacBook Pro running GarageBand, the whole nine yards," he said. "This is a recording studio set up to look like a club. Just add audience and comic."

"I have to admit, even from a psycho, that's actually a pretty clever idea."

"Yeah, I — shit!"

There was a *thud* and a staccato squeal of feedback though the speakers.

"Holy crap, are you all right? Should I run?"

No answer.

"Tap once on the microphone if you think I should run!"

"No . . . no. . . . Hold on. Sorry, sorry. There's just . . . I guess Dave's-Not-Here has a dog. There's a food bowl and water dish in here and I walked right into them. Made quite a mess."

"I haven't seen a dog at all . . ." Zoe wrinkled her nose. "Have you?"

"Nah. It's probably dead anyway."

She scowled. "Why would you say that?"

"You've never seen a horror movie before? The pets always die first."

Zoe blanched.

Finding a crumpled-up paper towel on the sound board, Steve sopped up the water as best he could. He wasn't sure why he cared about housekeeping on Murder Island; he did it more out of habit than anything else.

He hopped down the stairs, saying, "Yeah, whenever a family moves into a haunted house, you can pretty much kiss the dog or cat goodbye. It drags out the first act until the people deaths start happening. I had a writing partner for a long time, and we talked about doing one of those low-budget *Paranormal Activity* things as a spec. They're so formulaic . . ."

When he emerged from the stairs, he looked around the studio and realized he had been talking to himself for some time.

Zoe Schwartz was gone.

VII

Ruby Ng was no fool. She knew a trap when she saw one. She had forged her whole career by laying traps.

But as she shut the library door behind

151

her, she felt safe and confident for a number of reasons, not the least of which was that she had convinced herself of the cosmic truth of her bond with Yvette, the love that had brought her up from the dark, self-destructive flailing her life had been until that point. Their shared destiny gave Ruby an unshakable belief in her own invulnerability, that she was somehow fated to continue existing on this Earth as long as Yvette was there to share her life. This was why she was able to enter the library without fear.

Or much fear.

Also, and most importantly, she agreed with Meredith Ladipo, so adorable otherwise in her cluelessness, that they were alone on the island. It wasn't big enough for anyone to hide on for long. Ergo, it was someone among them who had texted her. And she'd been outwitting the motley collection of insecure misfits and head cases that comprised the comedy community for years.

All this of course begged the question, Which inmate of this particular asylum of emotional cripples had reached out? Ruby had her suspicions, but she didn't really consider them for too long because that person would soon present himself. And she was almost positive it was a he.

She wasn't completely self-delusional. She knew how unpopular she was among her colleagues. They thought she could be a bit too extreme in her criticisms, too strident in her politics. Well, boo-freaking-hoo. Comics should march in unity, arm in arm, as the Anti-Bullshit Army, and she had no problem calling out soldiers who weren't pulling their weight.

Besides, how many whining that she took it too far had gotten called a "gook dyke bitch" by twentysomething frat douches in red caps the week after Trump won the election? Had Twitter mentions full of rape threats and promises you were going to get deported? Give me a break.

She considered it a personal triumph that Dustin Walker had been driven mad by the realization that the straight white bros' hegemony was at last slipping through their fingers, as perilous as that may have rendered her own personal circumstances. The last gasp of a fading tyrant, killing himself, and poisoning the food and drink he provided for his guests. That was probably his plan, in the end: to starve the comics out.

Or have them turn on one another.

While she waited in a *Masterpiece Theatre* armchair in a corner of the room Ruby at-

153

tempted to call up her email or a website, any website, on the Wi-Fi-connected phone, but failed. This antique from 2003 was connected not to the wider internet but to some kind of in-house intranet.

After fifteen minutes or so Ruby began to feel like she was being made a fool of. Ruby did not appreciate being made a fool of. Her thumbs at this point were so limber and dextrous, she could type twice as fast on her phone as she could on a regular keyboard:

Where the hell are you?

The room had the overwhelmingly dull smell of cheap leather. She glanced idly at the leather-bound tomes on each shelf and saw that many had the word book stenciled in gold on the spine.

Frowning, she tipped one spine back, and the entire row of spines came with it — behind them was only Styrofoam. They were the fake books you'd find on bookcases displayed at Ikea.

The flip phone buzzed, startling her half to death. She looked at its narrow screen:

For the first time since she landed on the island, an icicle of fear lanced through Ruby Ng's heart.

She didn't move.

She didn't turn around.

VIII

The pier faced west, and as Dante Dupree descended the dizzying wooden stairs along the side of the sheer cliffs, he could watch the sun touch the Caribbean's distant horizon in an orange burst of glory.

Encroaching dusk had triggered the light-sensitive lamps mounted on the railing running around the pier. The guests' luggage lay scattered about the dock, unzipped, locks cut off, shirts and blouses and skirts and jeans strewn everywhere. A couple of bags were already drifting out with the tide.

Dante cursed under his breath and descended the few remaining steps. His own suitcase was one of those currently heading out to sea. Southern Comfort that he could be relatively certain hadn't been poisoned was safely ensconced inside.

155

He nudged a few of the disemboweled bags with his foot, seeing nothing illuminating.

One corner of the lid to Janet's enormous trunk was stuck upside down on a post at the end of the dock, as if someone had tried to pitch it into the water but it caught itself there. He reached down and tried to pull it up, but the inside was slippery and clammy. He struggled to get a grip.

"Holy shit, what'd you do, dude?"

"Goddamn!" Dante leapt to his feet. He dropped the huge trunk, which he had just managed to free from the top of the post. It fell into the water, sinking beneath the waves with *Titanic*-esque majesty.

Dante turned to face TJ, who had materialized behind him, surveying the luggage massacre. "I knew you had a lot of pent-up anger, man, but I don't know why you had to take it out on everybody's bags. I should beat your ass; some of my best shirts were in there. You just lucky I got bigger things to worry about."

"I didn't do shit," Dante said. "I found them like this. Where the hell did you come from?"

TJ held up the elevator's OUT OF ORDER sign. "I tried it and it worked fine, though it's super slow. You may not trust me, but I do not trust that Meredith Ladipo chick, man. Absolutely nothing she says has checked out."

"I don't know. I think that just makes her more in the dark than the rest of us."

"Yeah, right. You just want down her pants."

Dante shrugged. "You said it — I got other things on my mind."

TJ looked at the bags and shook his head. "This is not looking good, man."

"No," Dante said. "It most definitely is not."

They looked at each other.

"Well," Dante said, "let's give the others the good news."

Neither of them moved.

TJ said:

"How about you take the stairs, and I'll take the elevator. Nothing personal."

IX

When the shotgun blast came, it was indescribably loud.

X

Dustin Walker's estate did not simply have a pool. No, that would have been far too pedestrian. Instead, it had pools — three — each set on manmade steppes behind the house, each spilling over into the next in gentle waterfalls and draining into the largest pool at the very bottom, a steaming whirlpool jutting out over a sea cliff and surrounded by cabana chairs. The sun had set completely by the time the blast rang out, and the ankle-high lamps lining the paths and steps around the pool burned on.

By the time a witness arrived at the uppermost patio to investigate the gunshot they all had heard, the corpse had already drifted down from the top pool to the second one. It was lying facedown, an amorphous cloud of blood billowing from where its face used to be, trailing up to the highest pool, where bits of bloody bandage and gauze still floated.

Or maybe that wasn't gauze.

Maybe that was skin.

"Oh, my holy God," Meredith Ladipo said, emerging from the sliding glass doors leading into the playroom. A narrow concrete causeway jutted into the top pool and stopped at a central octagonal platform appointed with cushions and a fire pit. Meredith walked out to the pit and peered over the edge at the fully clothed figure. "Are you — are you all right?" she called out, rather unnecessarily.

The body drifted over the edge of the waterfall and flipped onto its back. As it dropped to the lowest level, it was obvious that Janet Kahn would never respond to anyone's query ever again.

THAT'S RACIST

So I want to talk about racism for just a bit.

Wait — no! Don't leave. Come on back now, hear a brother out. It's still gonna be funny. I promise. There you go. Thank you, thank you. There will be a ton of dick jokes afterward as a reward. I swear. Come on back now. Okay.

No, race is a funny thing, man. Used to be people would be all like, "Americans don't like to talk about race. Black and white Americans need to have a conversation on race. We need to talk about race. We got to talk it out. Confront that shit. Don't leave it repressed. Americans are repressed about race."

I just don't feel like that's true anymore, man. I feel like now people won't shut the fuck up about it, you know what I'm saying?

Like, are you like me? Do you have white friends that are a million times quicker to accuse other motherfuckers of being racist than you are? Like every day on Twitter is the March on Washington and they're Dr. King with a melanin deficiency?

White people *love* to call other white people

160

racist, man. They fucking looooooove that shit. "How can you make that joke? That's racist. How can you sing that song? That's racist. How can you not serve that guy at that lunch counter just because —"

Oh, wait. That *is* racist. Sorry. My bad.

But it sends a blast of white endorphins through their white brains, man! It gives them little white goose bumps on their white skin. They love it. 'Cause they know that means they're okay. They're one of the good people. Ahhh, yeah. It feels so good.

Only goes to prove one thing.

White people will steal anything.

I'm serious! I mean any goddamn thing! Calling out other people's racism, we used to have a monopoly on that. And they just swooped right in and straight-up jacked that shit.

The Vikings, Christopher Columbus, Elvis Presley. Land. Culture. Kardashians. If it's not nailed down and weighed with giant chains, white people will fucking take that shit and say it was theirs all along. And if it didn't start out being theirs, they'll say they do it better than you anyway, so you didn't deserve it in the first place.

How do you think we got enslaved, man? "Say, Chip, what are these Negroes doing, running around Africa like they own it? Well we'll just put a stop to that . . . Okay, Cody, bring the boat around! Load 'em up!"

Like what's her name, Rachel Gazelle? Rachel Dizzy Gillespie? Hell is her name? The Before pictures make her look like Hee-Haw Barbie.

Then she darkens her hair, darkens her skin, marries a brother. Says she "identifies" as black.

I wanna identify my foot with the crack of her ass!

Being black ain't like putting on a Halloween costume! You can't put on a skin mask like Hannibal Lecter! You can't steal that shit! What's wrong with you, woman? Don't you realize your husband liked you better when you were white?

That is a black man's worst nightmare. Marry a white bitch, then wake up one morning, turn over in bed and be like, "*Aaaaah! What happened?* How did I not notice that before? Was I drunk the whole time we was dating?

"She changed races on me after the wedding. That ain't fair, Your Honor. She took my virtue under false pretenses. That's false advertising and shit. So I got to ask you to please give me one of them no-fault divorces, or if there's her-fault divorce, I would rather have one of them because it's more accurate, Your Honor, sir."

I mean, you got to hand it to this lady. You just *got* to. She put on blackface to join the NAACP and go on TV and accuse other white people of being racist. In blackface! That is some next-level shit, man.

When you think about it, Rachel Dolezal is the whitest white person in the history of white people.

Shit. I don't even know, man. I don't even know.

I see at least . . . what? Four . . . seven white people in the club tonight. What happen, you click on the wrong Yelp directions?

No, no, I'm kidding. I'm glad to see you. When I say that white people are a race of congenital thieves, I don't mean you; I mean those other white people. The ones who didn't pay money to come see me. Yeah, the ones you call racist on Twitter. Yeah, no, you guys can stay.

See, the white people here are smiling and nodding. They're like, no, it's the *other* white people who are racist. Not us. We're the good ones. We own *The Wire* on BluRay, all five seasons.

We saw that Jackie Robinson documentary on PBS last night, and at the end, when we let him play baseball, we kinda choked up a little.

When Martin Lawrence played that black tomcat in *Help! I Married a Cat 4,* we all joined in the protest against hacky Dustin Walker.

We felt so proud of America. Fulfilling her *promise.*

But all the other tables around them — identify the white people, and how close you are to them — and the black people in the tables sitting near them, *hold on to your wallets and do not let go of that shit no matter what!*

— Dante Dupree
Uptown Comedy Club, Atlanta, GA
November 12, 2015 (third set)

CHAPTER FIVE

I

People gathered at the top of the pool, but in the twilight gloom no one could make out who arrived when.

"I waited for you!" Dante said when TJ appeared.

TJ's brow furrowed imperiously. Dante wondered how many hapless *2nite* PAs had been on the receiving end of that brow. "Who told you to do that? You're not my *abuela.*"

"It was for both of our protection, stupid. I got sick of waiting for you at the top of the stairs."

"If you were waiting for me, how did you get here first?"

"How did you *not* get here first?"

"I told you, man, that elevator is really damn slow!"

"Where did you go?" Steve asked Zoe

166

when he saw her gaping on the other side of the top pool.

She couldn't take her eyes off Janet's floating body. "I had to take care of a thing."

"A thing? What thing?"

Finally she looked up at him. "A *thing,* all right?" she said. "And it's fine now."

"Oh, good. I'm so very relieved."

Ollie Rees said, "I sat down to rest on the sundeck over there. I guess I fell asleep." He waited for someone to challenge him, or to express any interest whatsoever in his whereabouts. When no one did, he added, "The shot woke me up. I came as soon as I heard it."

"We all did." Steve looked at each of the remaining six comics. "Was anyone with Janet? Did anyone see anything?"

They all looked at him and said nothing.

Dante made his way down the steps along the side of the pools. On the bottom level he tried to grab onto the body from the side but couldn't quite reach. He found a long-handled net mounted along the railing and used it to hook Janet's left foot, pulling her closer. Zoe and Ruby headed down to join him.

"Was anyone with anyone else at all?" Steve threw up his hands, incredulous. "You guys! That was the whole point of searching in teams!"

Meredith pointed at Ruby. "We split up to look for Ruby! She wandered off by herself! It was her idea, I might add!"

Ruby yelled back, "And I left you with Janet! While she was still alive!"

Everyone looked at Meredith Ladipo.

"Does anybody see the gun?" Dante called to the others as he dragged Janet toward the submerged pool steps. "Look for the gun!"

He grabbed Janet's body by the wrist to pull it out of the pool and grimaced. She was cold — so very cold, made especially notable by the whirlpool's heated water.

The others paced up and down the stairs in the dim ankle-level light, looking in bushes. Zoe and Ruby pulled Janet's body out of Dante's hands as well as the water. They lay her on the bordering tile without looking at what was once her face, which now had the appearance of a corned beef brisket that had been backed over several times by an SUV.

Once Janet was lying on her back, bloody water puddling around her, Dante reached out again with the net to snag a pool chair floating in the deep end. It was light as a feather, and he was able to pick it up with one hand.

168

"Found it!" Meredith called. She stood up among some ferns beside the uppermost pool and held up a shotgun by its twin barrels.

"Great," said TJ, who was up there with her. He stepped toward her, beckoning. "Give it here."

"Oh no, you get the hell away from me, you spank!" She turned the gun in his direction.

TJ raised his hands and stepped back. "Yeah, that's making you look so much less guilty."

"Exactly my point! None of you trusts me! One of you has already attacked me! You obviously won't believe me, no matter what I say, so I'm going to take proper steps to defend myself!"

"Oh my God," Steve said suddenly. His eyes widened, but he wasn't looking at anything particular. "Wait — wait!"

"Nobody move!" Meredith turned the gun on him. "Everyone just calm —"

Steve turned and sprinted into the house without another word.

Meredith stamped a foot. "I have the gun! That means you have to listen to me!"

Steve emerged again, ashen-faced.

"What the hell was that about?" TJ said.

"It's gone," Steve said.

"What's gone?"

"Janet's photo. It's not on the wall anymore. Somebody took it. After killing the Shotgun with a shotgun. There's seven pictures left."

No one had any idea what to say to that.

II

Oliver Rees was scared of dead things, but he was more scared of getting yelled at for not pulling his weight. So when Dante Dupree asked for help wrapping Janet's body in a blue tarp he'd found in a plastic trunk by the bottom pool, Ollie volunteered first, followed by Ruby Ng.

Janet reminded him of his mother, in the sense that she was a woman and old, so he knew she should be treated with dignity. He tried not to get his hands anywhere near her HBO parts when they rolled her up.

He tried not to think about how stiff she was, rigor mortis making her limbs unyielding and aquiver whenever you tried to move them, like leafless branches on a rotting tree.

He tried not to notice the bruising on her already gray skin, gravity dragging the blood toward the lower extremities as soon as her heart had stopped beating. He didn't want to think that this implied the whole universe

170

was ready and waiting for you to die. That your existence was a mistake the natural order was eager to rectify as soon as was allowable.

And he most definitely did not look at the red snarl on the front of her head where her face used to be.

Fortunately they wrapped her quickly and she weighed very little, so he and Dante were able to carry her up the stairs with ease. Soon she was lying on the floor of the writers' room, next to William Griffith. Dante left as soon as possible, muttering something about washing his hands, which struck Ollie as a pretty good idea.

As he was leaving, however, something on the table caught his eye: the Orange Baby Man Theatre binder he had found in his bedroom and forgotten in the writers' room, after the whole weekend turned way murderier than the original invitation had led him to expect.

He took the binder and went into the kitchen. He turned on a light and flipped through its pages, looking for comfort in the familiar. But although it was formatted exactly like one of the handbooks he distributed to his satellite franchises, the contents were completely different.

And what he found surprised him.

III

Zoe Schwartz broke into tears when Ollie and Dante walked past her on the top patio bearing Janet Kahn, a legend and even a hero of hers who deserved way, way better than to end her story wrapped up in a blue pool tarp like a frigging human burrito.

Hell, they all did.

Her cry lasted only a minute, and once she rubbed the tears from her eyes, TJ Martinez was in front of her, beckoning her close.

Snorting back snot she said, "What the hell do you want?"

Looking around to make sure everyone else's attention was focused on the impromptu pallbearers and their damp, crinkling cargo, TJ hissed:

"You and me? I think we should form an alliance."

IV

"All of you! Stay where I can see you!"

The gaping barrel of the shotgun bobbed in Steve Gordon's direction as Meredith Ladipo backed through the patio entrance into the playroom. "So, what is your theory, Meredith? That one of us is working with

Dustin to enact his judgment on our hacki-
ness from beyond the grave?"

"I don't have any theory," Meredith said.
"I'm just saying two people have been
murdered on this island and I'm looking at
the only people who could have bloody
murdered them because we are the only
bloody people on this bloody island!"

"Well, except you," Ollie said.

"Except I know I didn't do it!" Meredith
said.

Ollie said, "No, I meant you're not looking at yourself, and you're also one of the
only people on the island —"

"Shut the fuck up, Ollie," said Meredith
and Steve at the exact same time.

"You guys are mean," Ollie said.

"Look, *I* know I didn't do it, either," Steve
said, "but my saying it doesn't make you
believe me any more, does it? Just like you
declaring you're innocent doesn't get you
off the hook."

"That's your problem, not mine," Meredith said.

"I also know I'm the last person on Earth
who would help Dustin Walker do anything
criminal, period, much less murder a bunch
of total strangers. Which is a lot less than I
can say about you, since he was helping you
with your career and all."

"She didn't do it," Ruby said.

"How do you know?" Ollie said.

"I just do," Ruby said.

"Thank you," Meredith said, "but I don't know where you were when Janet was shot, so that doesn't let you off the duff either."

"I get it," Ruby said. "Just stating facts."

Ruby knew Meredith couldn't have killed Janet because she received the texts from her mystery correspondent while Meredith and Janet were busy bickering over the panic room door. And there was no doubt in Ruby's mind that he (and of course it was going to turn out to be a he, I mean really) and Janet's killer were the same person.

But she hoped there was doubt in the killer's mind that she knew this, so she didn't say it out loud. She had narrowed down the suspects to a group she could count on one hand, but she couldn't put a name or a face to the perpetrator. She was confident she could get him to reveal himself, but she needed to buy time until she figured out what form that unmasking might take.

"There's another possibility," said a voice from outside the door, and everyone jumped.

Dante Dupree stepped in from the darkness of the patio. The first thing he saw was Meredith's shotgun swiveling at him, so he jumped back, too.

"Goddamn, girl, point that thing somewhere else, huh? I'm trying to exonerate your ass."

He held up a shattered jumble of wood clinging to rusty wire.

"What is that?" Meredith asked, still pointing the gun at him. "What have you got there?"

"It was in the flower beds over by where you found the gun," Dante said. "Some kind of trip wire."

Ruby groaned. "Oh, you've gotta be fucking kidding me."

"Yeah," Dante said. "One of those bar tables on the patio is all scratched up. And there was a patio chair in the pool with her."

Steve's forehead creased. "And that means . . ."

"Janet walks across the patio, all innocent as can be, then sits in the chair to take a load off. That triggers the wire; the gun fires remotely. The shot knocks her and the chair into the pool, while the kickback blows the gun and the doodad into the bushes."

"Wow," Steve said.

"Crazy-ass Dustin Walker could have poisoned Billy's — William's — beer weeks ago. He could have booby-trapped this whole island before he went off to meet with Lenny and Richard and Carlin."

"Wait," Meredith said. "What are you saying?"

"That Walker turned this whole damn island into a death trap while you were in L.A., killed himself, and then dumped us all here to die. Either we go batshit and kill each other off, or we starve to death because we don't know whether or not the food is poisoned, or we end up on the receiving end of one of the fun little party favors he left for us."

"But a boat is coming tomorrow morning, right?" Ollie said.

"That's what Captain Harry said," Meredith said.

"You believe him?" Dante said.

"I don't know what to believe," Meredith said. "I can't believe any of this is happening." She dropped into a nearby armchair and held the shotgun between her legs, with the stock on the ground and her hands folded over the barrel. She laid an exhausted cheek on it.

"Uh," Ruby said, "should you really be doing that?"

"It's not loaded," Meredith said.

"What?" Steve said.

Meredith sniffled and wiped her nose, then held the shotgun horizontally. She cracked open the barrel from the stock so they could see she was right. "This antique is for shooting clay pigeons. The skeet setup was left over from the island's previous owners. We only tried it once, then Dustin mothballed the whole apparatus, but I know this gun fires just two shots at a time."

"Wait," Steve said, turning to Dante. "If no one's helping Dustin, who's taking the photos off the wall?"

"You know who."

"Who?"

"Someone who thinks it's funny." Dante said. "Think about the degenerates you're surrounded by."

Steve frowned but said nothing.

Ruby reached for the remains of the trip wire in Dante's hand. "Let me see that thing."

Dante handed it to her. It was an abstract jumble of broken wood and rusty wire. Still.

"It's such a . . ." Ruby started to say, then trailed off.

"What?" Dante said.

Ruby tried not to look directly at Ollie.

She stopped herself before she could say, "It's such a *prop.*"

V

"What do you have against Steve?" Zoe asked TJ once they were alone. He had steered her outside by the front fountain. A water element, bordered by perfectly square flagstones that formed another path, gurgled out of the base of the fountain through a tall curtain of bamboo that obscured the view of the cabana beyond.

"Who?" TJ asked.

"Steve Gordon. Gordo. Why do you pretend you never met him before?"

"Forget Gordo. I want to talk about who's behind all this insanity."

"Who do you think it is?"

"I got a pretty good idea."

Zoe put her face in her hands. "This isn't frigging *Clue,* dude. Take the answer out of the little paper sleeve. Who killed Billy the Contractor in the Clown Lounge with the tallboy?"

"I don't know for sure, but that Dante Dupree, man, he's got a lot of issues."

"Really, you're going straight for the unidentified black male? That only works when you're trying to blame somebody else for the crime. Oh, wait, maybe you are."

"Don't dump your white guilt shit on me, lady. I'm Spanish, I got no dog in that fight.

178

Dude has a reputation as a nasty drunk. We wouldn't let him on my show because he messed up a line producer on Craig Ferguson while he was lit. He thinks I don't know. But I do."

Zoe blinked. "Everyone knows Dante's a drinker, but it's kind of a leap from trashing a green room to being the supervillain mastermind behind Death Island."

"Hey, whoever arranged this has to be some Dexter-level whack-a-doo, a psycho who looks mostly normal on the outside. I don't know enough to say definitely yes or no; all I'm saying is, you and I trust each other, so we should be watching each other's back. I know you, you know me, we've worked together before. We're — I know you have the FX thing, I'm in between TV things. Now that Janet's gone" — he crossed himself — "may she rest in peace, you and I are, no offense to them, the only ones with real careers here. We have something at *stake*. We need to look out for our best interests. We should be watching Dupree. Together. Make sure he doesn't try anything, you know? Particularly against me. Because he really does seem to have it out for me, man. I find it kind of frightening, for real, being stuck on this island with him."

"There is just a slight problem with this plan."

"What?"

"I don't trust you, TJ."

"*What?* You, too? Come on, why not?"

Zoe shook her head. "I can't even."

"What? Was it that thing I tweeted? Look, how was I supposed to know you can't say 'gaybird' no more? We used to say it all the time as kids! I don't even know what it really means, much less why it's supposed to be so offensive!"

Zoe held up a hand. "I'm curious: does this whole clueless hey-let's-be-pals act actually work on other people? Does *no one* call you out on your nonsense?"

"You lost me."

Zoe's face froze in disbelief. "You're actually going to make me say it out loud?"

"If you want me to know what the hell you're talking about, yeah!"

She took a deep breath. "The last time I was on your show, you came into my dressing room, locked the door, whipped your dick out, and jerked off in front of me."

TJ laughed. "What? That? Aw — really? No! C'mon. Zoe. Babe. That was a joke."

"No. No." Zoe got right in his face, her finger pointing:

"A Hasidic Jew walks into a bar with a

frog on his shoulder. Bartender says, 'Where'd you get that?' Frog says, 'Brooklyn. They're everywhere.'

"That — *that,* dumbass — is a joke. Trapping a woman in a corner and jizzing on her shoes is some kind of weird sexual dominance game and indecent exposure and sexual assault all combined into one, which I would have a lawyer look into if remembering it didn't make my frontal lobe want to vomit."

The smile faded from TJ's face. "Hey, now. You shouldn't . . . you shouldn't talk to me like that, kiddo."

"Really? And why is that?"

"I'm just saying. You should get a hold of yourself."

Zoe laughed and shook her head. "Oh. My God. That's why you wanted to 'ally' with me, isn't it? Because you think I'll keep my mouth shut. Well, I guess that's my fault. I haven't given you any reason to think any different."

"No, I —"

"You don't get it, do you? You're off the air, genius. Your show is gone. No one is going to enable you anymore. No one is going to look the other way because you can't do anything for anyone. I am ashamed to admit it, but that is why I didn't tell anyone. Other

181

than it being just weird enough to be borderline unbelievable — kudos, by the way, for coming up with a kink so specific and bizarre — you were scary powerful, TJ, you were. And I kept my mouth shut. Because I was a coward."

Her voice quavered with oncoming tears. "I don't know how many women you've done that to. Knowing you, scores. Hundreds? But it's all over for you, TJ. No one is going to protect you anymore. No one is going to pay for your lawyers but you. All you had going for you was that stupid talk show, with your stupid laugh track, and now that it's gone there's nothing to keep those chickens coming home to roost.

"So when I get back, *if* I get back, I'm going to tell everyone about you. In my act, in interviews. Your time is over, motherfucker. Just like poor crazy Dustin Walker. You stayed on stage too long, man. I'm going to ruin you, you smug little shit. When I'm through with you, no one will be able to hear your name without thinking, 'Oh, yeah, the Shoe Jizzer.'

"I'm going to do the worse thing I can possibly think to do to you, TJ.

"I'm going to make you a punchline."

As she spoke, the smug smile slowly crawled back onto TJ's face. "I see. I get it.

This is a stressful situation we're in, for everybody. I can't talk to you when you're hysterical."

"Sure. Sure. The woman is hysterical. Shocking, *shocking* that's your takeaway from all this."

A figure, backlit by the lights from the house, appeared in the arched doorway to the front gallery.

"What are you guys up to?" Steve Gordon asked.

"Nothing," Zoe said. "Hopping and skipping down memory lane is all."

She swung her arm back and slapped TJ so hard between his shoulder blades that he staggered forward a couple steps.

Steve didn't say anything for a second.

Then he asked:

"Hungry?"

VI

The kitchen, on closer inspection, lent support to the theory that no one had been on the island in a week or more. A loaf of bread spotted with mold was removed from the pantry. Deflated vegetables lay rotting in the fridge's crisper drawer, marinating in pools of their own viscous slime.

Nevertheless, they found canned diced

tomatoes and dried peaches, several varieties of Hot Pockets in the freezer along with a small box of frost-shrouded peas. They stacked every edible item on the marble-topped island in the center of the room.

Zoe picked up a can of sliced beets and inspected it closely, even going so far as to rip off the label. "Take a look," she said, handing the can to Dante, "there's not a mark on it. I have no idea how anyone could poison that."

"Or why anyone would bother," Ruby said. "They're already canned beets."

They all just stared at the meager collection of food.

"I am frigging starved," TJ said.

"I haven't had a bite since that Fruit Roll-Up at the airport," Ollie said.

"Our host deigned to leave us a can opener," Steve said, holding it up.

"Who wants to dig in first?" Dante said.

No one said anything.

"Fine, whatever, I'll do it," Ruby said. "Though no Hot Pockets. Those things are nasty."

"Pick your poison," Steve said, handing her the can opener.

She shot him a look.

"Sorry, poor choice of words."

Ruby chose a can of sweet corn and

opened it, took a spork and barely filled the tip. She nibbled at it like a bird for three bites while the others watched.

She set the spork aside and looked at them with a shrug. "Seems okay to me. Anybody want to see if the microwave is booby-trapped?"

VII

The microwave was not booby-trapped.

Various canned and frozen foods were heated, particularly for the Hot Pocket–allied and Hot Pocket–curious. The dirty sporks and plates were piled in the kitchen for later, in the unspoken hope there would be a later.

For obvious reasons, everyone prepared their own food, and they didn't let anything that was supposed to go into their mouths out of their sight.

A thin patina of normalcy settled over the evening for about half an hour.

Steve broke it by saying:

"Meredith, how well do you know Dave's-Not-Here?"

"Who?" Meredith said.

"That's the in-joke name we made up for the caretaker," Zoe said.

"Aw, you guys came up with in-jokes

without me?" Ollie said.

Meredith considered the question. "I mean . . . not a whole lot. He's from Maine. Or Vermont? Some place cold and American. Moved to the West Indies to solve a midlife crisis. Real beach-bum type. Dustin met him on one of the islands somewhere. He's divorced, with kids back in the States, I think."

"When's the last time you talked to him?"

"I emailed him this morning. I've been arranging the trip with him all week. Or so I thought."

"Why you thinking about Dave's-Not-Here?" Dante asked.

Steve pointed through the wall. "Because that house that's supposed to be his house, it's really a recording studio made to look like a comedy club. Except I found in the very back, where the dressing rooms would normally be, a little tiny room with a cot and a bureau in it, and a bathroom just big enough for a toilet. Dusty made Dave's-Not-Here live in a servant's quarters inside the servants' quarters."

"So what's your point?"

"My point is he's the only person who was supposed to be on the island who's not accounted for. We searched the island, and Meredith searched the island before us, and

186

nobody found nobody. But who would know better where to hide than the grounds-keeper?"

"The butler did it?" Ollie gasped.

"I don't know. Seems like Dusty went out of his way to make Dave's-Not-Here feel like a second-class citizen. Like a pet, almost. Doing its master's bidding."

"I feel like you're overstating the situation just a bit," Meredith said.

"C'mon, the situation we're in? The only way to accurately describe it is hyperbole."

"Except," Ruby said, "Meredith insists there's no one else on the island but us."

"There isn't," Meredith said.

"And Dante says there doesn't need to be anyone else on the island for us to get knocked off by the booby traps."

"So far, that's right," Dante said.

"So what you're saying is, either one of us did it . . . or no one did it . . . or some other person we haven't found yet did it."

"That about covers it," Steve said.

"You're a frigging genius," Ruby said.

At that moment the last bit of air seemed to squeak out of the balloon of the group, which was now thoroughly deflated.

Ruby said, "Should we think about maybe going to bed? I am so sick of looking at your goddamn faces. No offense."

Zoe Schwartz said, "My first thought is, you're crazy, who can sleep at a time like this? My second thought is, I feel like I'm buried under an avalanche. I can barely keep my eyes open."

Meredith looked at the digital clock on the stove and said, "It's nearly eleven."

"The doors and shutters of my room lock from the inside," TJ said. "I checked."

"Maybe a break would be good." Steve nodded. "We can tackle these problems fresh in the morning."

"Those of us that are still here," Zoe said, and much of the group laughed mirthlessly.

"Captain Harry usually arrives around ten," Meredith said.

Ollie said, "Maybe we'll all wake up, and we'll all be back in our beds at home and find out this was all just a terrible dream."

Everyone else shared the impulse to mock his childish sincerity, but no one could because they all wanted it to be true.

VIII

Ruby and Meredith filed upstairs first, followed by Zoe and Dante and Steve. They entered and closed and locked their doors as if they had synchronized it.

As Ollie started up the stairs, a hand

grabbed him by the arm. He nearly screamed, but another hand clapped over his mouth.

"Dude, it's just me," TJ whispered. "C'mere, I want to talk to you real quick."

TJ pulled Ollie back into the clown lounge. His eyes darted in all directions. "I feel like you're the only one of this bunch I can trust, man. You and me, we're both entrepreneurs. We both came from nothing. We built empires out of nothing except our own willpower and balls."

Ollie covered his mouth so TJ wouldn't see him giggle at the word "balls."

"We're in a tough spot, you know? All these people — they're all comics, man. Iffy types.

"Connie Chung Junior up there, she's just itching to put a shiv between the ribs of anyone more famous than her, which is everybody.

"Projects poseur, bargain-basement Chris Rock, he's a real thug. I mean, violent. Watch your ass around him. Keep the booze far, far away.

"Zoe Schwartz, she's a blonde Jew, what's that all about? You can't believe a word out of her mouth.

"The Nubian Princess, she's been full of shit from the get-go. For all I know she's carrying out Dusty's crazy-ass plan because it's a requirement for her to inherit all his dough.

"And that Gordo . . . he's a straight-up criminal, man. Believe me, I know from experience. He's the worst of the bunch, man. Watch your back around him."

Ollie clutched his hands together and got more and more excited the more TJ talked. "O. M. G. Mr. Martinez, are you saying what I think you're saying?"

TJ said, "You . . . shouldn't actually say text abbreviations out loud, man, but yeah, I think we should . . ."

"Form an alliance?!" Ollie hopped up and down and grabbed TJ's hands. "Yes! Yes! Yes!"

"*Sssh,* dude, keep your voice down. Yeah, that's the idea. Good, we got to watch out for each other. Particularly against Dante and Zoe. Remember, you can't believe a word that bitch says."

"I was thinking, we could probably scrounge up enough materials to build a raft. My construction skills are excellent. The voyage could be pretty easy as long as we had the weather with us. We could steer back to Saint Martin by the stars. Unless . . . that might bring back painful memories for you."

"Painful . . . what? Why?"

"Of how you and your family came to America."

"Dude. That's racist."

"Oh, no! I'm so sorry."

"Yeah, man, you're thinking of Cubans. Puerto Ricans come on airplanes like normal people. Don't mix up the two. It's very offensive.

"But that doesn't matter right now. The raft idea — I like it. You're thinking along the right lines. I feel like this partnership is already paying dividends. But hitting the open water is more of a Hail Mary pass. I think the smart play is to stay put. Even if Meredith has double-crossed us and the boat that brought us here isn't coming back, somebody is going to come looking for us. Or at least they're going to come looking for me. You, I'm not so sure about. No offense."

Ollie shook his head. "I'm supposed to inspect the Orange Baby Man Theatre at Sandals Virgin Islands on Tuesday. If I'm not there, my company will definitely want to know why. I'm not just their boss. I'm their inspiration."

TJ felt queasy — maybe it was Ollie's sickening earnestness, or perhaps it was the Hot Pockets bloating in his stomach — but he pressed on. "So we're agreed. The important thing is staying alive until we get rescued. I need you to not let Zoe out of your sights. Or Dante. Or any of them, really."

Ollie nodded sagely, considering this request. "Or maybe it would be easier and safer if we just spent the rest of the weekend in the panic room." He arched an eyebrow.

TJ had no visible reaction. Very slowly and very coolly, he said:

"How about you show me where that is, partner."

IX

Steve locked his door behind him and bolted the hurricane shutters. He had no idea if he could fall asleep with imminent violent death lurking in every shadow and around every corner, but he was genuinely exhausted.

He lay on his back still in his clothes, on top of the bedspread, in case any murder sounds needed investigating in a jiffy. He kicked off his shoes, closed his eyes, and folded his hands on top of his chest.

Like a body in a coffin.

Once that thought occurred to him, he dropped his hands to his sides.

Just beyond the shutters, a group of small frogs or large bugs, some invisible mass of crawling vermin, hummed and hummed and hummed like the quickening pulse of night.

The dread weighing down every fiber of Steve's being sank into his eyelids.

He was just about to drift off when a knock at the door snapped him to attention.

He froze, then turned his head to one side: "Who is it?"

"Zoe," came the whispered response through the door. "C'mon, open up!"

He got up. He unlocked the door and opened it just a crack. On the other side she was fidgeting in gym shorts and a gray T-shirt that depicted a generic human outline shooting both hands up in triumph and the words I POOPED TODAY!

"Let me in, let me in." She pushed him to get inside.

Steve looked out onto the land didn't see anyone. All the doors belvedere were closed. "Is som you?"

"Not *yet.*"

He locked the door an her. Zoe was wringing h ing bashful.

193

"What's wrong?" he said.

"Can I, ah, spend the night here? I really — I tried it by myself in there, and I, I didn't like it. Not at all."

"Sure," he said, "but how do you know I'm not the killer?"

"How do you know I'm not?"

"Your jammies don't look like they could conceal a weapon. Unless you're planning on snapping my neck Steven Seagal–style."

"No, I've never been able to generate that much torque with my wrists."

Still, he didn't take his hand off the doorknob. "You sure you wouldn't rather be with TJ?"

She looked askance. "I thought you looked funny when you found us together. Look — that was nothing. He's still an asshole. He wanted us to work together. Form an alliance."

"Against me?"

"Oddly, no. He hates Dante Dupree more for some reason. Your name didn't come up."

"Oh, so I'm nice and nonthreatening? Is that why you're here?"

"Dude. Are you . . . are you actually offended that I don't think you're the killer? Seriously?"

"Look, my masculinity is in a tender state

at the moment, sorry."

She sat on the bed. "You have this ador-able sad-puppy quality about you."

"You're not helping."

"Sad puppies are hot. I think you're . . . well, I can't lie. I've been fantasizing about you since tenth grade."

"Those must have been some reruns."

"To a girl who wanted to be funny? You bet your ass they were. And I don't know . . . this whole experience . . . it's kind of hot, right? Fight Thanatos with Eros? That's a natural impulse, isn't it?"

She patted the bed next to her.

He took his hand off the doorknob.

Steve said:

"Natural or not, I'm going to encourage it."

X

At midnight the wind off the ocean grew noticeably, punitively cooler. And stronger. The hushed sounds of the palms brushing against one another grew louder, bolder; wordless voices rising in mounting panic.

Nevertheless, Ruby Ng kept her hurricane shutters open. She faced the night sitting cross-legged on her bed and thumbed her way through every conceivable level of the flip phone's primitive settings until she confirmed its network connection was entirely one way. She couldn't get on any external website or app. Apparently all she could do was contact one specific other phone.

So that's what she did, typing:

We need to talk

She waited a full minute for the response:

U didnt come to libary u werent there

She frowned, considering her response, before thumbing:

I was there. Then Janet got shot.

No answer for a while, then she added:

I still want to hear what you have to say. Can you still meet tonight?

This time the response came much

quicker:

> U no were playroom is

She quickly sent:

> Yes. Meet you there in thirty minutes?
> 1am?

> K

Instantly she jackknifed off the bed and collected a small travel-size can of mace out of her purse. Until Janet was shot, she'd thought it was overkill to come back to the room and get it, but hell no, not anymore.

From her purse she also grabbed a "personal alarm," a big black button at the end of a lanyard that, when pressed, emitted the world's loudest, most annoying sound. Basically, it was a rape whistle on steroids. Her mom had ordered it for her on Amazon when she moved into that apartment in Koreatown because everyone (Mom said) knew that Koreans were a racist people who looked down on Vietnamese and didn't they

197

have gangs there and you can't let them think they can mess with you and maybe you'll meet a nice Korean doctor with a penis and get married and carry on the family bloodline as God and nature intended?

Ruby was also armed with a vague knowledge of aikido acquired two years ago during a series of weekly classes at the Long Beach LGBTQ Center. She was pretty good about going for five weeks, until her tour schedule heated up and she never went back. Other than not quite being able to shake the nagging feeling she was personally legitimizing a Euro-American stereotype by learning martial arts, Ruby discovered that the step-step-grab-throw-pivot movements required to kick someone's ass without actually kicking their ass — per aikido's philosophy of nonviolence — was so complicated it was like memorizing VCR instructions for her own body. She was pretty sure that when confronted by a rapist in a dark parking lot, trying to remember some Olympic-level gymnastics routine instead of just sending a non-nonviolent kick straight to his balls was going to get her killed, or worse. Also, all aikido moves seemed to dump your opponent on his back, looking right up at your highly punchable crotch, which was the area she was generally trying to protect in the first place. That seemed like a design flaw in this whole system of self-defense, if you asked her.

That said, if the Dustin Walker Island Killer came at her with a knife (and not a shotgun or a bazooka), and the mace nozzle jammed, and her personal alarm failed, she was fairly confident she could grab her assailant by the wrist, flip him onto his back, and then run like hell for help.

Ruby put both her phones on silent (no vibrate) and took off her shoes, slipping barefoot onto the belvedere landing and closing the door silently behind her. She padded downstairs, quickly, making sure she was alone. She was. She couldn't see anyone on the grounds either. The pool, the fountain, the distant cabana were all pretty well lit by a few scattered lampposts. Palm shadows bobbed like scythes against the white plaster walls. There was no sound but sighing trees.

She stole into the playroom a full twenty-five minutes prior to the agreed-upon meeting with her mystery correspondent.

Of course, he wasn't much of a mystery to her.

She had figured out it was Oliver Rees.

For one thing, Ruby had been a psychology major in college. For another, she had been a woman her entire life. It was obvious to anyone with half a brain and an entire vagina that Ollie was a classic aggrieved male, underdeveloped sexually as well as emotionally. A textbook case of someone acting out perverse domination fantasies on a cohort largely comprised of people of color and women and queers. And if he could prove to the handful of cis straight men he had invited along that he was superior to them (even if he did look as though Danny DeVito had asexually budded off a smaller, completely hairless Danny DeVito), well, then so much the better.

Also: she had seen him carrying around one of those Orange Baby Man franchise binders, which she had recognized from the time she'd intercepted him for *Comedy Ambush.* Clearly he had some kind of business arrangement with Dustin Walker and the two were in cahoots.

Double-also: Ruby knew enough about Ollie's Orange Baby Man operation that his elaborate prop gags, puerile though they may be, required a formidable amount of tactical planning and technical expertise to execute. Exactly what was required to pull off something as insane and insanely complicated as what they were being subjected to here.

She looked around to satisfy herself that she was alone. Then she climbed into the ball pit and burrowed her petite body as far as possible beneath the surface of the multi-chromatic spheres, making sure she could still survey the room through tiny gaps in the top layer.

She was not afraid to die. Not for a cause that was right — and outsmarting this ass-hole who was terrorizing her and her colleagues, oppressing them, making them live in fear, was the rightest cause she had ever been involved in.

Ruby had a natural, assured patience honed from many, many hours lying in wait for the unsuspecting. Tipping your hand too soon was the gravest sin in the hunter's religion. Usually she passed the time by go-ing over her stand-up routines in her head, attacking each joke word by word, weeding out stray adjectives, practicing the length of pauses.

In this instance she worked on her vows for her wedding, which she knew in her heart of hearts she would be saying out loud soon.

Hey, 'Vette. Look at us, standing here at last. I can tell by your face you hardly believe it? Well, makes two of us. You finally won. You finally wore me down. And I've never been happier to lose any fight ever.

She didn't check the time. She never did. Any anticipatory movement could give the game away.

You used to say all the time that comedy was my real wife, that you felt like my mistress. And putting up with all my touring and traveling and career bullshit — can you say bullshit during wedding vows? If not, sorry, bring me a time machine — I hope you know now how not true that is.

You are my one true love, 'Vette, now, then, and always.

She did not know when, exactly, the sliding glass door to the pool area slowly opened. She just flexed her grip on the mace and made sure she knew where the button of the personal alarm was by her clavicle.

The door opened all the way and a figure stood in the opening. It was outlined in black by light streaming in from the patio beyond, so she couldn't make out who it was. She would know for certain soon enough.

She braced herself to leap out of the pit, but the balls beneath her feet simply shifted; she moved her legs a little but still found no stable foundation off which to leap out — a foundation that had been there just moments before.

Ruby didn't want to cry out and give away her position, but she heard the metallic shudder of gears beneath her and suddenly realized she was kicking her legs and not finding purchase — there was no beneath beneath them. The mass of balls she was encased in was falling down as the floor of a pit yawned open below, and she was going with them.

She let out a little cry and released both the mace and the alarm at the same time, lashing her hands outward for the edge of the pit. But it was already too late. She was sinking far away from the rim. All her clawing fingers found were more plastic balls falling in the same direction as she was.

In an instant, her bravery cratered: she *was* afraid to die. She was fearless only if her death meant something, if it was to strike a blow against her enemies and her community's enemies. She was afraid to die stupidly, or to die pointlessly, to die anonymously, like any other faceless schmuck, which is what she had convinced herself she was not, because that was what she needed to give her life meaning.

TOK, TOK, TOK. She could hear the balls dropping a considerable distance and bouncing at the terminus of the pit far below.

In her animal panic she made several stark, staccato sounds, almost like barks, and the figure approached the edge of the pit. Ruby saw her outline — oh my God, she was wrong, it was a her. *It was a her!*

Then the balls, like sand through the hourglass, smothered her vision, and she realized the figure she had been looking at wasn't a real thing at all, but Yvette, in her flowing white wedding dress, holding her bouquet and shaking her head at the tragic fact that Ruby didn't listen to her and came here over her objections — that Ruby never listened to her at all, in fact. Never in their entire relationship. It was always comedy first. Always career. Yvette knew who Ruby's true love really was.

She opened her mouth to say *I'm sorry, I'll always be sorry, now I'm coming back to your side and never leaving,* but the last of the balls in the pit beneath her fell away and then there was nothing between her and the void and into it she dropped.

When Ruby Ng landed, she at last learned where all the blades in the house had gone.

You know what else I hate?

Yeah, there's more than one thing. I know. I'm as shocked as you are. Yeah.

Actually, I do hate a lot of things. It's true. My mother says it's to keep more room in my heart for love.

(Beat)

God, I hate my mother.

But that's not relevant to the current discussion.

And I have to warn you, when I tell you this, you'll never get it out of your head. It's like the video from *The Ring.* You'll see it everywhere. It's like a curse. Seriously. This happens in movies and TV all the time.

Like, I was watching this classic film, *The Adventures of Cosmic Carson.* Dustin Walker. Yeah. Anybody see it?

One . . . two of you?

Huh.

All three of us must have been on the same flight.

Anyway, in this movie, there's this one person sitting in a room.

You know, like they do in movies.

And then another person comes into the room, and sits across from her, and says, "We need to talk."

"We need to talk."

I mean, is that line really necessary? When you need to talk to someone, you never go up to them and say, "We need to talk."

Because, for one thing, by saying that four-word phrase, you're already talking to them. So by making the statement "We need to talk," you're already doing the thing you're declaring you need to do. You're not even waiting for permission or acknowledgment from the other person. It's a real microaggression. It's like verbal mini-rape.

Yeah.

I know.

You don't say, "We need to talk." You just talk. Because you're a real person. You're not fictional.

At least, I hope you're not.

Otherwise I'd be doing this show to an empty room.

And that would be weird.

(Beat)

I don't understand what screenwriters are thinking. The first guy is already in a room eating a sandwich or examining the naked corpse on the slab or staring out through the bridge screen at the empty vastness of space.

You know, depending on what kind of movie it is.

So then the second guy comes in and says, "We need to talk." Are we at home on the couch now supposed to be like, "Oooooh, talking. They let us know that's gonna happen. In a fictional scene. Now I'm interested. I thought maybe they were going to play hacky sack for twenty-five minutes. But no, there's going to be *talking*. Awesome sauce. Quick, bring

Grandma in from the bathroom.

I don't care if she *is* in mid-dump.

No. Get Bà Nôi off the toilet right now, I said. She specifically said to come get her the *second* any *talking* happens."

"We need to talk."

Really? Do you *need* to talk? Are you sure? Why? Is this like that movie *Crank* where you've been injected with some kind of poison that will kill you if your lips stop moving?

In kung-fu movies, two guys don't come in and say, "We need to kick."

In horror movies, the maniac in the mask doesn't say, "We need to stab."

In pornos they don't say, "We need to screw."

Well.

Maybe in some pornos they do.

I don't know if you've noticed, but the writing in porno movies is really bad.

Hollywood, don't be like pornos.

"We need to talk."

You don't need to pump the gas, man! I'm already watching. My ass is in the seat. I am ready and willing to be entered by, you know, your thoroughly focus-grouped and committee-conceived corporate entertainment product. Don't say "We need to talk," just start talking. Geez.

It makes me want to go all Elvis on my TV.

Except I'm very anti-gun. Very anti-gun. I don't own a gun. I can't shoot the TV.

(Beat)

I do own a vibrator, though. I could throw my vibrator at the TV.

My vibrator is industrial strength. Yeah. I sprung for the Leviathan™. It's powered by sixteen D batteries. Yeah. It's like being finger-blasted by an entire WNBA team at the same time.

Except in, you know, more convenient portable form.

The Leviathan™ people did not pay for that

endorsement, by the way. No. I don't do that. I do not do corporate sponsorships. That was a purely spontaneous testimonial.

There is one big difference between the Leviathan™ and a WNBA team, though, which is that you can't bring the Leviathan™ into the bathtub with you. Otherwise . . . no, it's just not a good scene. It'll ruin your day. Believe me. I know. I tried. Yeah. I'm not proud about it, either.

Yeah, that Leviathan™ is gonna do some serious damage to our plasma screen when I chuck it at it like a spear. Yup. My girlfriend is gonna be super-pissed.

But c'mon, honey. What was I supposed to do?

Bones chick said, "We need to talk."

— Ruby Ng
Meltdown Comics, Los Angeles, CA
October 3, 2016

CHAPTER SIX

I

The idea to kill TJ Martinez entered Zoe Schwartz's mind not long after dawn.

She awoke well before Steve Gordon. He lay on his back with his mouth open and occasionally made sounds that threatened to become snoring, but then went right back to breathing regularly again.

Murder popped into her head as she turned away to face the door. She was having these thoughts not for the first time since Martinez had frightened and humiliated her in the dressing room at *2nite,* but this time she did not immediately discard them as she had every time before. Instead she considered killing him in an academic, practical sense, as opposed to the idle cathartic fantasy it otherwise had always been. For the first time, the thought occurred in a place where she could commit the crime — one murder amid many — and theoretically get away with it. TJ was too megalomaniacal and stupid to be threatened by her, either physically or mentally, by her threats of exposure. It was that same smug feeling of invincibility that let him do what he did to women. It might even be worth it, risking jail, distracting herself from her own survival, not to mention costing her her own soul, just to see the look on his face when he realized she was about to end him. It might be the only time in TJ Martinez's life that he would be capable of experiencing something resembling remorse.

But a thought of murder was an uninspiring thought nevertheless. And after a few minutes of cursory examination, when the logistical absurdity of doing it without a weapon (*push him off a cliff*) in such a way that didn't tip off the others (*after midnight*) and get her blamed for all the other murders (*they would all support you because they hate him, too*), became plain, she put the thought away. Besides, she fancied herself a good person. She could no more kill another human being in cold blood, even a human being with so few upsides as TJ Martinez, than she could, well, cum on somebody's shoe when they weren't asking for it.

Steve stirred and nuzzled the back of her head:

"Good morning," he said.

"Good morning."

"What are you thinking about?"

"Nothing," she said.

II

The idea to kill Zoe Schwartz began as an offhanded aside in TJ Martinez's mind, easily batted away: no, don't be ridiculous.

He wasn't really aware of sleeping or wakefulness, dreaming or conscious thought. Before murder had occurred to him, his mind had been transfixed by the panic room in the wine cellar, with its steel vault door and keypad lock. Any idiot could see it was not only the safest room in the house, it was also the likeliest hiding place for whoever was knocking them off one by one.

Well, if you were going to kill her, this would be the best place to do it, right, because it would just get blamed on Dusty Walker.

Shut up! his mind roared. I can't worry about this. Dusty is trying to kill me *and* her.

But what if he's not? What if this is all just an elaborate scheme to get at you?

213

That's loco.

You are trapped on a tropical island by a man who said he was going to kill you. Traditional standards of "loco" do not apply.

TJ thought, I can't worry about Zoe fucking Schwartz and whether she may or may not have the balls to tank my career. I've got to worry about keeping my own ass alive. Concentrate on the matter at hand:

Ollie Rees said that the code to open the panic room was six digits, but he also said there was no indication, in his binder at least, of what the combination might be. TJ tried to remember back to the early '90s, when he and Dusty would be wingmanning each other in the clubs, how they identified the girls they wanted, the girls they wanted at the same time, the girls they let each other have, but nothing came to mind that could be reduced to a numerical code.

Would Ollie let him see the binder? Noooooo, of course not. "I'm sorry, Mr. Martinez, but this is something private between me and Mr. Walker," he'd said. "I know his ghost may be trying to kill us, but I am a strong believer in comic/potential backer confidentiality." That tub of guts was the biggest comedy criminal of all of them, about this TJ had no doubt. He charged for childlike wonder by the hour, plus overtime on weekends and bank holidays.

That was the problem with losers, really. They never get what made winners different. They assumed it was some trick, some conspiracy, a blow job to the right person. So full of resentment and envy, they never realized that the only difference between winners and losers was that winners won. That was it.

Exactly. So you are going to get out of here. But what if Zoe gets out of here, too? Then it'll be too late.

I thought I told you to shut up.

What are the chances Dusty actually kills all of you?

He's doing a pretty damn good job so far.

Bullshit. An old lady and a snob with his head up his butt he caught by surprise. But now you're forewarned. Now you know better.

Exactly. And if I get caught trying to do in Zoe, I'll be blamed for all the others.

So don't get caught, genius.

TJ willed the thought away, tried to think about something else, some other clue what the combination to the panic room might be. Ollie said it was originally the date his album *Can't Help Myself* dropped, so had it been changed to some other significant date? The date *What Just Happened?* went on the air — or, more likely, the date it went

215

off? The date he met his wife . . . but which one of the three? The date his kids were born? If he had any kids? TJ couldn't remember.

Maybe you could sneak into her room.

No, it'll be locked. Besides, we have no weapons. I'd have to smother her with a pillow. Can I do that? Physically, I mean? She looks like she works out.

Steal the shotgun from Meredith Ladipo? Even if I could, it's not loaded.

Push her down the stairs? No, too good a chance she survives.

Lure her to the cliffs and push her off? *Now, we're talking.* But (a) how could I get her to come out alone with me, and (b) out in the open it's pretty likely I'll get spotted.

Unless you did it late at night.

TJ lay on his back and stared at the ceiling. The mahogany fan in the center of the white-painted slats listed slightly on its axis, so it sounded like it kept muttering "rutabaga rutabaga rutabaga" as it wobbled in place.

Unless I did it late at night, he thought.

III

Dante Dupree did not wake so much as come very slowly back online. He was fully

216

dressed, crumpled in a heap over the still-made comforter on the bed in his room.

He rolled onto one side and, for a brief, glorious moment, was grateful how hungover he wasn't; but then he sat up and the pain dropped on his head like a cartoon piano. He felt exhausted and empty, like his body had been drained of some vital fluid. Invisible cobwebs extended from him to the rest of the world, and they kept his movements slow and sluggish.

As he rose to check that his door and shutters were locked, his stomach did a Chinese acrobat routine. He had thoroughly examined the seal on the cap of the whiskey bottle rediscovered on his end table when he came upstairs to go to bed, seeing no puncture anywhere, and decided it couldn't have been poisoned. He swore he'd only try a taste, but a taste became a cup, and a cup became a third, and a third became fuck it. Now he was awake and convinced that someone had tried to murder him overnight with witchcraft, his head was so compressed and his body so abused.

Why did tasty beverages have to be so tasty?

Why couldn't he have just one? Why was booze going to force him to give up booze altogether? Didn't booze understand that he loved booze with the fire of a billion blazing suns? He and moderation were not very well acquainted. It's all or nothing with this drinking thing, Dante, in both drinking and *not* drinking. You're kidding yourself to think you can ease up on the throttle. You just got to sell the whole damn car.

Except it had yet to hurt him so badly that he felt he absolutely needed to get help. He was aware of the bottom's existence without having reached it yet. He could find it on the map, he had met people who had been there, he had seen pictures of it, he had read about it in school, but he had never actually been there. He was aware he was drifting toward it, but until he landed, he could still persuade himself it was just a mirage, a rumor, and he could continue falling weightless forever without consequence.

Dear baby Jesus, if you're really there, I swear, if you help me get off this island, I will join the hundreds of comics already in the program. I will take the thirty-nine steps, or whatever they call it. I will stand up in a church basement and use a fake name and tell strangers a credible lie about how long it's been since my last drink. I promise to never shut the fuck up about how many days or months or years I have been sober, just like every other tired old

218

comic I ever met.

Unless Dustin Walker kills me, in which case, screw you. I'm getting hammered in heaven every goddamn day.

He shuffled back to the bed from his morning pee and accidentally kicked the empty Scotch bottle, sending it bolting across the floor and bouncing off the dresser. It rattled harshly as it rolled, and when Dante picked it up, saw something he hadn't noticed in his binge the night before:

A small key on a wire-thin ring was lying inside.

He upended the bottle and with purposeful jiggling managed to drop the key into his palm.

Now what the hell does this open? he wondered.

IV

By seven-thirty the birds beyond the closed hurricane shutters were dueling songs in earnest, so Zoe Schwartz decided it was safe to return to her room. She reasoned it was too late in the morning for anyone to be murdered without alerting the others, which made sense to Steve, too, allowing for the fact that making sense was not the primary quality of the situation in which they found themselves.

Steve stayed in bed while she put on her gym shorts and the I POOPED TODAY! T-shirt.

"You know, if we get out of here alive, this would be a good project to pitch Apatow," he said.

"You're from Canada, huh?"

"You read my Wikipedia page?"

"Didn't need to. You pronounce project '*proh*-ject.' "

"Yeah. You ever heard of Kitchener, Ontario?"

"Has *anyone* ever heard of Kitchener, Ontario?"

"No. It was just me and my parents. Three-person town. We elected our cat mayor every year."

Zoe laughed.

"Anyway, that's where I'm from. Came to the States to go to Northwestern and ended up at Second City. Though I guess the more accurate way of putting it is that I wanted to go to Second City, and Northwestern was the excuse to have my parents pay for me to leave the country."

"Big *SNL* fan, huh?"

"I have lived my whole life by Lorne Michaels's teachings. He's Canadian, too, you know."

"Really. I've never met a Canadian in comedy who's mentioned that."

"Are these also Canadians in comedy you've slept with or . . . ?"

"Yo, don't slut-shame me, bro."

"I'm Canadian. I'm far too polite to slut-shame anyone."

"You know, Canadians and the word 'polite,' this is like Americans and the word 'freedom.' It's a buzzword you like to repeat over and over to puff yourselves up but that you don't actually like living up to. Most of the time when we say 'freedom,' we mean 'do it my way or I'll shoot you.' Most of the time when you say 'polite,' you mean 'passive-aggressive.' "

He laughed. "Think what it's like growing up there."

"I bet I would have liked it better than Long Island. There people are aggressive-aggressive."

She went to the door, put her hand on the knob, but otherwise didn't move.

"You think we're going to get out of this okay?" Zoe asked.

"I wish I knew, Zoe," Steve said, looking at the ceiling. "I hope so."

"I mean," she said with a nervous chuckle, "we're the pretty white people. We always come out ahead."

Steve didn't laugh. He looked at her and said:

"I don't know. I don't think that applies here. It's not like this is a job interview or anything."

Zoe didn't know what to say to that, so she just stepped into the belvedere gallery and closed his door as quietly as she could.

Immediately she had the sense that she wasn't alone, even though, looking up and down the hallway, she saw no one.

Her own door was still closed, but she just realized that she had no way of locking it from the outside, so someone could have slipped in there during the night.

And was in there now.

Waiting for her return.

It was then that she saw the shadow retreat down the stairs.

"Hey! Hey there! Who is that?" she called down.

The shadow froze for just a second, then instantly receded.

"Stop! Stop, you fucker! Stop!" Without considering if this plan was smart one way or the other, Zoe sprinted barefoot to the top of the stairs then ran down them two at a time. "I see you, fucker! Steve! Everybody! Come on! I've got him! I see him!"

When she reached ground level she saw

the shadow retreat outside through the front gallery. She ran after it, braking outside by the fountain. Looking right, through a line of bamboo, she saw a robed figure loping up the slope to the cabana.

Zoe Schwartz had been a cheerleader and a member of the track team in high school. Just a few months ago she had hired a personal trainer to help her drop her usual twenty-five before the press tour for her Netflix special, and she hadn't yet had the opportunity to stuff it all back into her mouth in the form of cheesy-crust Domino's and vats of Neapolitan ice cream — a common postpartum aftereffect to fill the void left when she wrapped up a major project like an hourlong.

So she bounded like a gazelle over the water element extending from the fountain and through the curtain of bamboo and up the hill after the bobbing silk robe, yelling "Stop, fucker, stop!" the whole time. And when she hurled herself at his torso, he went down with a crash like a lumpy mattress.

"Ow! Ow! Stop it! Gross! Get off of me!" cried Oliver Rees, rolling out from under her. "I'm sorry, all right? I'm sorry! Just leave me alone!"

"What? Are? You? Doing? You? Fat? Fuck?" Zoe gasped, more winded from her sprint than she anticipated.

"Don't call me an eff, you bee!" Ollie said, rising on his knees. "My doctor says binge-eating is triggered by stress. And I don't know if you noticed but this is a very stressful situation we're in, Zoe!"

"If you don't start making sense right now, I'm going to murder you myself, then blame it on Walker," Zoe said, getting back to her feet. "What were you thinking, creeping around like that?"

"I couldn't sleep," Ollie whined. "And when I'm upset, I eat. I wanted to get back to my room before anyone caught me."

The others started to arrive. Steve was in just his boxers; Dante in the clothes he had on the night before. TJ had on a *2nite*-branded tank top and pajama bottoms. Meredith Ladipo slipped on a taffeta robe over some kind of one-piece nighty thing and carried the empty shotgun in both hands.

"How much did you eat?" Steve said.

"I'm not sure," Ollie said. "I fell asleep in the middle of the night at the kitchen table, and when I woke up I forgot how much I ate so I ate the rest of it, just to be sure."

"How much?" Zoe said.

"A-all of it, I think . . ." Ollie said, and then flinched as Zoe cocked a fist to hit him.

She pulled back at the last minute.

"I should hit you just for scaring the crap out of me," she said.

"Sorry," he said.

"That was all of the food we had," Meredith groaned, shaking her head.

"What in God's name are you wearing?" Dante couldn't take his eyes off Ollie's orange silk robe with gold trim. "You look like the Pillsbury Pimp-Boy."

"It's from my boxing sketch. Have none of you seen my act?"

"I prefer comedy," Dante said.

TJ Martinez looked at all of them, then back at the house:

"What happened to the podcasting chick? She's the only one who didn't come down."

V

"Ruby?" Zoe called as they reentered the gallery. "Ruby?"

Steve sighed, gesturing at the wall with the headshots:

"Save your breath."

Meredith, Zoe, Ollie, TJ, and Dante gathered around them, too. There were five photos remaining on the wall.

Not one of them was Ruby's.

Dante Dupree roared:

"Fuck this fucking shit!"

He yanked the frames off the wall and piled them in his arms and marched outside.

"Should you — ?" Ollie started to say while running after him, but TJ stopped him by touching his arm.

"What did I tell you about this guy?" he said to Ollie under his breath.

Ollie just looked at him before running after the others.

Meredith followed Dante outside, calling for him to stop, followed by Zoe and Steve. He just kept yelling some variation of "Fuck this fucking shit" over and over.

"Can you see this, Dusty? Huh? From out there?" he called up to the sky, then, looking to the ground: "Or down there? Your act? It sucks. It's not funny, dude. Not funny. And I'm not gonna sit here all polite and shit in the audience while you do it, neither! No way! You're not gonna ignore me! I'm gonna make you break!"

When Dante reached the cliff edge overlooking the rocks and surging surf he took one frame and hurled it, discus-style, into the sea.

"Gonna get you off your game, baby! You ain't seen no heckle like a Dante Dupree heckle!"

He cast out another headshot. It arced

briefly skyward before plummeting seaward, disappearing from view before even hitting the waves.

"Sick of this unfunny shit! You hear me? Sick of it!"

He twisted his waist as far as he could before pitching the remaining three photos over the edge.

"We're not gonna play by your script, motherfucker! Try doing the act with no props, huh? Who's the hack? You're the hack! You are! You are! Yeah! That's right!"

By this point Dante was just yelling and pointing at the water. When he finished, he was out of breath. He turned back panting to his audience of three.

"Feel better now?" Zoe said.

He thought about it, then grinned.

"You know, actually I do."

Ollie came running over, breathless. "Hey, hey, wait, you guys! Dante! I just realized! If we put someone or hid a camera or iPhone pointed at the photos, we could catch whoever's taking them away red-handed!"

Dante looked down at the surf and its distinct lack of photos.

"Now I feel worse," he said.

VI

As soon as Oliver Rees left the courtyard, TJ Martinez dashed upstairs, two steps at a time, until he reached Ollie's door, whose location he had noted when they went to bed the night before.

Although Ollie had stayed in the room for less than twenty-four hours, it looked like a toddler had been locked inside for a week. Clothes were strewn everywhere. However, the traffic-cone-colored binder was impossible to miss, lying atop the spectacularly unmade bed, its sheets tangled into knotty cords as if the occupant had been trying to make rope in his sleep.

Through the window TJ could see the others at the edge of the cliff, counted all five of them, then snatched up the binder and flipped through to learn what advantages it had given Ollie.

The graphics were nigh-incomprehensible blueprints for elaborately staged prop gags, among them the shotgun-in-the-patio bit that took out Janet and a schematic for some kind of hatch underneath the bouncy castle. After flipping past these he discovered a precise architectural drawing of the panic room, with columns of dense text describing . . .

TJ groaned and closed his eyes.
The text said:

Egg keeky dipshuh bliddle little bey unt
ten u glib gamma mamma pama boo blpp
blpp glx

The whole book was written in Baby-Rap®, the cloying Pig Latin babbled by Rees's Orange Baby Man character onstage. And apparently it was . . . an actual language? That someone could replicate in letters and characters? That Rees could read? Or was he just trying to put one over on him?

TJ found it hard to believe that Ollie had the cranial capacity to deceive him like this, but who knew? Maybe there was some animal cunning going on in that perfectly round gumball of a head.

He noticed the others returning from the cliff's edge, so TJ tossed the binder back on the bed and hurriedly left Ollie's room to get downstairs before they arrived.

But they were quicker than he anticipated. "Where'd Martinez go?" he heard someone say just as he was closing the door.

Inspiration struck instantaneously.

"Up here!" he called. "Look what I found!"

He opened and closed doors until he found a room with a still-made bed. He left it open and stepped inside. Ruby Ng's driver's license lay inside her Hothead Paisan duct-tape wallet, which was inside the metal Wonder Woman faux-vintage lunchbox she used as a purse.

"You wanna see this!" he yelled through the open door, and soon the others joined him in Ruby's room.

"Thought I'd do something useful while you were acting out," TJ said.

"Fuck you, man," Dante said.

"See, Ruby's bed hasn't been slept in. At least that's what it looks like."

They all looked at the bed.

"Search the house?" Steve said.

"Again?" Ollie groaned.

"We haven't searched this floor yet," Meredith said. "We were interrupted by . . . Ms. Ng sneaking away. And Ms. Kahn dying."

Zoe said, "Why bother? You're the one who keeps saying there's no one else on the island."

"There isn't," Meredith said. "But now Ms. Ng is unaccounted for."

"It's more likely one of us killed her than the other way around," TJ said. "Shit she's talked about all of us, she's the most hated comic on this island."

"She was definitely the most hated *woman*," Zoe said, looking pointedly at TJ.

"Fuck you, too," he said merrily.

"Enough of that," Steve said. "Let's start looking and get this over with. Same pairs as before? Sorry, Ollie, you go with Meredith."

"Okay," Ollie muttered.

"No one is looking in my room," Zoe said. "Sorry. But no."

"Zoe . . ." Steve frowned. "We have to."

"No way." Zoe shook her head. "I'm not letting you."

Dante said, "Babe, I think you got to file this under 'tough shit.' "

"No, 'babe,' " Zoe said, "forget it."

Meredith Ladipo said, "Doxy this rank right frogger," walked out of the room, and turned the knob of the room next door.

"What'd she say?" TJ said.

Zoe let out a cry of protest and rushed past Meredith down the belvedere gallery. This, and the fact that the bed in the room also hadn't been slept in, indicated to Meredith that this wasn't Zoe's room.

She turned to leave when her brain processed an image her eyes had registered on the bedside table.

Meredith stepped back into the room,

closing the door almost all the way. A Dior handbag was thrown in an armchair, suggesting that, by process of elimination, this had been Janet Kahn's room.

What caught Meredith's eye was a squarish box on the end table.

It was full of shotgun shells.

She could hear the others arguing outside. Stepping out of sight of the landing, she loaded a pair of shells into the gun, then slipped the box into her robe pocket.

She rejoined the others outside, saying, "There's nothing in Janet's room," but no one was listening. The four men were arguing with Zoe, who stood in her doorway, refusing entry in an ever-higher octave.

Meredith Ladipo elbowed past Dante Dupree and Steve Gordon and hit Zoe in the stomach as hard as she could with the butt of the shotgun.

When Zoe doubled over, wheezing "Bitch!" Meredith reached past her, opened the door, and went inside.

"Now we're even," she said.

Zoe's bed hadn't been slept in either, though a few clothes from her carry-on had been tossed about. Meredith wondered what the big fuss was when suddenly something small and gray darted around the side of the bed, unleashing a cascade of barking much louder than one would have thought possible from such a tiny animal.

"Holy shit, Jesus," Meredith cried and leapt back, shotgun raised. Fortunately she had the wherewithal not to pull the trigger at what looked like a large rat that had survived multiple attempts to drown it.

"Asshole! Asshole!" Zoe cried, muscling past the others and putting herself between the barrel of the shotgun and the tiny dog.

"Why you calling me names, bitch?" TJ said. "I didn't lay a hand on you."

"Asshole is the *dog's* name," Dante said.

"How'd you know that?"

"Netflix," Dante said.

Meredith said, "You brought a dog? Here? In clear violation of your contract?"

"I never could bear to be separated from my baby," Zoe said, lifting the dog in both arms. Asshole bathed her cheek with kisses from his microscopic lizard tongue. "He's basically a service dog. He helps with my anxiety. I'm between therapists right now or I would have made them write you a note."

"Did you think we were going to eat him or something?" Dante said. "Why all the secrecy?"

"And how did you keep him so quiet while smuggling him onto the island?" Steve said.

"I gave him Puppy Ambien® right before

we got on the plane," she said. "It knocks him out for hours and hours. But once I got here and I saw the house was open to the rest of the island, with the sea and the cliffs and everything, I kept him in here and fed him and petted him. He's very well trained. He pee-peed on this copy of the *New York Post,* and I've been carefully disposing of his doo-doos."

Ollie covered his mouth and giggled at "doo-doos."

"I wish you had told us sooner," Steve said.

"I didn't want the murderer knowing he was here! That's why I ran back from the cabana to check on him. *You* said the pets always die first!"

"I meant they always die first in horror movies," Steve said. "And they're usually killed by ghosts, not stepped on by accident, which is probably how that pathetic mutt is going to check out."

"Did you find that thing stuck in the hair-catcher in your tub?" Dante said.

"*Is* that a dog, or did one of your pubes get hit by lighting and come to life?" TJ said.

"Don't listen to them, Asshole," Zoe whispered to the dog. "They're just a bunch of real jerkie jerk-face comics, yes they are, aren't they?" Then she licked the dog's face while he licked hers.

"Eeyyughh," Meredith Ladipo said.

VII

Ultimately Steve's splitting-up-and-searching plan was shouted down by the unlikely alliance of Dante Dupree and TJ Martinez. Since the last attempt was a spectacular failure, they decided to look for Ruby as a group, never letting one another out of their sight.

A wan and shuffling mass, they looked in all eight guest rooms, Meredith's room, the unslept-in master bedroom, the clown lounge, the faux library, the pool patio, the kitchen, the writers' room, the dining room, the playroom, the wine cellar, the bouncy house, the cabana, the elevator hut, and the dock, uncovering the following details:

The master bedroom, Dustin Walker's room, was spartan and anonymous and covered in dust. A plasma screen and PC tower sat on a desk, lying dormant in sleep mode. When Zoe hit the space bar to bring it back to life, the group was challenged for a password that no one had the energy to puzzle out.

Meredith Ladipo's room had a Basquiat print on one wall and a laptop (with no internet access) on the makeup table. They made her wait in the hallway, fidgeting with the shotgun, while they searched her room and bathroom.

It was nigh impossible for anyone to be in the writers' room for longer than a few seconds because the two corpses had begun to reek.

The only food left on the island appeared to be the half dozen packets of gourmet dog food Zoe had smuggled inside Asshole's carrier.

And no trace of Ruby Ng was found.

VIII

When the search concluded and the group returned to the front gallery, Meredith said, "I am going to wait for Captain Harry. He's about an hour late, but that's not unusual."

"His boat runs on CPT," Dante said. When she frowned at him he added, "Colored people's time."

Meredith wrinkled her nose. "I don't know what that means, but it sounds offensive."

"It's an American thing. Also an ironic thing — *you* not understanding what *I* say for once."

As Meredith walked toward the fountain,

Steve stepped in front of her.

"We can't separate," he said. "Not anymore. We have to stick together at all times. It's the only way to be sure we don't keep getting picked off one by one . . . and to make sure we aren't the ones doing the picking. Strength in numbers, et cetera."

"Fine," Meredith said. "*We* are all going to the dock, then, to pray for Captain Harry's cromulent return."

She brushed past him and headed for the stairs; the others looked at each other before following in a loose pack a few steps behind.

"Should we really let her have that gun?" TJ said to no one in particular.

"Where's the harm," Dante said, "if it's not loaded?"

"Can you be sure it's not loaded?"

"Why don't you grab it from her and find out?"

"I bet you'd like that."

Dante sighed. "Honestly, dude? I'm pretty sick and tired of lugging around dead bodies."

IX

To the surprise of exactly no one, Captain Harry's boat never showed up on the horizon, nor did anyone else's boat either.

At noon, something resembling a commercial airliner appeared in the sky far away, but it shortly disappeared behind the clouds.

When it vanished, the group agreed to leave the dock. They loaded on to the surprisingly huge and excruciatingly slow elevator and returned to the estate.

The Red Skelton Memorial Clown Lounge seemed the most defensible and comfortable room in which to hunker down, with its lockable doors and comfy divans, not to mention a bathroom just outside. They could take turns sleeping on the couches while others kept watch. They had no spoken plan and no endgame, except for the vague notion that if they held out long enough, somebody associated with one of their various businesses would become sufficiently disturbed by their absence to attempt a rescue.

Steve and Zoe sat side-by-side on one sofa in the sunken fireplace pit, smiling at each other and whispering and holding hands.

TJ sat near Ollie at the bar across the room. There was still a pittance of booze to be had, but after what had happened to Billy the Contractor, nobody wanted to risk the chance that it might be poisoned.

After making a disgusted snort in Steve

and Zoe's direction, TJ turned to Ollie, who was poring over the Orange Baby Man binder in his lap. "What are you getting out of your magic book there?"

"Well, I'm working my way through it and translating — it really shows that whoever wrote this really gets me, really gets the worldwide revolution in positivity I'm trying to spark with my art —"

"There's a pretty high profit margin on that, from what I hear."

"You see, TJ, it's that kind of cynicism that makes me not want to trust you. There are secrets in here, secrets of how the house was built and when many of the gags — well, he calls them gags in the same way as, you know, stuntmen call them gags —"

"Yeah, from what I've seen so far, they're hilarious."

"— but I don't feel comfortable sharing them with someone like yourself, who hasn't embraced the Radical Yes."

"Right. I haven't drunk the Kool-Aid. Or, in your case, the Tang."

Ollie shook his head. "Do you remember the exact moment all hope inside your soul died?"

"Yeah, the first moment the priest passed around the collection plate in Mass. These people who insist you have a soul, they always want you to pay for the privilege of cleaning it. And I'm sorry but I like being dirty. Most people like being dirty. I'm just not afraid to admit it."

"There's good in you, TJ Martinez. I'm just not sure how to draw it out."

"Take a number. Listen, I think we need — well, we need a code of our own."

"I'm not going to teach you BabyRap®. That's proprietary."

"God no, please don't. I can already feel myself losing what little's left of my marbles. No, I mean more like —" He looked around to make sure they weren't being observed. "In case I need you to help me out with, like, a diversion."

"A diversion?"

"Yeah, you zig when I zag, that sort of thing."

"I like it, I like it."

"Like when I call out a code word, you go for it. You draw them away."

"Like what? What were you thinking?"

"Like . . . how about . . . Tang."

"Tang?"

"Yeah. What's wrong with Tang?"

Ollie shook his head. "Nothing. I like Tang. Tang is good."

X

Meredith Ladipo felt a hand on her shoulder. She sat up in the clown lounge armchair she had kicked her feet back in, hands fumbling for the shotgun at her side.

"Chill, girl, chill. You fell asleep." Dante Dupree stood over her.

She groaned and rubbed her eyes, the weariness of the past twenty-four hours making her thin frame feel a thousand pounds heavier. "What time is it?"

"Little past five."

"Bloody hell." She'd been out for over four hours. "Boat's not coming, is it?"

"Who, Captain Harry? No, he came and dropped off stuff at three. You just missed him."

"What? Really?"

"No, of course not, dummy."

"Oh." She chuckled uneasily.

Dante peered at her with a crooked grin. "You know, no offense, girl, but for a stand-up you're the most gullible person I've ever met."

"That just means I'm a breath of fresh air," she said.

He pulled up a nearby footstool and sat next to her. "You get to do any actual gigs yet or . . . ?"

"Just some open mics, mostly back in London. A couple after I moved to L.A."

"You kill? I bet you killed."

"I . . . I wouldn't say I killed. I . . . lightly wounded. Once." She smiled bashfully and looked away. "All the other times, I bombed, to be honest."

"But you still went out, though, right? That takes guts. You should be proud of yourself."

"Then I met Dustin and I went to work for him, and I just haven't had time to get back on stage."

"For real?" Dante frowned. "If Dustin's mentoring you, he should be encouraging you to get on stage more, not less."

"No, of course. He is mentoring — he — he *was* mentoring me, but . . . I had certain . . . issues he was helping me get over, in my performance. And the job was a lot more involved than either of us had anticipated. I mean, organizing this weekend, it took quite a lot of time."

"His little murder party, you mean."

"I had no idea that's what it was —"

"I know, it's okay, I just . . ." He squinted. "How'd you meet him, you say? He see you perform across the pond or what?"

For a while Meredith looked like she was going to answer, but instead she said, "You

242

are asking a lot of questions, Mr. Dupree."

He flashed her a bright grin. "Sorry. Just naturally nosy, I guess. Get it from Grandma."

Somebody clapped their hands, and they turned to see Steve Gordon standing up.

"Okay, everybody, get up. Come on, on your feet."

They all just looked at him. Not even Zoe moved.

"Seriously, guys, if we die here it doesn't have to be of boredom," Steve said. "We'll do a super-quick, easy, and fun game I do to warm up my improv students."

Everyone groaned.

"Man, don't make us do improv," Dante said. "That makes you a Hitler."

"Once again, I am just making a suggestion," Steve said. "If you absolutely don't want to play, you don't have to." He said this as he took the two tall bar chairs TJ and Ollie weren't sitting on and dragged them to the front of the room, spacing them about six feet apart.

He stood between the chairs and said, "This game is called Goalie."

Zoe laughed. "My God, could you be any more Canadian?"

"I've been an American citizen since 1999, but thank you for playing. Anyway, here's how this works. I'm the hockey goalie, and you guys are trying to take shots and score off me."

"You're ugly," TJ said. "Like simultaneously ugly and really forgettable at the same time. I don't know how you pull it off. It's almost magical."

"Thank you, TJ, but I'm not done explaining the game. The idea is you guys come over and initiate a scene or a character or a bit, and I have to respond in kind almost immediately. If I hesitate or stumble in any way, you score. The idea is to turn off thinking, and instead of trying to be clever or funny, you just go with your instincts. Once we go all the way around the room, someone else becomes the goalie, and we keep going until everyone's had a chance in the net. Okay?"

Ollie leapt out of his chair, clapping his hands. "This sounds so *awesome.*"

"Your endorsement isn't helping, Ollie, but since you're the eager beaver, you get to go first."

Ollie pranced and danced like a fairy, pointing and *ooh*ing and *ahh*ing at various imaginary objects around the room.

"You're supposed to do this quickly, Ollie," Steve said. "Hence the hockey analogy."

"Which is a sport," TJ added, just in case Ollie didn't know.

Ollie reached down and plucked an invisible flower out of the ground and skipped over to Steve. "Good sir, would you accept this gift of a lovely flower?" he falsettoed.

Steve whipped out an imaginary can and sprayed it in Ollie's face. "Mace!" Ollie clawed at his eyes and screamed and fell away.

Steve turned to an imaginary camera and said, "Remember, kids, never accept gifts from bald people. People without hair are fundamentally evil and regularly inject their flowers with AIDS. This message has been brought to you by the Coalition Against Bald People."

TJ was next in line and marched up to Steve and said, "You are a huge loser and you should do the world a favor and kill yourself."

Steve raised his hands wide. "Oh, Mom, you shouldn't have! What a kind birthday message. How's prison treating you?"

TJ turned and sat down and Zoe went next. She minced over to Steve, holding an imaginary scepter and waving to the others with a robotically cupped hand. "Pardon me, young man," she said in a high-pitched posh English accent, "I am the Queen of

England. Could you tell me what I'm doing in this biker bar?"

Steve swishily waved a limp wrist at her and said, "Girl, it's your lucky day! All queens drink for free on Flaming Queens Thursdays!"

"Yay!" Zoe cried, clicked her heels, and sat down as Dante bounded over to Steve. He grabbed the man's shoulder and pointed to the heavens:

"Doctor!" The movement of his lips didn't match the words coming out of his mouth. "That eight-hundred-foot tall erection is laying waste to the city! What can we do?"

"Never fear, Timmy," Steve said, pushing Dante aside and stepping forward. "This is the city's lucky day. I may have been kicked out of the Justice League for being, quote, totally useless — thanks a lot, Aquaman — but this looks like a job for Vaseline Man!" He tore his shirt open, revealing nothing beneath. "I know how to make that boner limp and flaccid and easily subdued by our armed forces, but I warn you . . . First you'll have to bring me the biggest tube sock you can find and every damn box of Kleenex in the city."

Even Dante chuckled at that one, then slapped Steve on the back and sat back down next to Meredith, who sat wide-eyed in her armchair, not moving.

"Come on, Meredith, your turn," Steve said.

"Let's go, girl. We know you're not just a pretty face," Zoe said in a tone that made it clear she did not in fact know that.

Meredith stood up, slightly, and wavered about coming forward.

Then she whispered something and dashed from the room, near tears.

"Did she just say 'limburger'?" Ollie said. "I thought she said limburger. That's *kind* of funny . . ."

"Whoa, dude! You broke her brain," TJ said, looking to Steve. "I didn't think you had it in you, bro, but that was some ruthless shit. Kudos."

Steve spread his hands. "I didn't mean to! I thought she was one of us."

Dante frowned at the doorway. "Don't sweat it. I'm sure she'll be fine."

Then they heard her screaming.

AIR TRAVEL/HECKLER

Can I tell you something? Can I?

I flew in from New York on the red-eye to make this show and I swear to God, are you with me? Doesn't it seem like the airlines are actively trying to make flying the most physically and mentally traumatic experience possible? Like they're doing future research for the Fourth Reich or something? Like it's like that Broadway show *The Producers* where they're trying to do such a bad job the companies tank and they can pocket the insurance money?

Case in point:

Last night, after I got my federally mandated cancer at the security checkpoint, I made way to the gate, and I was running a little late, and . . .

And, uh . . .

Just a second. Just a second.

I'm sorry, I have unexpected competition here in the front row. This table thinks they're the second stage.

Pardon me? Sir? Sir? Can I tell you something?

Yes, of course you! Honey, there's only two people talking in this theater. One of us has a huge pair of boobs and the other is me.

Just in case you don't quite comprehend the situation here, see, I'm the one with a mic in my hand. I'm the one these nice people paid money to see. So how about you pipe down and let me do my job, huh?

What's that? What? You don't think I'm funny?

Wow, if I gave a crap what you thought about anything, that might really bother me.

Look, I don't come down to where you work in SeaWorld entertaining tourists and tell you how to eat fish or flip through a hoop or whatever, do I? No, I don't. So show me the same courtesy, huh? Or, in words you understand:

(Flaps palms together, barks like a sea lion)

Ar ar ar ar ar ar ar!

Oh, my God, he's still at it. Buddy, have people ever made the mistake of listening to whatever annoying nonsense dribbles out of your mouth? Ever? Really? Has anyone ever said you were funny?

Yes? They were lying. All the laughs you get are fake, just like her orgasms.

What's that? Don't bring your wife into it? I'm trying to help this poor woman. How long have you been with this fat bastard, sweetie?

Not the full sentence — just tell me when you're up for parole.

Did he tell you how long it took him to flatten the other ones? Where they're all buried?

He's got a long ways to go with you, I see.

Can we get this guy a ticket to the buffet next door? I've got a feeling the only time he's not moving his lips is when he's moving his teeth, and it must be way beyond feeding time.

Stop. Just stop. You already lost. No, you did. I can trace it back to the exact moment, you know when it was? All the way back when your mother said:

"I refuse to have an abortion on moral grounds."

It's been all downhill since then, hasn't it? You peaked real early, mister. It's a shame.

I'd almost feel sorry for you if you'd shut up for five seconds so my hatred could subside.

No, really, you're a terrible person. I know you think otherwise because you're a man, and men spend their entire lives being mollycoddled and having their egos stroked and their sensitive little tuchuses wiped, but I'm sick of doing it for men. I'm sick of it!

Am I right, ladies? Right? Hear those cheers. They know what I'm talking about. And I'm just not doing it anymore. There's nothing any of you men can do for me that an extra-large cucumber from Krogers can't do just as well, and I can make a nice salad out of it afterwards.

What? It's shrink-wrapped in plastic! What's the big deal? I don't know what's wrong with you people. Prudes. You disgust me.

Look, buddy, your mistake was, when you woke up this morning, in your tank at Sea-

World, it didn't occur to you, in your teeny-tiny walnut brain, that maybe sitting in the front row of the Shotgun's show, and proceeding to talk through it, and then trying to out-insult her, that maybe that was not the wisest course of action. Insult the insult comic? Yeah, that's a good plan.

I know that kind of planning and strategic thinking will make you a success at whatever you attempt to do with your life.

You know, once Greenpeace finally succeeds in freeing you.

Oh, up they go, that did it. Okay, bye-bye! Have a nice evening! There they go! Watch *Free Willy* go! Waddling like the wind.

Hey, you know, I think *Help! I Married the Cat 3* is playing at the Cineplex next door. That might be entertainment more up to your speed.

What? What's with the groans?

I love these cat movies, these Dusty Walker movies. They're like the whorehouses across town:

They make money hand over fist, but nobody ever admits to going there.

— Janet Kahn
Venetian Showroom, Las Vegas, NV
June 20, 2000
(On YouTube as "Janet Kahn Epic Pwns
Heckler," 3.4M views)

CHAPTER SEVEN

I

The other five came running to Meredith Ladipo in the front gallery.

"What's all the yelling about?" Steve Gordon asked. "And why did you run . . ."

When he saw what all the yelling was about, he stopped in his tracks. Everyone did.

The six photographs of the six remaining comics were back on the wall, in the exact same position from which Dante had torn them down four hours earlier.

"How . . . ?" Zoe said.

TJ said, "We all went out for bathroom breaks! Any one of you could have run back here and replaced them!"

"Or *you* could have," Dante said.

Steve's face was a red mask of fury. Without saying a word, he stepped forward and grabbed each photo off the wall and hurled it as hard as he could to the tiles beneath his feet, shattering them. He started with his own, then threw down Zoe's, then Dante's.

He'd taken Ollie's and was about to smash it when Dante grabbed his arm.

"Hold on just a second."

Dante bent down among the shards of glass and cheap plastic littering the floor. One frame hit the ground so hard that it split apart, and now the white back of its photo faced upward.

"There's something written on it."

Dante pulled the photo free of the cracked glass. In the picture, he was standing on stage with a microphone.

"Looks like . . . Atlanta, maybe? Uptown Comedy?"

Written on the other side in black Sharpie were the numbers 11-12-15.

"What does that mean?" TJ said.

"Someone has trouble counting," Ollie said.

"It's got to be a date," Steve said. "Does November the twelfth mean anything to you?"

Dante shook his head.

"Could it be when the photo was taken?"

Dante looked at it. "Maybe. I was touring the South in the fall of 2015. Sixteen cities." He thought about it some more. "Maybe. But there's nothing about any of the dates that was all that . . . significant." He looked to Meredith Ladipo. "You didn't write these, did you?"

She shook her head fiercely. "Absolutely not."

Zoe pulled her own photo from the rubble and removed the backing of the frame. "02-02-17," she read aloud.

"Oh, it all makes sense now!" she cried.

They looked at her.

"No, I'm kidding, I have no clue what this means."

TJ said, "I wish motherfuckers would stop trying to be funny all the time."

"Can't Help Myself," Steve Gordon muttered, staring at his own photo on the floor.

"Then try harder," TJ snapped at him.

TJ lifted his headshot off the wall, then wrested the photo out of the frame.

"What's it say?" Dante asked.

He held it up so the others could see: "09-10-01."

"That have any special significance to you?"

"It's the day before 9/11," Zoe said.

TJ Martinez looked at the photo of him on the *2nite* set. It could have been taken any weeknight over a twenty-year span.

256

Except it wasn't.

"We were off the air for the rest of the week after 9/11," he said. "The attacks were on a Tuesday, and we did a show the night before." He thought about it. "Larry David and . . . the White Stripes? I think?"

"Quite the memory," Meredith said.

"Ask me what I had for breakfast this morning and I couldn't tell you," TJ chuckled.

"Sure you could — it was nothing, just like the rest of us," Zoe said, and she shot a look at Ollie, who had finally succeeded in opening his photo's frame.

He gave a little cry when he looked at the back: "Oh, yeah! I know exactly what this is! This is Orange Baby Man's birthday! January 4, 2006, the first time I tried the character out on stage, at Carolines. I immortalize the date in all my Playbills and historical literature."

"What about your photo, Steve. What does it say?" Dante said.

"I don't have a burning desire to know," Steve said.

Dante looked down and saw that Steve had put his foot over the photo.

"You already know, don't you?" Dante said. "Why don't you clue in the rest of us?"

"Oh, shit," TJ said. "Oh, shit." Revelation

rippled across his face.

Steve looked at TJ. Their eyes met briefly, and TJ just guffawed.

"C'mon, Steve, stop being weird," Zoe said, arms crossed.

Steve Gordon had been the person throwing the frames to the floor in the first place, so he was closest to the wall where one framed photo remained: Meredith Ladipo's. He pulled the photo sideways out of the frame, looked at the back, then showed it to the rest of them:

It was blank.

"What's the significance of that, Meredith?" Steve said, looking right at her.

"I don't know," she said, and then stomped her foot. Tears were on their way again. "It's the same answer for any question you want to ask me! I don't know! I don't know what's happening here any more than you do. How many times do I have to say it before you'll believe me?"

"Tang," TJ said.

"Huh?"

"Tang."

"Shit, dude, are you having a stroke?" Dante said.

"Tang!" TJ said, and he looked right at Ollie.

Steve sighed. "Ollie, do you have any idea

258

what he's —"

Before he could finish, Ollie dashed out of the gallery and toward the fountain with a hearty cry of *"Taaaaaaaaaaaaang!"*

Almost all the others looked in his direction as he receded into the distance.

"What the hell was that about?" Dante said.

Zoe turned around and yelled:

"Look!"

They caught a glimpse of TJ Martinez running away in the opposite direction.

II

Ollie lost his breath running up the hill to the cabana, but halfway there he looked around and saw that no one was following him.

"Eff me in the a-hole," he said out loud, then bounded down the hill to look for the others.

III

TJ Martinez overshot the cellar door under the grand staircase in the central hallway by a few paces but grabbed the doorframe, righted himself, and descended the stairs two at a time. His heart pounded, his limbs trembled. When he reached the bottom, he crashed into the huge center cabinet.

He could hear the others at the top of the stairs. They were right outside the wine cellar door.

In two strides he made it to the keypad.

He typed in 0 then 9 then 1 then 0 then 0 again then 1 again: the sequence on the back of his gallery headshot.

The panic-room door popped open with a beep and a hiss.

The door was steel and a foot thick, and TJ had just managed to get inside and pull it shut as the other comics reached the cellar and threw themselves after him.

But they were too late. The door slammed shut and TJ bolted it manually with a metal wheel on the inside, like the hatch on a submarine.

"Ha, ha! Take that, motherfuckers!" TJ whooped and hollered and jumped up and down when the full import of his triumph sank in. It was a Hail Mary pass, guessing that the passcode had changed from one date to another, but his theory turned about to be correct. Why was the combo now that particular date? Would any of the dates on the back of the photos have worked? TJ didn't know. Nor did he particularly care. What mattered was that he had made it inside, and the others hadn't.

TJ looked around. The room was perfectly soundproof and as silent as the inside of a grave, not that he could have heard anything over his heaving chest and pounding heartbeat. His eye was immediately drawn to a movement on one of the four wall-mounted monitors. From a camera in a corner of the wine cellar he could see Zoe, Meredith, and Dante banging soundlessly on the locked panic-room door.

An intercom mic and buttons were located under each monitor. He hit the Listen button under the wine cellar camera and was nearly deafened by the invective and blows directed his way.

He pressed the Speak button and said: "Hey, hey, you guys. Come on, chill out, this is great. I can work this to our advantage."

The speaker must have been mounted near the camera because his trio of pursuers turned and looked in its direction, with none of them figuring out exactly where his voice was coming from.

"This is bullshit, TJ. Let us in, man," Dante said.

"I don't think so, potential murderer," TJ said into the intercom. "Hey, look on the bright side. Now you guys know I didn't do it because the murderer would not hunker down and wait for rescue instead of, uh, you know. Murdering you."

"None of us thought you were the killer," Zoe said.

"Yeah, you're way too much of a dumbass to pull this off," Dante said.

"Gee, that really hurts my feelings. Now I'm definitely not letting you inside my private bunker.

"Aw, who am I kidding? I was never gonna let you in anyway."

IV

Ollie reentered the house and stuck his head in a couple rooms. He surprised himself by feeling relieved when he did not find the others.

He was just effing sick of it all, sick of all their effing bee ess. At first he was scared to be trapped here, where he might be murdered like Billy or Janet, but now he was more angry at being stuck here with the living — people who were saying or doing nasty things to him *all the time.* It was the same suffocating claustrophobia he had experienced on the school basketball court before first bell. On that wide, flat tarmac he had nowhere to hide, just like here. And no bell to release him from the jungle into the semi-safety of the company of adults and teachers.

Except . . . that wasn't technically true, was it?

About him having nowhere to hide.

He did know a place, thanks to the orange binder that Dustin Walker had so generously left him, to signal he was better than the others, that their host also had sympathy with his pursuit of the Radical Yes. One of the blueprints in the book said that there were a bunch of hidden gags around the island, like the secret switch that turned the elevator on and off and made the bottom fall out of the lift. Ollie thought that seemed more cruel than funny, but to each his own — he wasn't going to question how another performer designed his act.

He knew of another gag, though, that was highly applicable to his current predicament.

Ollie retrieved the binder from the bar in the clown lounge. He went into the library and pulled the false bookcase "door" that seemed to open to a blank wall, with the cartoon outline of a figure running through it. That was a clue, the binder told him, because, in a double-ironic twist that appealed to Ollie's professionalism, the fake door opened to a fake wall that was actually a real door, which opened when he pushed on its edge near the lower left-hand corner. He felt the release and heard the *click* and discovered he was able to slide the panel to the right, into the wall, revealing a small recess beyond. And inside that was a narrow unpainted metal staircase that spiraled up claustrophobically in a narrow shaft behind the wall.

He suppressed a squeal of delight and went inside; behind him the bookcase swung shut with a *thump,* startling him. For a moment his knees buckled in fear, and he thought about calling out.

But he didn't want to call out. He didn't want the others to know where he was. He didn't want to share his discovery with them. The best he could ever hope for from those bees and dees was that they would ignore him. He'd hide where they couldn't get him. They'll think Walker got him — or maybe that he was the killer. Wouldn't that be something! That would show them. All he wanted to do was inspire love and laughter in the world, but dee-bags like these other comics, who made money making fun of other people and putting them down, they would never understand that. All they responded to was fear. So that's what he would give them.

He took a deep breath and climbed the spiral staircase alone.

V

A kind of cushioned metal bench that could act as a bed or a sofa was attached by hinges to the panic-room wall opposite the bank of monitors. TJ Martinez lifted the seat and discovered a wide variety of goodies in the cabinet beneath, including a cloth first-responder case full of medical supplies, three neatly folded blankets, a tray of 100-hour ReadyCandles, a shrink-wrapped case of iodine pills, and a briefcase filled with neatly stacked thousand-euro bills on one side and thousand-U.S.-dollar bills on the other.

Returning to the Speak button he said, "You all have ill will toward me. Particularly you, Zoe, and you, Dante. But maybe we can reach some kind of arrangement."

"Take your arrangement," Zoe said, "and please shove it sideways up your ass."

"Don't answer too quickly." TJ looked around the room. There was a sink, a plastic toilet, and a shelf stocked with cardboard boxes stamped SELF-HEATING EMERGENCY MEALS (LOW SODIUM).

"I got all kinds of things you could use in here, like, gee, I don't know, off the top of my head, *food*. So let's see how this shakes out, and maybe I can figure some way to send food out to you guys so you don't starve. At the same time, I need to maintain my, you know, personal security and shit.

"And that means you explaining what your deal is, chickstick. Yeah, you, Meredith. You're still the likeliest guilty party among all these freaks and basket cases, so as long as you're around, I'm not inclined to open this door for nobody."

Meredith didn't say anything. She just shook her head wearily and turned her back to the camera.

VI

Oliver Rees knew he could never be completely safe, not on this island, and his nerves were all aflutter, like when he was awaiting the arrival of a Grindr date. But the unknown was also exciting, yawing before him and eager to be explored, like when he was awaiting the arrival of a Grindr date. And maybe his detractors were right. Maybe he was greedy. He wanted the glory — and the discovery — all to himself. Serves those dee-bags right, for all they made fun of him.

The staircase spiraled up through the building inside a stuffy, hollow tube until it reached a square opening with light streaming in from above. With considerable difficulty he squeezed his rotundity through the aperture and found himself in a garret with no windows. If he had to, he would have guessed there was a secret third attic level, above the belvedere gallery but accessible only from the library on the ground floor. The ceiling was barely seven feet above the carpeted floor. The air inside was sun baked and dead. The only visible movement came from the dust spiraling through the light thrown off by a single overhead bulb.

The room was empty save for a leather armchair, a small table with a dorm fridge underneath and a flat gray Ikea desk with a plasma screen on top and a tower CPU below.

Ollie went for the fridge immediately, and was somewhat disappointed to find a few pieces of fruit — a banana, some ripe plums, and a Granny Smith apple — and two small bottles of Poland Spring water. He would have preferred candy. Then he remembered that fruit, of course, was nature's candy, and he grabbed a plum and instantly bit into it, sweet juice squirting down his chin.

He tapped the keyboard and the monitor burned to life, showing some kind of chat app that displayed a text conversation:

We need to talk.

U didnt come to libary u werent there

I was there. Then Janet got shot.
I still want to hear what you have to say.
Can you still meet tonight?

U no were playroom is

Yes. Meet you there in thirty minutes?
1am?

K

Boring, Ollie thought, and then quit the message app.

He had finished the plum and was looking around for someplace to throw away the pit, or perhaps a napkin to wipe the sticky ichor off his hands and chin, when he saw them stacked on one side of the room:

Framed photos. Two or three sets, on the floor. He went over and picked them up. They were copies of the same headshots from the front gallery.

This seemed significant, in ways that weren't immediately apparent to him, until another thought bounded into his head and pushed all others out:

Messaging.

Someone was messaging from the computer.

He whirled back to the monitor just as it darkened in sleep mode. He immediately slapped the space bar with a finger, and if anyone had a problem with the keyboard being all sticky with plum juice they could just kiss his grits.

The monitor came back to life and he found the full-barred broadcast symbol in the status bar indicating that this thing did, in fact, have a Wi-Fi signal.

He chuckled deeply, in a way that he hoped made him sound like a comic book supervillain, because he had achieved what the others couldn't. He did the first thing he always did whenever he got online.

He checked his horoscope.

Some benefits are definitely coming your way, Gemini, although everything isn't quite as promising as it seems.

"Pshaw, thanks for nothing, Kreskin," Ollie said out loud. "Tell me something I *don't* know."

VII

TJ realized that if he could press the Speak button and lock it in place, he could broadcast his voice through every camera on the grounds.

"Hey, Ollie, buddy, we did it! Come on out, wherever you are!"

"Aw, not Ollie, too," Dante groaned.

"You didn't really rope him into your stupidity, did you?" Zoe said.

"What do you care?" TJ said. "I was the only who didn't treat him like dog dirt."

"Except, you know, when it matters. Like now," Dante said.

TJ said into the intercom, "Listen, Ollie, I can't let you inside the panic room, okay?

270

It'd be a tight fit, buddy. And besides, how could I open the door to let you in without these *pendejos* pushing their way inside, too? Listen, you're far more valuable to me out there, being my eyes and ears, making sure they're not plotting against me. Keep 'em honest, Ollie, and I'll fulfill my end, I promise."

With that, the others in the wine cellar groaned and headed single file up the stairs.

VIII

Ensconced in the attic garret, Ollie couldn't hear the speakers at all. Even if he could, he was too entranced by his Yahoo homepage, which said there was a terrorist attack in one of those poor countries he'd never heard of, and it seemed that during his time here stocks had fallen, then risen, then fallen again. He was already getting bored and ready to grab the Granny Smith from the mini fridge when it occurred to him that he should probably get word about their predicament to somebody in the outside world.

But who? The local authorities? Who were they, and how was he supposed to get in touch with them? He didn't know how to make phone calls on this thing. Hadn't William Griffith gone on and on about how this island was sort of owned by the Netherlands and sort of owned by France? Which country should he call?

Should he email the FBI? How long would that take? And what was their email address?

Maybe he could contact his agent or manager? Like everyone else in Hollywood, they were taking the month of August off for vacation, and he wasn't entirely sure how to get a hold of them. Plus they both had a tendency to yell at him when he got himself into trouble, which was a lot, so he was more than a little scared of them.

Then he knew — he knew exactly who to contact, and who would respond immediately.

A small spherical camera was mounted on top of the monitor, so he scrolled through the applications on the desktop and found the one that controlled it. He passed an open window showing views from various cameras planted around the island — the library, a sound booth of some kind, the dock — but these meant nothing to him, so he shut down the app.

At last he figured out how to turn on the camera, and when the light burned green and the on-screen numbers counted down to zero, he looked in it and said:

"Hello, Sandals, this is Oliver Rees, but you know me better as Orange Baby Man. I am the creator of Orange Baby Man and the president and CEO of Orange Baby, LLC. I am supposed to be in Saint Thomas, with you, inspecting our theater on Tuesday. But I am not going to be there because I have been kidnapped. I have been trapped with a whole bunch of famous people on Dustin Walker's private island and we are getting killed off one by one. Janet Kahn, she's dead. Billy the Contractor, he's dead.

"I am pretty sure Ruby Ng is dead, but I'm not sure how famous she is anyway, so never mind.

"But look! I am still here. TJ Martinez is still here, and even though he is kind of a giant dee, I have no desire to see him dead. I have no desire to see any more people here die. I'm just not that kind of a person. It takes too much energy to be vindictive, you know?

"Dante Dupree is here — he is black. And so is Zoe Schwartz.

"I mean that she's here, not that she's black. Not that that would be anything to be ashamed of if she was black. I am just saying, for the record, she isn't.

"A couple of other not-famous people are

here, but I do not remember their names.

"We are almost out of food, and more importantly there is a crazy person trying to kill us in all sorts of different ways, with guns and poisons and nooses and things. We need help. And food.

"Well, no, we need to be rescued and brought to a place where there is a more reliable supply of food. Like Sandals Virgin Islands! If you took us back to Sandals, that would be great. I don't really know where I am, though. It's this teeny-tiny island off the coast of, uh . . . Saint Croix? Saint Louis? One of those saints that are named after islands. Look, I'm sure you'll be able to talk to somebody who can find out."

As Ollie talked, it became increasingly impossible to ignore that not only was he rambling, but to any rational listener, what he was saying probably sounded like the ranting of a crazy man. So he tried to look as serious as possible, like the old man who introduced his favorite classic movies on TCM, and said:

"Look, I know you think of me as hilariously, hilariously funny. Which I am. Most of the time. But you have to believe me, owners and operators of the Sandals Orange Baby Man Theatre. In this particular instance I am being one hundred million

274

percent deadly serious.

"Pun *not* intended."

Much to his surprise, he found himself tearing up.

"I shouldn't have to die just because my whole life I've been funny and I look funny and I talk funny and everything about me is funny. Because it took me a long time before I figured out how to make that *work* for me, and if it now killed me after I got all rich and famous, well that would suck. It would really, really suck big veiny bulbous donkey dee."

He wiped snot from his nose and tears from his eyes. "We are fighting for our lives here. We really need your help. Please. This isn't a joke. Don't wait until I don't show up on Tuesday. Do something now."

He took a deep breath. He searched for something else worth saying and came up empty.

"Thank you in advance. This is Orange Baby Man, aka Oliver Rees, saying good-bye."

IX

Ollie turned off the camera and scrolled through the Contacts in his phone until he found the email for the Sandals people in

275

the U.S. Virgin Islands, slowly typing out the address with his sticky fingertips on the keyboard.

He wondered whether he should hit Send. The whole thing, when you said it out loud, just sounded so . . . preposterous. Stupid. Like a weird setup to a surrealistic prank.

But he hit Send anyway, and was surprised at how long it took the video to upload to the email. He guessed the file was pretty big. He did talk for a long, long time.

He hit the Cancel button a few times, but the window froze. It seemed as though every iota of the computer's processor was being used to compress his massive, rambling cry for help. So maybe the message would go through, and the computer would recognize his cancel command after it was too late; or maybe it would cancel it before the fact, like he had intended.

He pushed away from the desk in despair. He couldn't find the right words to make the outside world believe him. His brain wasn't wired that way. He was going to have to swallow his pride and ask someone for help — probably the black girl who wasn't famous and had a British accent for some reason, who had not, to his memory, made fun of him (yet) — because the idea of admitting to the others that he was exactly as inadequate as they thought was something he just could not bear.

He thudded down the stairs and unlocked the false-wall door from the inside.

The door was halfway open when the sledgehammer swung out from behind the wall.

Ollie didn't have time to comprehend what he was looking at until it slammed into the bridge of his nose and his eye sockets, and caved in his skull, and ended his vision for all time.

X

TJ realized he could switch the three monitors to different views from cameras around the estate by flicking the dial to the side of each screen. He flipped through to the clown lounge, then the pool patio.

Steve Gordon, noticeably absent from the wine cellar contingent, had managed to light the fire pit in the concrete island in the middle of the pool and was holding his own headshot to the flame, making sure it was thoroughly burned.

TJ giggled to himself and spoke into the intercom. "What do you think you're doing, Gordo?"

The voice in the patio made Steve drop

the photo into the fire pit, where it was quickly consumed.

"I see you," TJ laughed into the mic. "You're not getting away with it. You never get away with anything. You just don't have it in you, Gordo."

Steve's eyes found the camera in the corner of the patio. "TJ," he said, "I *knew* you knew who I was."

"No shit, Sherlock," TJ said. "I always knew who you were. And *what* you are. And I got eyes on you now, buddy. Eyes everywhere. I'm gonna make you pine for the days when I acted like you didn't even exist."

DOG PERSON

I know you may find this hard to believe just by looking at me, or obsessively reading about me on TMZ.com.

Which all of you do, right?

(Laughs)

Okay, good. Just checking.

So you know, from all your research you did before the show, right, I'm an iconoclast. I defy a lot of stereotypes in a lot of ways. For one thing, most people assume women like cats, and men like dogs. But I don't. I like dogs. I'm a dog person.

Whoo-whoo, right? Give it up for the dog people. I'll drink to that.

Or anything, really.

That's the kind of subtle, pervasive sexism in society that really annoys the hell out of me — assuming that, just because you're a girl, you're a cat person.

Cat owners can get really uptight about it

when you assume their cat's a girl, too:

"Oh, what a beautiful kitty! What's her name?"

"IT'S A BOY, GENDER FASCIST."

"Okay, okay, so it's a guy, what's his name?"

"His name is Smooshy Lovey-Dovey Cotton-Face."

(Laughs)

"I know. I know, his name suits him; he's very butch. We almost called him Mr. Puffytail, but that was the name from the cat in those *I Married a Cat* movies, and you can take this cat-lover thing too far. I mean Dustin Walker should be tried at The Hague for that last one, you know what I mean?"

I mean, I am a dog person, but that doesn't mean I want to round up cat people and put them in camps or anything.

Make them wear a felt Hello Kitty outline on the front of their jackets. No, no, that's going too far.

They did that to my nana in Poland and I know

my history well enough not to repeat it. No, no.

(Laughs)

I'm not one of these people, you know, who only cares about her side, her team, and just goes, you know, it's my way or the highway, buster. I'm not like that. I didn't just leap into this whole dog-person thing with eyes wide shut. No, I took cats in one hand, and dogs in the other, and weighed them against each other, like this. And that's how I made my decision. And I totally get, and respect, if you came to a different conclusion.

On the one hand, you have an animal that doesn't come when it's called, likes being touched intermittently at best, and spends all its time eating, sleeping, and staring out the window. And has just terrible, terrible mood swings.

I don't need that in a pet. No.

Because I already own a mirror.

Hello! I just described me! Don't call me, don't touch me, eat, eat, eat, oh God why did I eat all that and why won't anyone call me? Why don't I have a boyfriend? I know, I'll have a bottle of sauv blanc and two Ambien and we'll see if anything has changed in the morning. Gulp. Glug. *Snore . . .*

Individuals in relationships need to complement each other, you know? Provide what the other lacks. Don't double personality traits! Otherwise you're just another one of you. You might as well get one of those full-body pillows girls at Comic Con have that has a nude photo of you silk-screened on it and walk around with that.

Then you never have to let you go.

I just got a dog. You want to meet him? Yeah, of course you do.

Come here! Come here, boy! Come out on stage! You see the treats? You know what that means, right?

Yes, come on out here, Asshole! C'mere! That's a good Asshole!

Oh, sorry, yeah: I named my dog Asshole. I know, I know, some of you are judging me right now. "Oh, that bitch is so awful, how can she do that?" But just hear me out. When I brought him home from the shelter —

Yes, he's a rescue. I know, I'm so awesome and caring, right? But I hate that word, it's so bourgie. Poor people get their dogs from a *pound* while hipsters *rescue* their dogs, like they were in a fire, or strapped beneath a laser by a supervillain.

That's a good Asshole. Who's a good boy? You're Mommy's special little boy, aren't you?

Uh-oh. He's peeing. He's . . . peeing. Can we get someone out here? Whoo. Yeah, no, that's definitely got an odor. Did you have asparagus for lunch? Can we get a mop or . . . ? Thanks.

Can you get of him out of here? Here, thanks. Bye, sweetie! See you back in Mommy's dressing room after the show! Eat my Valium and I'll kill you!

See why he's called Asshole? When I "rescued" him from the pound he was named Buster.

But then I got to know him.

And he ate my Louis Vuitton bag.

And then he pooped in it.

I realized then that you shouldn't name dogs immediately. You should wait and observe their personalities for a while and then settle on a name, like Native Americans used to. Or like Kevin Costner has taught me: Dances with Wolves . . . Wind in His Hair . . . Stands with a Fist . . .

Or if *I* was Native American:

Struggles with Credit Card Debt.

But to know Asshole is to love Asshole. No, really. He is thrilled every time he sees me; he runs up to me when I walk through the door or come home from a shoot or from being on tour. He looks like he's going to die whenever I leave, like he can't live without me. Anytime I talk, he looks like every word coming out of my mouth is the most brilliant thing he's ever heard, dumb tail wagging, dumb mouth panting.

He loves me so much.

Or so I thought.

I was getting my hair done at what must be

the same place Neil deGrasse Tyson goes to, because they had some, I don't know, some science-y magazine on the table. What do I know? And I was reading in it that people think that dogs are naturally more affectionate than cats but that's not true. What's really going on is that dogs have been with humans tens of thousands years longer. So dogs have actually evolved to react to our human cues. Asshole knows, hardwired into the DNA inherited from hundreds upon hundreds of ancestors dating back to the Stone Age, he knows that his survival, his meals, his shelter, his safety, his everything really, is entirely dependent on keeping on my good side.

So that's not love.

That's pure calculation.

And I'm like, yes, *thank you, God*!

That is actually what someone like me, with a bottomless roaring void where her self-esteem should be, needs in a relationship. Mindless, unquestioning loyalty. Not codependence, but *uni*-dependence. One person is totally obsessed with meeting the other person's needs, with the other person ready to send him back to the pound if he messes up another four-digit handbag, I am not kidding around this time, Asshole, no I'm not, you hear me backstage, Asshole, do you?

Sure, sometimes I still hate being single, and my mother texts me to remind me that I am at the same time every day when she sees her neighbors leave the house to take their kids to school. But not as much, since I got Asshole.

In fact, there's only one thing keeping me from going, "You know what? Asshole is all I need. He is fulfilling eight or nine out of the ten things I could get from a man." And there's · only one thing preventing me from saying, "You know, what? I'm deleting the JDate app off my phone. I will be happy with Asshole and this Channing Tatum swimsuit spread from *Us Weekly* as my only life partners."

And it's sad. Yeah, you know where I'm going with this. It's sad.

But it's the whole lifespan issue, you know? There's no way he's going to live as long as I am. Asshole, at best — and I mean, like, at *best* — he's going to live to be twenty years old. And if that happens he'll have local news crews around him going, "We were wondering what you eat to keep you so, well, *young* is the wrong word, but you know . . . alive? Is it a special gourmet form of dog shit you eat? Like, do you only eat the dog shit of virgins? Of French dogs? Is there a specific kind of butt you sniff? What's your secret? And can we get a doggie-diet best seller out of it?"

(Laughs)

Sometimes, I just get in these moods, where I look at Asshole and I can't think about anything else but him dying. Really! It's awful. I know one day I'm gonna come home, and he's not going to be asleep; he's going to be dead. Or, even worse, he's going to get cancer or kidney failure or something and I'm going to have to bring him to the vet and put him to sleep, and the vet's going to be like, "Do you want to be here for it?" and I know no, I don't really want to, but then she's going to judge me — that I'm cruel or a pussy or whatever — and so then I'm like okay and I'll just stand there and watch as my dog dies right there, on the slab, in front of me, licking my fingers.

And when I think that, it's the only time I ever get really mad at Asshole. I'm all like:

287

You selfish dick.

Why can't you ever think about how your decisions will affect *me*?!

— *Zoe Schwartz*
Paramount Theatre, Seattle, WA
February 2, 2017
(*Filmed as* Laughs Like a Girl *for Netflix*)

CHAPTER EIGHT

I

TJ flipped through the monitors in the panic room, familiarizing himself with every camera and every conceivable view:

In all the guest bedrooms and Meredith's room, but not the master bedroom.

In the kitchen looking at the fridge and the pantry; outside in the wine cellar.

There were two in the playroom, both aimed at the ball pit.

One was aimed at the stage in the groundskeeper's cabana.

One was in the writers' room, which encompassed the veranda outside.

One in the clown lounge, but none in the library.

A camera looked up at the bottom pool and another looked down on the top pool.

He was surprised there weren't more cameras directed at the grounds — none pointing at the bouncy castle, for example. He was not surprised there was no camera in the entry gallery, where their headshots once hung, since that definitely worked to the killer's advantage.

In addition to cycling through the news using the dials beside each monitor, TJ could rotate each camera with a small joystick in a one-hundred-degree parabola.

He figured this out when he caught Dante Dupree creeping around the grounds. He watched as the comic meandered near the entrance to the dock elevator, waiting for him to do anything the least bit interesting. Finally TJ got bored and spoke into the microphone:

"I see you with your guilty thoughts, tough guy. Don't try anything you don't want me to see."

"I wouldn't dream of it, dude," Dante said, looking around but seeing nothing.

"Over here, jackass," TJ said, and on-screen Dante turned, looked up, and walked toward the camera, which presumably was mounted on one of the lampposts lining the fountain walk.

"Moves, huh?" he said.

"Keep it all on the up-and-up and you don't have anything to worry about," TJ said.

"I wouldn't dream of being anything but up, I swear," Dante said, and he backed out of the frame, keeping one eye on the camera the whole time.

"That's a lame bit, dude," TJ said, munching on an MRE. He hadn't eaten all day, and to him, its au gratin potatoes tasted like heaven.

II

The afternoon dragged on across TJ's monitors.

He saw Zoe Schwartz in her room, opening one of her dog's vacuum-packed treat cups. Asshole ran over to her, tail wagging.

She set the plastic cup under his nose and he scarfed down most of the food. As soon as he raised his snout to lick his chops, she picked up the cup.

She looked around. Gordo was in the bathroom. She had no reason to think she wasn't alone, since neither of them had discovered the camera in her room yet.

Zoe put two fingers into the dog food, scooped it out. If TJ hadn't just eaten a bag of Skittles from the MRE stash, dog food might have made his stomach grumble a bit, too.

Asshole barked at her impatiently.

Zoe shushed him, putting her other hand around his muzzle.

She popped the dog food in her mouth with her fingers.

She chewed briefly, swallowed, swished her tongue in her mouth.

Then she stuck her fingers back in for another bite. Asshole flanked her on the left, then the right, staring at the food, his tail a worried blur.

The toilet flushed and Gordo emerged unexpectedly from the bathroom. Zoe made a little cry and tossed the doggie cup across the room. Asshole pounced on it.

"Jesus!" she said. "Didn't you wash your hands?"

"What, I —"

"Don't even think about touching me until you wash your hands!"

"Okay, okay, I'll wash my hands," he said, returning to the bathroom. *"Again,"* he added, unconvincingly.

TJ covered his mouth and laughed his ass off.

III

The monitors were black and white with light enhancement, so it was hard to gauge the day ending from eyeballing the screens alone. The digital clock on the panic-room tablet computer said it was half past six when TJ spied Meredith Ladipo frantically looking around her room.

He pressed the intercom: "If it's your conscience that's missing, I'm pretty sure you left it behind on the mainland, hon."

Meredith jumped up, looked at the ceiling, started to say something, stopped, then stalked out of the room.

IV

At 7:25 pm Dante Dupree appeared in the wine cellar. He had a small key that he used to open one of the Plexiglas shelves.

"Dude, where'd you get that?" TJ said into the intercom.

Dante didn't answer. He grabbed a bottle, put a second under his arm, and took a third in hand.

"Dude, if you let me have one I will totally give you a spaghetti in meat sauce. I've got a half-dozen kinds of MREs in here. I got chili, tacos, ravioli, ready-to-eat breakfast with bacon and hash browns, man."

Dante turned toward the camera and gave it the finger.

"C'mon, dude, don't be like that. That ain't right. C'mon."

Dante grabbed a fourth wine bottle and walked up the stairs toward the kitchen.

V

Night fell at last and as TJ flipped through the cameras, there was one person he didn't see.

"Hey, guys," he said in an intercom broadcast throughout the island, "anybody see Ollie?"

No answer.

"I mean, I haven't seen him for, like, a long time."

Zoe, still sitting at the foot of her bed playing with her dog, looked up at the camera.

Then she looked down, ignoring him.

"Can somebody maybe organize a search?"

Gordo sat by Zoe's open window and smoked, using an empty can of beets as an ashtray.

"I mean, I would go, you know, but . . . uh. You know."

Dante drank glass after glass of wine in the kitchen.

"I'm just worried about him, is all."

He didn't know where Meredith was.

The white-noise buzz of the fluorescent

lights in the tiny room was really starting to drive him crazy.

VI

At 9:35 pm, Meredith Ladipo entered the kitchen and found Dante Dupree sitting at the center island, finishing off three or four bottles of wine. They were pretty obviously from Mr. Walker's private stash, which begged the question how he got into the locked cabinets, but her expression indicated that she was beyond the point of caring about such things.

"Where've you been?" he asked her.

"On the docks, hoping to signal a boat. Or a plane. Or a mermaid."

"Oh," Dante said, and he poured himself another glass.

She leaned her shotgun against the fridge and got a glass out of the cabinet and filled it with ice water. She sat at the counter and drank it, trying to ignore her whining stomach.

Suddenly, Dante looked up at her and said:

"Do you think I'm an alcoholic?"

Meredith blinked. "How should I know?"

"I don't know if I'm an alcoholic or not. You know why? I've never tried to quit. So who knows, maybe I could. But if I did, I'd have to go cold turkey. Give it up all at once. Because, you know, I've tried having only one drink. When you're sober, one drink seems totally doable. Takes the edge off. Lets you wind down the day. My grandmother had happy hour as one of her nightly rituals. She could only have one. A glass of Southern Comfort on the rocks, that was her favorite. Or a glass of white wine. But that was it. I always admired that about her. She could have just the one; you'd offer her more and she'd say, 'No, I'm good.' And she would never reach for that bottle herself.

"I don't understand why I never got that ability from her. For me, one drink always becomes two. And it is true, there are some nights I can just do two. Like if I'm at a restaurant and it's late or I know I have to drive a long way home or back to the hotel.

"Usually, though, if I'm going to stop, it's after just three. That's where the bladder gets unsealed, and then we start wearing out a path between the bar and the men's room. But three is fine; three gets me just toasty enough to last me until I go to bed or whatever.

"But if I'm honest I get only three a few times a week. Much more often I just keep going, you know? I'm on a roll. I'm just so full of excitement and energy and the drink is a way of channeling it, you know? You're tired or you're depressed or you're bored and . . . and after you haven't done it for a day, you forget. You just want to keep that buzz, that euphoria going, and then when you've gone too far it's too late, or you've gone to bed after it's already too late, and you wake up with a caved-in brain and cottonmouth."

He picked up the last unopened wine bottle, stood up, paced the room, looking for the bottle opener. "Hell I put that thing?"

"You seem to have given this a lot of brat york," Meredith said.

"Huh?" he squinted at her blearily.

"Thought," Meredith said, her expression changing not one iota. "You seem to have given this a lot of thought."

"Yeah, I guess. I think that if I had kids, I wouldn't drink so much. Not because I'm worried what I might do to them, but because I'd have less time on my hands. Less time to marinate in my own shit, you know? Running this way and that for things that don't involve writing my act, practicing my act, driving to do my act, doing radio to promote my act, hustling to get the next act. If I had kids, I'd just be outside myself more, you know?"

"Was that a choice, not to have kids, or . . . ?"

"Yeah, you know, it was never really something that entered my head. I think that's partly from being raised by an old lady, my own parents long gone. In my head, that was just something people did in their retirement, like raising roses or something, you know? Raising roses, raising people. I know that don't make no damn sense, but that was just my upbringing.

"In a way it's for the best, I guess. I can get, you know, overly exuberant when toasted. Sometimes it's hard for me to control my temper. Hasn't caused me too much trouble.

"Except, you know, when it has."

He started opening random drawers with a deafening rattle. "I mean, the goddamn wine opener was right here. You take it?"

Meredith shook her head.

Dante said, "You know, the thing that worries me the most, though, is that nervous energy, though, that darkness; the drinking keeps it, you know, from overwhelming me. All the comics struggle with it. Lenny. Pryor. Robin. They fucked their own shit up but good. I'm not saying I'm anywhere near their category, but it's hard not to notice that to do this job, you've got to be a little off.

"Like, I mean, look at Dustin Walker — talk about off. You know what I mean? Talk about being full of darkness."

"I guess," Meredith Ladipo said.

"Did *he* have kids? Walker?"

Meredith shook her head.

"Huh. Then I wonder . . . remember that trophy Ruby found, when we were looking for weapons? 'Dorothy Walker Clear-Mind Clinic.' Who was that named after? Sister? Wife?"

"Mother," Meredith said.

"And that was what, for rehab, right? A place to stash rich junkies while they get clean?"

"No," Meredith said sharply. "It was . . ." Realizing she had reacted a bit more emotionally than she had meant to, she took a breath. "Mrs. Walker had Alzheimer's, and her son founded the clinic to study that and other neurological diseases and disorders. To look for a cure."

"Oh." Dante sounded disappointed. "I mean, good on him, I guess, but I guess I'm in the market for a rehab. Though, I ain't gonna lie to you, I am worried — if I go full teetotaler, that'd be a little like getting my

299

balls cut off, you know? Domesticate me a little too much, like I'd been spayed. Would I still be able to tap into that darkness, or would it get, like, I don't know, sealed off, behind glass, where I couldn't get to it anymore? Like natural Xanax or some shit?"

He stopped and stood in the middle of the room and flailed his arms helplessly:

"Goddamnit, Dupree, where the fuck did you put that motherfucking cock-sucking bottle opener?"

Meredith slid off the stool and reached for Dante. "Here."

She took the wine bottle from him, screwed off the cap, and handed it back.

Dante looked at the open bottle.

He looked at Meredith.

He looked at the bottle again.

"Thank you," he said.

"You're welcome," she said.

VII

TJ watched Meredith and Dante's exchange in the kitchen until he got bored. He thought maybe they would fuck, which might be cool to see, or might be gross, hard to tell. But when it became obvious they weren't going to do anything, he switched to the feed in Zoe Schwartz's room.

300

Asshole stood quivering before the door-way, every strand of fur vibrating in anticipation of the adventures to be discovered in the hallway.

The dog ignored the two humans rolling around and kissing on the bed.

"Is it weird we're fooling around so much?" Steve said. "I feel like maybe it's weird."

"That's survivor's guilt," Zoe said.

"I haven't technically survived anything yet."

"Then it's Canadian's guilt. You feel bad we're having a good time while everyone else is miserable."

"Actually, I'm pretty miserable, too."

"Makes two of us. So let's stop talking about it. Or about anything. Fuck me until I forget where I am, please."

As she was pulling his shirt out of his jeans and up over his arms, they both heard, very loud and very close:

"Do you guys do requests, or is this going to be ten minutes of boring missionary-position white-people sex?"

The voice came out of nowhere and both Steve and Zoe simultaneously but independently jackknifed off the bed to look for its source. Asshole ran in tiny circles and barked in a way he presumably thought was helpful.

"Hey, if you get the dog in, like, a three-some, there could be some money in it for you."

TJ's cackle was unmistakable, and it appeared to be coming from the light fixture in the fan rotating overhead.

"You are such a piece of shit, TJ," Zoe said. She turned to Steve: "Let's go somewhere else."

"You can't get away from me in this place, girl. I got eyes everywhere."

"Why do you have to be such a hateful douche, TJ?" Steve said as he shoved his shirt back in his pants.

"Why do you have to be a joke thief, Gordo?" the ceiling fan said.

Steve's jaw dropped as if he had been struck across the face.

"What nonsense are you yammering on about?" Zoe said. "You expect me to believe that?"

TJ said, "No more secrets. I hear that's your new policy, right, Zoe? Well, I'll go first. You think I'm a piece of shit? What about your new fuck-buddy? You know why I said I didn't know him when I first got here? Because he's dead to me. Dead to everybody. Dusty made sure of that."

"You're a lying sack of shit," Zoe said. She turned to Steve: "Isn't he?"

TJ laughed. "He knows. He knows it's true. He knows he deserves this."

Steve turned toward Zoe. "Listen. What happened was —"

"What happened, Zoe, was that Dusty used to warm up the studio audiences before tapings of *What Just Happened?* He didn't really have a lot of time to go out on tour, or do the Store or anything, so that was his outlet for stand-up. Most of the time the producers hired a comic to warm up the crowd, but a couple times a week Dusty would do it himself — all-new material, original stuff he came up with on his own."

"Sometimes," Steve said to her, "there's parallel thinking. There's only so many premises for jokes somebody can come up with —"

Zoe's face fell. "Oh, Jesus, Steve, really?"

"And sometimes motherfuckers just rip you off," TJ said. "Steve heard those jokes, and he remembered them, and he started going out and doing them as his own. It wasn't until he went on his *SNL* audition that Dusty really came down on him."

Zoe looked like she might throw up. "My God."

"This was right after *What Just Happened?*

went off the air. Dusty threatened to sue NBC and HBO, and they killed the special they were going to do with him before it got too far down the pipeline. Then Dusty went to every single club owner who was anybody, every agent, every manager, every booker for every late-night show, and made it very clear that if they ever wanted to have anything to do with world-famous funnyman Dustin Walker ever again, the last thing they should do is book joke thief Steve 'Gordo' Gordon."

Zoe didn't need to ask Steve if it was true. She could see on his gray, wan face that it was.

"That's not on your Wikipedia page," Zoe whispered accusingly.

Without looking at her Steve said, "It kinda fell in that gray area in the early aughts, before every single thing that happened to every single celebrity, no matter how minor, was captured online. And then, you know, I never did anything afterward worth writing about. I basically had to break into the industry again. And I didn't. There's one thing you can never be more than once, Zoe. And that's *new*."

"You got what you deserved, *pendejo*," the light fixture said.

"Oh, like you would know what getting

what you deserve looks like," Zoe barked up at it. "Shoe Jizzer."

Steve started to say, "I wanted to tell you before — I mean, after the photo thing, but I —"

Zoe held up a hand and took a breath.

"Look, Steve, even though the source is a loathsome, shit-caked human sphincter . . ."

"You're welcome," the ceiling fan said.

"I mean, you get that this is some heavy stuff here, right? I'm a comedian. It's what I've wanted to be since I was nine. I've based my whole life on it. This . . . I gotta process this. It's like a rabbi going out with a Holocaust denier. If this is your rep . . . I mean, that's a problem on a whole bunch of levels. Sorry. But it just is, you know?"

"No, I know. I know." Shoulders slumped, Steve made his way to the door and opened it. Before walking out, he turned and said, "For what it's worth, Zoe, I really do admire and respect your comedy —"

"Asshole!" she cried.

His head drooped. "I get it, I'll go."

"No, dumbass, you're letting the dog out!"

The anemic mutt bolted between Steve's legs and into the belvedere gallery before he could react.

Zoe pushed past and ran after him. "Asshole, come back here!"

305

TJ's cackle bounced off the walls. "That went even better than I could have possibly hoped."

Steve sighed. "Do you have to be such a hateful piece of shit 24/7?"

"It's not personal, Gordo. Well, maybe it is, just a little."

"Why do you care so much? I mean, they weren't even your jokes."

"You may find this hard to believe, Gordo, but every man's gotta have a code. And I strongly believe in the comics' code. Never, ever steal another guy's material. Never, ever. Makes you — what do they call them in India? — untouchable. You been dead to me since that day, man."

"Yeah, you're right, TJ," Steve said to the fan, "I do find that hard to believe. You being Mr. Integrity, with that laugh track on *2nite* and all."

"I keep telling you, that was different."

"Yeah. It's always different when *you* do it. Choke on a bag of dicks, TJ."

Steve turned to leave, but before he did, he saw on the end table a small vacuum-sealed cup of foie gras treats for dogs. He grabbed it and put it in his pocket, hoping this minor chivalrous gesture would go some way toward getting him back in his lady friend's good graces.

VIII

Zoe bolted onto the landing just as Asshole hit the stairs. His legs were short and his claws were long, so he skittered down the steps, allowing her to close within a few yards of him.

Asshole skidded across the hallway floor at the bottom of the stairs. She was almost on top of him, but he gained traction just as she reached for him. He accelerated away from her, tongue lolling, into the front gallery, where he stopped and cocked his ear.

She called out his name and he started to turn her way — but then he heard something else, something she couldn't hear.

He ran in that direction, his legs moving so fast that at first the rest of him didn't move at all, like a cartoon character revving up before taking off.

The front gallery really slowed her down. The floor was still covered in glass from the photo frames smashed there and she was barefoot.

She stepped across the minefield of shards as carefully as she could, stopping only to remove a triangular bit from the side of her heel with a curse.

Asshole sat on the grass near the fountain, looking into the gallery, watching her, head cocked, as she approached.

She sort of saw that a third set of head-shots was back on the wall to her right, materializing as mysteriously as the second set that had appeared after Dante Dupree cast the first set into the sea. She, Gordo, Dante, TJ, and Meredith were all still there. Ollie wasn't anymore, but she didn't notice. She had other things on her mind.

As soon as she made it to the other side of the room, Asshole turned and dashed away, darting diagonally past the fountain and into the wall of swaying bamboo to his right.

She followed the dog through the bamboo, along the brick walkway between of the leafy curtain.

Her first thought was that if she wanted this level of aggravation, she would have gotten a cat.

Her second thought was the dim realization that, up on the hill by the cabana, someone was holding what appeared to be a whistle to their face. She thought, *I know them — but wait, I've got to have that wrong because —*

The thought was neither completed nor retained, because it was replaced with the sensation of being unable to breathe, as the inability of breath tends to do to all thoughts that do not directly relate to regaining the ability to breathe.

She dropped onto her back on the stone path and felt a sharp pain in her throat, which, she began to realize, came from something she had run into while cutting through the bamboo. Placed exactly at the level of her Adam's apple, it dug into the flesh of her neck, practically cutting it in half, and then detached from the metal poles she could now sort of see in the green bamboo on both sides of her. It was a taut garrote that, once she ran into it, had detached from its moorings and spooled around her neck like a tentacle.

Asshole stood over her, barking and barking like the whole damn thing was her fault in the first place.

IX

TJ Martinez watched in silent horror as Zoe dropped into the mud as though her strings had been cut. He squinted at her gritty image until he realized that the glint around her neck must be a wire, strung along the bamboo curtain just at neck level. When they collided, it didn't just nearly crush her larynx, it was released from brackets that he could now see shining on mounts attached to poles in the bamboo. Her fingernails clawed at the garrote so hard, she was tearing the skin of her throat to ribbons. Her feet kicked out beneath her like they hadn't yet gotten the message they were no longer running on the ground.

The idea then seized him fully formed:

He would save her.

He would save her, and even if that didn't cause her to give up her vendetta against him, it might weaken her resolve, maybe give a counternarrative to the one she planned to deploy against him. Did he get carried away with his specific kink? Sure. Did he regret it? You bet. But did he deserve to have his life ruined over it? No, sir. He wasn't a bad guy. Look, it sounds cliché, but Hollywood was the real victimizer here. He hadn't been refused a thing for so long, he had forgotten what that was like. The bottom line was, being rich was awesome, but fame sucked. Not being able to go out and just be a person in the world, it was a lot to give up. The kink, as he called it, that was his release, being able to use that power for his own ends for once. Sure, it might have freaked out some girls, but who knows, maybe it benefited some of them in the long run. Toughened them up. Or loosened them up. One of the two.

He would save Zoe Schwartz's life, right at her lowest ebb, and that would prove, to himself at least, what he knew to be true: he was one of the good guys.

TJ threw himself at the wheel to retract the bar across the panic-room door.

It would not move.

He tried a few more times, then wrenched the wheel again, but succeeded only in wrenching his shoulder.

He banged on the door and called out futilely; he could see on the monitor that no one was in the wine cellar beyond.

On the other monitor, Zoe's struggles with the wire around her neck began to weaken.

X

Asshole's barks were becoming more and more distant in Zoe's hearing. She began to lose the strength to reach up and pull the wire out of her throat.

As the world contracted into darkness around her, she became aware of a light in the center of it, warm and inviting.

It was so obvious to her now. All the striving and worrying, all the career maneuvering. All the fretting about her weight, about her hair, about her makeup, about her clothes, her general attractiveness. Did men

311

like how she looked? Did women dislike it? She would have laughed, if she had the breath to spare and the airway to expel it out of, at how absurd it all was.

So that was life's great truth: You're holding on too much. Let go. Let it all go.

For the first time in her adult life, Zoe Schwartz felt calm. At peace.

Her mouth turned upward in a smile.

MY IMPORTANT CHARITY WORK

So, I don't know if you heard or not, but:

I've become kind of a big deal.

Yeah, right? Thank you, thank you kindly. Bless your redneck hearts. That's kind of you.

As a result, it would seem that the financial recompense that has eluded me all my misspent life has finally arrived, with bells on.

But I'm still the good ol' boy you know and love. Or if not love, then mildly tolerate. I'm not gonna be one of these celebrities who forgets where he comes from, or gets too big for his britches.

For one thing, I get my britches at Sons-O-Britches. That's the tall-and-wide britches store in the britches outlet mall just outside Jacksonville, Alabama.

In the britches district, yeah, that's the place. You got it. Still gonna shop there.

I'm gonna be more like them rappers, you know, who bring all the homies with 'em from the hood even after their records go platinum.

I'm gonna be just like that. I still got my entourage from down in 'Bama, when I used to do construction down there. Cooter, Rebel, Pondscum, Li'l Big George, Big Li'l George, General Lee, Leavenworth Jim, Stutterin' Sam the Flimflam Man, Liver-Eatin' Jones — yeah, they're my boys. They always will be.

Gotta hose 'em down every night or they really start to stink up the place, but they're still with me.

But I'm not gonna live like no monk or nothin', 'cause I already got myself a pool.

Hitched its trailer up to the back of the one my house is on and everything.

There is one thing, though, you know — that once you get money, there are certain things you're expected to do.

With great power comes great responsibility.

You know who said that?

Spider-Man. That's right. Spider-Man. My second favorite philosopher, next to Jesus.

I always listen to a man covered in cobwebs. Yeah.

Reminds me of Grandpa.

So, this didn't really occur to me during my years of deprivation and struggle, but once you become a big-time celebrity, you're expected to give back to the community and the world.

Like, you know how Bono, he's gonna grow a potato for every person in Africa?

Or I assume that's what he's gonna do, seeing as how he's an Irish fella and all.

Maybe he's gonna take Africa out to the pub and get it stinkin' drunk on Guinness so it forgets all its problems. That'd work, too.

I'll be honest with you, I'm not really sure what he's gonna do. I was watching his scraggly piehole flappin' away on CNN in the waiting room at the car wash — my kids were gettin' their weekly shower — and the subtitles were all messed up, so maybe I only got part of the story.

I do think Bono could afford a shave once in a

while, though, don't you?

"Bics for Bono," that's my new charity.

Some of these celebrities, man, some of their charities are really obscure.

Like, I saw Dustin Walker — yeah, the cat movie guy? Yeah, I saw he's raising money for, like, rare neurological diseases? You know, people who got seriously messed-up brains?

I mean, that's what he *says* he's doing.

Personally, I think he's just funding research to look into *his* brain and find why he ain't funny no more.

He's got to, say it with me:

Fix 'er uuuuuuuuuup!

Yeah, that's right. That's right. That's the thing about the catchphrase — you gotta spring it on people when they least expect it. Like a possum in a sack.

You shoulda seen the look on my son's face when I opened that sack. Boy, you'd just about mess yourself.

I mean, he's just six months old, so it's the same expression he has on his face most of the time anyway, but I still thought it was pretty dang funny.

Yeah, father of the year, that's ol' Billy.

So after a lot of soul-searching and cogitating and twelve-packs of Miller Lite, I hit upon the underrepresented, underprivileged, underserviced group that will be the beneficiaries of my newfound largesse.

Are you ready? I don't think you're ready. Because I'm thinking outside the box here. The cause I'm gonna champion is:

Sluts.

Yeah, sluts. You're laughing, but it's true — they get no respect. None. Women don't like 'em 'cause they steal all their men; men don't like 'em either.

The next morning, I mean. After those five clinic visits. All that cream and penicillin.

But sluts provide a valuable public service, which is giving hope to millions of ugly-ass, underendowed men all over the world, that even they, too, may one day get laid. It's hard being a man — no, it is. You ladies think we got it made, but we gotta pee standing up, just like everybody else.

What?

What's that?

Oh, yeah, maybe that wasn't the best analogy. Or metaphor.

I always get them two mixed up.

Sluts been giving so much for so long to so many people, after so many raspberry margaritas, that I think it is high time somebody gave something to them.

Repeatedly.

Night after night.

With gusto. And verve.

See, I don't know why you're laughing. This is important charity work I'm talkin' about here. Show some goldang respect, y'hear?

What my charity is, see, is a not-for-profit to

318

help them sluts at their most vulnerable, which is, statistically speaking, Saturday and Sunday mornings, when they wake up in the bed of whoever last night's fella was and, somehow, they gotta make their way back home.

The proverbial walk of shame, yeah, you got it. I plan to make the walk of shame a thing of the past.

Like polio.

I am going to take my excess income and invest it in a fleet of refurbished ambulances that drive around town looking for sluts on their walks of shame, pick 'em up, provide them with the morning-after pill, hangover cure, antibiotics, replacement thongs, whatever else they may require, and then bring them sluts on home, drop 'em right at their doorstep with no cost to them personally and, more importantly, no judgment. None. We don't do none of that "slut-shaming" I read about on the internet. No, no. We provide this service free of charge, no questions asked.

Except for their phone numbers.

What?

You think I'm gonna let this precious opportunity to meet the next Mrs. The Contractor go to waste, you're outta your goldang mind!

Fix 'er uuuuuuuuuuup!

— Billy the Contractor
Grand Ole Opry, Nashville, TN
April 12, 2010

CHAPTER NINE

I

TJ Martinez laughed despite the fact that he was horrified, not amused, by Zoe's dying on the monitors in front of him.

He banged on the bar, but it wouldn't move.

He laughed at that, too.

When he tried to look inside the jamb and discover where the bar was stuck inside the doorway, he started to laugh, too.

He started to feel light-headed and dizzy and staggered over to the bench to sit down, but his ass missed it and he crashed hard and painfully to the ground. And that caused him to erupt into a three-minute-long laughing jag that left his chest on fire.

It was becoming harder and harder to breathe. The whole situation reminded him of hanging out at the clubs with Dusty, and they'd get passed those small metal cylinders — what did you call them? whippets — to break open and snort and get all revved up before hitting the dance floor.

"Oh my," he said, and his voice was high and squeaky, like he had just inhaled a balloon.

He looked at the air vents and saw the slats waving like they were a mirage, and he realized the room must be flooding with gas.

Nitrous oxide?

Also known as laughing gas?

"Oh, shit, it's a trap," he squeaked.

He looked on the monitor where Zoe lay, eyes wide, staring up at the camera. Was she looking at him? Was that possible?

"See you in just a bit," he said, and then started laughing.

And laughing.

And laughing.

II

Two things happened more or less simultaneously, or at least that was how it appeared to those experiencing them in real time:

The lights went out, one by one, across the island.

And the laugh track started.

Steve Gordon stepped out of Zoe Schwartz's room with the dog treats in his pocket, trying to follow the *pat-pat-pat* of her bare footfalls on the tile floors but not moving very quickly, presuming it was wise to give her space to calm down.

He was halfway down the wide sweep of finely carved balustrade when the whole house abruptly plunged into darkness, punctuated by a snorting, nasal chuckle.

Steve froze on the stairs, gripping the railing until his fingers were white, but no other sound came. He could sort of sense, in the air, the nonvocal anticipation of an audience waiting to let loose.

He thought he saw movement in the gallery coming toward him. Not wanting to take any chances fighting blind, he stepped sideways into the library. What little moonlight seeping into the gloom outlined the edge of one bookcase-turned-door, slightly ajar.

He crossed to the door and opened it, and the corpse that had been leaning against it keeled all the way out. Its skull, barely held together with uneven strips of skin, broke open and smeared the front of his shirt with blood and bits of bone and brain.

Cruel peals of delight reverberated against the walls, appropriate for an unexpected pratfall, the ultimate slip-on-a-banana-peel response. Steve pushed the corpse away and stumbled back. The face was an inhuman cabbage of dark red splotches, but somewhere in his brain sparked the realization that its clothes had once been on Oliver Rees's body.

His mind had no use for this information. It just wanted to get away, away, away from here. Already his throat was tightening, his stomach churning. He scrambled away blindly from one body and collided with another.

This one was upright, moving, warm. He whirled as the air above him exploded with diaphragm-borne guffaws and aw-no-he-didn'ts rolling like hurricane waters.

He grabbed the shoulders of the intruder and saw the wide, white eyes of Meredith Ladipo.

III

Meredith Ladipo?

"Don't!" Steve said, backing up through the door she'd used to enter the room. "Don't make me hurt you! I don't want to!"

"Ha ha ha ha ha," the walls said. "Ha ha ha ha ha ha."

Out through the clown lounge he stumbled, leered and wept over by grease-painted gargoyles. He stumbled through the play-

324

room and fell out of the French doors in the direction of the pool, with the still-lit fire pit providing the only illumination as far as he could see. He fell on his knees and threw up into the top pool what little remained in his stomach. It was hardly more than ocher bile, but it drifted in a tendrily mass through the too-blue water like a unicellular organism grown to grotesquely impossible size.

His vomiting earned polite, go-along sympathy laughs. The kind you give your boss when he tells a bad joke but you still want to be employed; the kind that makes you feel less of the audience for having given it, and even less of yourself for eliciting it.

These mild chuckles he heard from the sliding glass door, from back inside the house, not that he needed any more persuasion not to go back there. Laboriously he stood up, one foot and then the other, and spit the remnants of the puke out of his mouth and into the pool.

He staggered around the side of the house to the edge of the cliff where the bouncy house stood. The inflated Dustin Walker danced on its gable in the moonlight as if in pagan ecstasy.

Another light burned in the distance, one he had to stare at for a good forty-five seconds to verify it was real and not some fear-crazed illusion.

IV

After Steve Gordon ran from her, Meredith Ladipo felt her way around the library; she discovered Oliver's remains and backed away breathlessly to the stairs. She fled upstairs to her bedroom, intending to lock the door behind her and not come out again until dawn, but she discovered Dante Dupree sitting at her desk, illuminated only by the screen of her open laptop, rocking back and forth in her rolling chair.

"Oliver Rees is dead," she said.

To her annoyance, the air quivered with closed-mouth chortling, ghost mockery from dark quarters. With a queasy feeling, she realized that the speakers must be here, along with the cameras, so anyone in the panic room could watch and listen to her sleeping, dressing, bathing, and doing God knows what else.

Dante looked at her when she spoke, his eyes heavy-lidded, and he moved his lips momentarily as if about to speak, then didn't.

So she continued:

"It looks like another booby trap. There

326

was a hidden staircase, it looks like, in the library, and, uh, when he opened I guess, from the inside, this sledgehammer, on a wall? Swung out and smashed him right in the face and, uh, it did not do his skull any favors. It does not look good. There's a huge bloodstain on the wall, and, and . . . I don't know that I'm ever going to recover. The hammer hit the wall so hard that the wooden handle, it shattered in half so . . . it's no longer useful as a weapon and — could you please stop looking at me like that? I would really prefer it if you would stop looking at me like that. Whatever is the matter?"

"When were you going to tell us about this?" he asked.

Between his right thumb and index finger was a small pill bottle with a prescription label wrapped around it. He shook it like a baby's rattle.

"I was never going to tell you about it," Meredith said, stiffening. "It's private. And you have no right to go through my things. Much less take prescription medicines which I need. I've been looking all over for them all day and I would ask you to give them here." She reached for the bottle.

Dante didn't move. " 'For anomic aphasia,' " he read off the side of the bottle.

"I had to look it up on your dictionary program here." He nodded at the laptop. "That's quite a list of symptoms."

He picked up a legal pad he had taken from the writers' room and showed her what he had written. "Look right to you?"

She looked at the pad and looked back at him, speechless.

" 'Consistent inability to use or recognize words correctly, particularly nouns, proper nouns, and verbs.' All that crazy stuff out of your mouth nobody understands — those aren't, like, weird British words we don't have in America. Those are super-special Meredith Ladipo words that absolutely nobody else on planet Earth uses, am I right?"

She started wringing her hands. "It's a very rare neurological condition even on the anomia spectrum. Substitution aphasia, it's called. I was born with a defect in my brain in the speech production center. Broca's area? I know what the correct word is to use in any given instance, but my brain can't find it. Instead it substitutes another. Especially under times of stress."

"Stress," Dante said. "Like, I don't know, doing stand-up in front of a crowd? Or an improv game with five other people? No one believes in the indomitability of the human spirit as much as yours truly, but one might suspect that the inability to use words correctly is, I don't know, a deal-breaker for someone claiming to want to be a comic. Using words, after all, is pretty much our entire fucking job description, unless you want to be the first black Marcel Marceau."

She took a deep breath and spoke as slowly as she could. "That's why I always wanted to be a comedian. They always know just the right words to use, and when to say them, and how high or how soft, how fast. How to not say anything and let the laughs build in the silence.

"When you have this condition, you feel like you're just this big, clumsy hippopotamus in a world made of glass. You're always bumping into things, knocking things over. Stand-ups are so graceful with their language. That was what I wanted for me.

"Dustin . . . Dustin believed in me. He thought I could overcome my disability. For someone like that, with his reputation, to give encouragement . . . hope? You have no idea what it meant to me."

"Enough that you'd kill for him?" Dante said.

V

The wall of the cabana facing Steve Gordon was lit up like the marquee on a comedy club in classic Old Vegas fashion, each letter illuminated one after the other before the whole thing blinked together before going dark again and starting the letter-by-letter cycle once more:

S-T-E-V-E G-O-R-D-O-N
F-r-o-m T-V's "W-h-a-t J-u-s-t
H-a-p-p-e-n-e-d?"
O-n-e N-i-g-h-t O-n-l-y

Was it a trap? he thought.

Don't be simple. Of course it was a trap. This whole island was a trap.

He walked toward the cabana without being conscious of having decided to do so. As he approached the small house, the laughter in the mansion receded to the background.

For that he was grateful.

VI

"I've never killed anyone in my whole life, or even thought about it," Meredith Ladipo said. "I'm not that sort of blunderface —"

She winced, like a needle skipping across a record. "I'm not that sort of person. I can't believe Mr. Walker was either, really."

"Then you haven't been paying attention," Dante said. "Or he sold you on a bunch of nonsense. But then it wouldn't be the first time, would it?"

"You're talking shite."

"Nah, nah. Not me. I'm a big fan of hope and encouragement, but it sounds like he was selling you a bill of goods in exchange for making you his mammy. Like he said you could climb Mount Everest with a plastic fork and a pair of earmuffs."

"No, no, you're being excessively negative. It's not as impossible as you're making it seem. Substitution aphasia is manageable with a variety of treatments, like picture association . . . naming therapy . . . and drugs."

"Drugs? Yeah, let's talk about drugs. I found this in your bathroom when we were searching it earlier." Dante returned his attention to the pill bottle label. "Draxamema . . . Draxamemapheti . . . I'm not even gonna try. All I care about is this list of side effects: Mood swings. Paranoid tendencies. Memory loss. Aggressive outbursts. Manic and grandiose thinking." He lowered the bottle and cocked a grin at Meredith. "Girl, there's a whole side of you we haven't even seen yet, isn't there?"

"No," Meredith said, her voice quavering.

"Dustin Walker didn't meet you in no open mic in the West End, did he?"

"No," Meredith said, then caught herself. "I mean . . ."

Dante leaned forward in his chair:

"Dustin Walker found you in his nut-house, didn't he?"

She wiped tears from her eyes. "I wish you wouldn't use words like that. They're very hurtful."

"I swear I will cry myself to sleep tonight for using such insensitive language, I swear to the Lord above," Dante said. "How about I say funny farm instead? Sounds like where they put our kind out to pasture. Dusty found you on one of the funny farms he gives money to as a tax write-off, and because you were a nice piece of ass, he made you his pet psycho."

"No! You're razzing it all around!"

"Am I now? Let me look at this file I found on this here computer — you really should password-protect your shit, girl; you never know what crazy motherfucker might come along and start rummaging through it — this Microsoft Word file marked 'Dustin Speech.' "

332

"I was supposed to give a speech at the Dorothy Walker Clear-Mind Clinic in Calabasas. I used to go there for treatment after I moved to Southern California. He helped me keep my green card."

"Yeah, I know that, girl. I read it here. You know what else I read? 'I owe Mr. Walker everything. Much more than my one true chance at a normal life, but my one true chance at my dreams.' That's laying it on a bit thick, but it sure sounds pretty. Here's the part I find interesting, though:

" 'None of you know the true Dustin Walker. The person who wants to help people not just by making them laugh, but by making them live. He's not the person other comics, other ungrateful comics, make jokes about. I am so sick of them making fun of him, he who gave them all so much laughter and inspiration. And one day, I hope to show them how wrong they are.' "

He turned to glower at Meredith. "You know, under the current circumstances, that sounds a little, I don't know, damning, don't you think?"

Meredith shook her head. "It sounds like you're being paranoid."

Dante shook his head. "Girl, I have just about had it with you lying to me. I truly have."

Meredith Ladipo gripped her elbows. "I need my pills; I'm way overdue for them. I would have taken them earlier but you wouldn't let me into my own room while you were searching it."

She reached for the bottle in Dante's hand but he put it in his breast pocket. Then he stood up. He was almost a full foot taller than she was, and broad shouldered. His eyes seemed to strain in their sockets.

"You tell me the truth, I give you your pills. Not a second before."

"I've been telling you the truth. This whole time."

"And now that he's dead, you're the person to carry on his work, 'cause you feel so indebted to him! To make sure the rest of us end up dead!"

"No!"

"How do you know? Sounds like you don't even know what's happening half the time when you're doped up on these things!"

"It's not like fugue, I swear."

He tore the top sheet off the legal pad and shoved it at her, along with a pen.

"Now you're gonna write down everything I want to know," he said, stepping toward her, "or you and me are gonna have issues."

She looked at the pad, then at him, and

started backing out of the room. "Why won't you just abaft me alone?"

A white kind of rage ignited behind Dante's eyes.

He picked up the bottle of shiraz off the desk.

"Fun fact: You know what makes these bottles different from any others in the house?"

He smashed the bottle on the side of the desk and it shattered into a thousand shards, leaving a jagged end in Dante's hand.

That was enough for Meredith. She ran screaming from the room.

VII

In the panic room, Meredith entered and exited one monitor after another in no linear fashion — she appeared in the camera's view on the right before dashing into a corner, only to reappear in the middle. Dante Dupree did the same thing, bellowing and waving the broken bottle, appearing all over the pattern of screens as if trapped in a constantly flipping channel.

In TJ's increasingly rheumy vision, with eyes watering from too many belly laughs and not enough oxygen, Meredith appeared to run out the door with the shotgun and trip over Zoe Schwartz's grinning corpse, while on the next monitor she was just leaving her bedroom screaming while on the next monitor she was dashing into the kitchen to grab the shotgun where she had left it, leaning against the fridge, while in the next monitor she was standing in the clown lounge, looking around in confusion, clearly trying to remember where the hell she had set down the shotgun.

He let out a side-splitting, gut-busting, stomach-clutching, gasping-for-air laugh that banged off the walls and echoed throughout the house and grounds, nearly blowing out the speakers. With that involuntary outburst, TJ had managed to expel most of the remaining oxygen in his lungs. Now the world before his eyes became a tunnel and in that tunnel was the bank of monitors.

In the leftmost screen, Meredith staggered to her feet after tripping over Zoe's inert ankles. She grabbed the shotgun again, just as Dante Dupree drunkenly lumbered into the frame. She ran off past the fountain, toward the elevator.

Dante followed close behind, yelling something at her, but TJ couldn't quite make it out over the hiss of the nitrous oxide filling the room, pushing out all the breath-able air.

VIII

Meredith reached the elevator and punched the button. When the doors opened, she nearly rushed inside, but at the last second before setting foot into empty air she pulled back from the open shaft. The elevator was far below, on dock level: another trap.

Dante reached her, panting, the jagged bottle in one limp hand. He dragged her away from the elevator, keeping one eye on the camera mounted on the lamppost. It did not move to follow them, but he made sure to pull her out of its range anyway.

She managed to squirrel away from his grasp and point the shotgun at him. At last he was the spitting image of the violent drunk people had described in whispers behind his back, a person she could never quite imagine, yet now he appeared before her.

"Cat the bird!" she cried.

"Put down that dumbass thing," he said. "We both know it's not loaded."

"You're wrong," Meredith said. "It is. I found shells in Janet's room when we were searching. She had a whole box of them.

Back off. I'm serious. This thing carries two shells, so the only way I can prove it's loaded is if I shoot you in the chest. It's better in this instance for you to trust me, yeah?"

At least that's what she wanted to say, inside her head.

What she actually said a loud was:

"Aright wrong. Kalpeen. Tither the dole in mudpie heyday when gramercy hawk earlier. Jardyloo max a whole razy chiosk. Pare off! I'm gilet. This areen only parcels two rubber, so the only skewerite ticket can athwart it's erewhile is if I gadzook you in the birdsong. So it's better in this caper for once for somebody on this bloody parfay to just masticate me, yeah?"

Dante started rubbing his eyes mid-gibberish and didn't stop until she did.

"I've just about had it with your foolishness."

He lunged forward and grabbed the barrel.

IX

The resulting shotgun blast was audible on the speakers in the panic room, along with argument that led up to it.

These sounds were audible but not heard,

for TJ Martinez had been asphyxiated seconds before they began.

In his final death spasms, he flipped to one side of the bench, his pelvic bone pressing onto the edge, causing a white fluid that squirted out of his penis to dribble down one pant leg and drip out the cuff and drop onto his shoe. This residue was not semen but rather seepage from his prostate gland, now that all of his muscles had relaxed post-death. Common enough upon the expiration of the human male, the whitish splotches looked like the other thing on his brown loafer.

Sadly, the irony of this moment would not be known to humanity at large or the weirder annals of show business history, for none who knew of TJ's secret identity as the Shoe Jizzer would ever see the loafer, and no one who saw the loafer would know of TJ's secret identity as the Shoe Jizzer.

So this joke had been told, like so many infinite others, solely for the private amusement of the universe.

X

Steve Gordon heard the shotgun fire when he was halfway to the cabana. It sounded exactly like the rolling, ringing blast that had felled Janet Kahn.

He thought momentarily about investigating, but the sound had come from the darkness in the direction of the dock. It felt more prudent to keep heading toward the light.

The light with his name on it.

The club was fully lit when he stepped inside, the plastic votives on the tables glowing, the disco ball spinning. An easel bearing a blowup of his headshot from the gallery stood on the stage. Outlined arrows on the faux-brick backdrop lit up a spot where the mic stood; the spotlight cycled through reds and greens at its base. Hip-hop throbbed from the ceiling to bury the hubbub of an audience gathering and settling.

Except there was no audience that he could see.

He got up on stage, and the music faded into silence. The lights narrowed into a spot on just him. The plastic-brick backdrop ceased its pulses.

He could see little more than the first few rows of tables beyond the glare of stage lights, but when he placed his hand over his eyes he thought he could see a figure standing inside the sound booth over the bar.

He stepped in that direction, but an electronically distorted voice spoke to him over the speakers:

"I wouldn't do that, Gordo."

He stopped moving.

"I've got good news and bad news," the voice said. "I'll start with the bad news: look down."

He did.

A small panel snapped open beneath his soles, staggering him a bit, but he straightened when he realized a covering had been retracted above a strip of Plexiglas upon which his feet still stood. Beneath the strip were three thick mud-colored discs with black-button centers, almost like the removable weights on barbells. The buttons had been depressed all the way to the level of the discs.

"Those are three American-made antipersonnel landmines, manufactured in beautiful Janesville, Wisconsin," the voice said. "Extremely illegal now — thank you, Princess Di — but still readily available at your local gun show. The entire stage is a pressure plate that has measured and set your weight, thereby arming the devices. If you get off the stage for any reason — or if anyone gets on the stage to help you — either addition or subtraction of weight will set them off. Any one of those mines by itself would blow your foot and most of your leg off, but all three of them detonating simultaneously will . . . Well, the best description I can come up with is that you will be instantly transformed into a substance not entirely unlike red finger paint."

Steve swallowed. A void roared through him. His movements became deliberate and restrained. He looked up again at the sound booth window. He couldn't see anyone there anymore. Was this a recording? A remote broadcast?

"But here's the good news," the voice continued. "Your fate is still technically in your hands.

"The stage is also on a timer. Your voice activates the timer. You may be headlining, but you're going to get the same length as an opener. You need to get through ten minutes of actual material, Gordo. Not stolen jokes. Real ones. Ones you wrote.

"If you stop talking for longer than ten seconds, the mines will go off.

"If you try to get off the stage for any reason, the mines will go off.

"If anyone tries to get on the stage with you, the pressure plate will register the difference in weight and the mines will go off.

"If I catch you using anybody else's material, the mines will go off.

"If any circumstances unforeseen by these guidelines occur, the mines will go off.

"Oh, I can also detonate the mines remotely. Did I not mention that? Sorry. I can detonate the mines remotely, too.

"So you'd better make me laugh. You'd better be funny. *Your own act* better be funny. Not a stolen one.

"Or you're going to . . .

"Do I have to say it?

"Screw it, I will anyway:

"Or you're gonna bomb, Gordo. You're gonna bomb.

"Ten solid minutes, do you understand me, Gordo? At the end of the intro."

Steve Gordon was preternaturally calm. He just stared ahead with his mouth set straight. He didn't sweat. He didn't tremble. He didn't cry.

"I said, do you understand me, Gordo?" the ceiling demanded.

Steve nodded:

"Let's do this."

The only response he got was a sudden shift in music — a whiplash segue from generic club hip-hop to the rhythmic vocal moan opening of Gin Wigmore's "Black Sheep" — and the speakers said:

"All right, Walker Island Comedy Club, put your hands together for a man so amazing he's his own opener, his own middle, your headliner, and quite possibly his own finisher — we'll see how he does — but you know him from a series so old it's not even in syndication anymore, *What Just Happened?* And . . . and . . . oh, who am I kidding, you don't know him from anything else at all!"

During his intro, Steve turned away from the mic stand and walked toward the faux-brick backdrop, taking care not to depart from the edges of the pressure plate, of course, which, now that he knew to look for them, self-evidently delineated the perimeter of the stage maybe ten centimeters from the edge, all the way around.

"Give it up for . . . *Steve 'Gordo' Gooor-rrrrrrrdooooonnnn!*"

Gin Wigmore's voice rose then faded, replaced by canned applause and cheers. Steve bounded downstage from the brick wall, waving and grinning, blew a kiss or two.

The clapping and the whistling subsided as he wrestled the mic off the top of the stand.

He looked out over the empty chairs and tables visible beyond the spotlights and breathed deep.

And he said:

TEN SOLID

Thank you, thank you so much for that incredibly meta introduction. Really. It's so, so great to be here on Murder Island, half-starved, in near-constant fear for my life, seeing friends and colleagues killed in front of me.

I did get laid here, though, so it hasn't been all bad, you know?

No, seriously, I had sex here for the first time in . . . about fifteen months, I'd say? Now if I had known that fear for their lives would get women to go to bed with me, I would have spent a lot more time in war zones and sites of ethnic cleansing. I need to update my Ok-Cupid profile:

"Looking for single female, any race . . . in regions controlled by genocidal warlord . . . must like . . . dogs. No . . . fatties." There. Now I just have to sit back and watch the emails roll in.

(00:42.21)

My day job for the past few years has been as an improv teacher in Chicago, which, I know this is hard to believe, is not really conducive to making it with the ladies.

The main problem, when you come right down to it, is that in improv you're supposed to begin every response with "Yes, and." You're supposed to both embrace what the other person is feeding you, then build on that with something of your own.

But in dating, that doesn't really work so well. You can come across as super needy. Or psychotic.

Girl says, "I had a really fun time tonight. I'd really like to see you again."

You say, "Yes, and our next date will be on a blimp."

"Well . . . I mean, maybe? But I was thinking dinner and a movie again?"

"Yes, and we will save the queen of England from ninjas."

"Is that . . . is that really something we can plan for?"

"Yes, and we will become like unto immortal gods who secure our place in legend with our amazing feats of strength and genius."

"You know what . . . never mind, I think this whole thing has gotten way too weird for me. Goodnight, have a good life, and . . . go get some help, okay?"

(Pause: second and a half)

"Yes, and I will now leap into a volcano."

See?

It's just not practical.

So I would like to thank my old bud Dustin Walker for inviting me here, if only for improving my love life. After all, he is responsible both for my being gone so long and for my standing before you now.

You see, Dustin and I go way back. We starred with another winner named TJ Martinez on a comedic television program called *What Just Happened?,* which both describes my feeling when I learned I got the gig, and also exactly describes the rest of my career after I lost it.

(02:21.35)

347

I never really understood why I got the job, I think I had just an exceptionally good night when the producers visited Second City to see me perform, looking for a bland white guy to round out the cast of an improv show.

Plus I am Canadian, which was even better. Blandness is to Canada what guns are for the U.S. It's what makes our fine nation simultaneously unique and horrifying.

I had a lot of fun making that show, I'm not going to lie. I felt like I was walking on clouds for four years.

Later, I found out those weren't clouds, those were my castmates' egos, but at the time I was just happy for the nice view of Studio City.

And I gotta tell you, I worshipped Dustin Walker. I mean, *Can't Help Myself* was only two or three years old by the time they started holding auditions for *What Just Happened?* and I had it memorized. I thought Dustin Walker was given to us by the comedy gods to save us from lame bits about dating and airplane food.

Then I made the mistake of meeting him.

I don't know about never meeting your heroes, but definitely, definitely never meet Dustin Walker.

Nonexistent ladies and gentlemen, Dustin Walker was a control freak, a moody S.O.B., mad at the world, and burning through interns and PAs like toilet paper, firing them or terrorizing them until they quit week after week. We started calling them goldfish because they'd be like the ones you won at the state fair. You'd never know when you'd walk in some morning and find them bobbing upside down in the tank.

(03:46.30)

Eventually, the show ended, and I don't care what anyone tells you, there is only one reason TV shows get canceled, and that is money. It's not creative differences, it's not the stars wanting to go pursue feature film work, it's money. Ninety-nine out of a hundred times the show ends because it's not making enough money.

Or, in *Seinfeld*'s case, it's making so much money they canceled it because the cast was running out of room to put the money in their house.

"Here's another hundred million, Jerry! Where do you want it?"

"Oh, I don't know, pile it in the corner there. Money! Do you ever wonder what the deal is with money, I mean, really?"

So the show was ending, TJ had already lined up the *2nite* gig, he was well on his way to sexually harassing his way to the top, and Dusty was bragging about all the big movie roles he had lined up, leaving the artistic kindergarten of television behind. He was going to do Shakespeare with Kenneth Branagh!

I, of course, didn't have shit, except for the bricks I was shitting every day contemplating my future. Comedy clubs were always asking me to perform because they knew a familiar face from TV packed in the plebes. I had about five minutes' worth of material, something like that, but that was it.

And Dusty, who, goddamn him, for all his many, many personal failings as a human being, was still the funniest person I ever met. He would warm up our audiences before our tapings. Normally, the studio would just hire two or three regular midlist comedians who weren't me to do that, but Dusty just started doing it for fun, and he made sure the stand-ups got paid. And he would just — I mean, he would just kill! But he said he hated stand-up, he was never going to do it again, the audiences were morons who didn't get him anymore, he was going to just concentrate on movies. And so he had no reason not to cast out these pearls to our two hundred-seat soundstage theater.

(05:35.32)

And he kept saying he was never going to use them again!

I'm not justifying what I'm about to tell you. I'm just telling you what happened, okay? Save your judging looks and catcalls for the end, nonexistent audience.

So I was terrified that this show was my only shot, and I couldn't handle going back to being a nobody again. I really couldn't. I was already the fifth wheel on a show that had a cast of three people. So I was not getting such great offers. And I had *some* stand-up material, but not enough after the grind of doing *What Just Happened?* for four years.

So, I took four or five of Dusty's best jokes.

(Pause: two seconds)

I can't even remember them very well.

One of them was about grunge, that's how incredibly relevant they are to today, you know?

Honestly, I didn't even think he'd care if he found out. He didn't want them, and I needed them. I needed them bad! Or so I thought.

Besides, how would he find out? I mean, who has spies at the Comedy Store for the midnight set?

Heh.

The joke, as they say, was on me.

And did he care?

Ooh boy, did he care.

(06:41.52)

I mean, I don't really know what I was thinking, ripping him off, just from the way he terrorized the interns alone, but he fixed me good. He made sure no studio or producer

352

would take a chance on me. No talent agency or management company would take me as a client. No tour or club would book me.

I mean, he fucked me so good I thought about changing my own name, but I couldn't afford the court fees.

My savings ran out so I fled back to Chicago, which is Hollywood for people who are afraid of success.

Oh, I'm sorry, Chicago, I'm sorry. I know you want to get drunk and kick my ass now.

But I thought that's what your kids were for?

I'm kidding. I kid you, Chicago, because I love you.

They are very pro-loser in Chicago, yes they are. I bet the Cubs are gonna be the only team in history to be *less* popular after winning the World Series. This is why they are my people.

No, I truly do love Chicago. Between the winters and the economy, it's the Stockholm syndrome of cities. So I don't really have a choice.

I'll tell people I fell down the stairs, Chicago, no really. Please don't leave me. It's not you, it's me. I can change, I promise.

You see, I learned the dirty little secret of success, which isn't much of a secret because every celebrity talks about it but nobody listens to them. Fame doesn't fill this emptiness you got inside of you, you know?

(08:00.90)

I really, truly, deeply wish that everybody could be famous, even for just a year or two, so they could really understand how little it changes you. You still got to get up every morning and look in that mirror and deal with that dopey-eyed sap staring back at you. Every single day.

That emptiness never gets filled up because, the public? They're never going to love you the way you want to be loved. Not because they don't really understand you or any shit like that, but because you'll never see *you* through *their* eyes, eyes that worship you. You still got your own to look through. And they knew what you were then, which is what you'll always be.

And so I found my peace with it. I convinced myself I was happy in my teaching jobs, as bad as they paid, as infrequent as they were, because even if I didn't get to stay on the mountaintop with Dusty and TJ, at least I had been there. At least I had seen the view, you know?

But now here's the *funny* part. My "closer," as we say in the biz.

Even after achieving that level of, I don't know, let's call it inner peace — sure, why not — even after I achieved it, and even after *knowing* what a vindictive son of a bitch Dusty Walker is, and to what lengths he will go to revenge himself on whoever he sees as having crossed him in the slightest, most innocuous way . . . Knowing all that, and having been on the receiving end of it in such a . . . such a profound and dramatic way that literally shaped the majority of my adult life . . .

. . . Knowing all that, *I agreed to come on this* fakakta *trip in the first place.*

(09:20.40)

Oh, come on. I know that if there was anyone here, the walls would be ringing with laughter. I would be absolutely deafened! I mean, it's

355

almost unbelievable that I would be the saddest of all sad clowns, that my life would be so pathetic that quite possibly being the only person who knew for a fact that Dustin Walker was capable of this craziness on this island, that I would still think this would be my best option to spend a weekend.

Because he knew, that son of a bitch, I was chasing the laugh. I wanted to get it back. And he knew I knew he could help me, if he wanted to. Because that laugh, it's stronger than smack to an addict, stronger than a flame to a moth. And I flew right into that flame, like the dumb, desperate schmuck moth that I am.

Heh.

So that's my whole sad story. You have to admit, that is some comedy gold. Really and truly.

Oh, wait! Wait!

I remembered. I remembered one of the Dusty Walker jokes I stole.

Yeah, it went something like . . .

"I recently bought a big house in the canyon. I

had always heard that fame really changes you, gives you a bunker mentality. I didn't believe it until I bought this monstrosity.

"It's like Alcatraz, but without the lovely sea view."

There.

See?

That totally seems like something worth dying for, right?

(10:27.22)

— Steve "Gordo" Gordon
Recording studio on Walker Island,
somewhere in the Caribbean Sea
Just now

CHAPTER TEN

I

When Steve Gordon finished the set, he tried to put the mic back on the stand. It wasn't easy because his hands were trembling — not from fear, but from the adrenaline surging through them. Though the circumstances were outré, he had not faced an audience, even a fake one — no students, no sketches, just him and his mouth and the mic — in twenty years. The blood pounded through his body and he could feel it pulsing in his forehead and he felt alive, truly alive, for the first time in two marriages, eight apartments, sixty-two fruitless meetings with agents, managers, producers, directors, and the like.

He looked out over the faux club to the sound booth.

"So what do you think? That was ten and change, right?"

No answer.

"And it was pretty good, right? Obviously, I need to tighten it up a lot more with, you know, an actual crowd, but that was some solid shit, man. That was solid. And most of it, I made it up right on the spot."

Silence and darkness from beyond the crowd.

Steve sighed.

"You're not even up there, are you? There's no one there. You're a recording — a 'party favor,' like Dante said. I might as well have done that whole routine in front of my mirror in my parents' house, like when I was a kid. Doing Carlin's *Class Clown* or *Live on the Sunset Strip*. Except what you just heard? That was all me, you cocksucker. All of it, every last word."

Nothing.

Steve swallowed. "The worst part? Is knowing I didn't need to do it. I didn't need to steal. I was good enough all by myself. Except I got scared. And so here I am."

He looked down at the seam delineating the pressure plate from the rest of the stage.

He thought about raising his foot and stepping off. Even if it was the end, so what? At least he'd be going out on a high note. He did a set. He did a good set. Sure, it sucked that no one else knew it but him.

But *he* knew. And he didn't before.

"Mr. Gordon? Steven?"

The voice didn't come from the ceiling, and it had no electronic distortion.

His throat tightened with fear, but after a second he was able to call out, "Yeah, in here!"

The front door to the club yawed open and Meredith Ladipo shuffled inside, dazed.

Steve held up his hands. "Meredith, don't come up here. I've been rigged — there's a mine — look, you know, it's too crazy to explain. Just don't come up onstage."

She kept walking as if she hadn't heard a word he said. When she entered the aureole of light from the ceiling, he could see she had been crying.

"What's wrong?"

"Clepe," Meredith said. "Clepe endlong."

"Uh . . . what?"

She swallowed and struggled to say very slowly: "He's dead."

"Who's dead?"

"I killed him."

"Who?"

"Dante," she said. She burst into tears and wiped her eyes. "I killed him."

Steve didn't know what to say, so he didn't say anything. After tamping down her sobs she said:

360

"He tried to grab the shotgun from me. I told him it was loaded, I *told* him, but he didn't believe me. *Why don't any of you ever believe me?*"

"I believe you, Meredith, I believe you. It sounds like an accident — you didn't mean it, right? It was an accident?"

"He's dead, Steve, it's my fault . . . The shot knocked him back, down the elevator shaft, and he's gone . . . he's gone!"

"Hey. Hey! No offense, kid, but I am still here and very much want to stay that way. Can you do me a favor?"

"What are you saying?"

"Meredith! Focus, man! Can you . . . look behind you, see the stairs beyond the bar?"

She sniffled. "You mean to the sound booth?"

"Yes! I forgot you work here. Yeah, could you go up there and see, uh, if there's anyone there?"

"What do you mean?"

"I mean, I thought I saw someone there, but now I'm not so sure."

"You mean like Zoe?"

"Sure, like her. Just — poke your head in and see. Pretty please?"

Meredith wiped her nose and her eyes and walked over.

She trotted up the stairs.

She could hear someone inside. Some sort of movement.

At first, she didn't know what to do. It was a scratching sound.

She stepped away from the door, gripped the knob, and threw it open.

She shrieked as something bolted out of the booth and past her feet, knocking over the water dish and food bowl from which it had just been partaking.

Asshole ran down the steps and right up to the stage. He stood there, looking up at Steve and wagging his tail.

"Meredith!" Steve shouted.

She stepped toward Asshole. The scruffy little dog stood, every fiber of its being aquiver, transfixed by the dog treats it could see sticking out of Steve's pocket, the dog treats neither Steve nor Meredith had noticed.

"Call him over, Meredith," Steve said, his voice cracking. "Please, Jesus God, call him over to you!"

Meredith opened her mouth, but it had been a long time since she had taken her pills.

"Trolley," she said.

"Yo-yo!

"Jam chaser!

"Forby yede!"

"What is wrong with you?" Steve said.

She held up a hand for him to wait a second.

"Are you fucking serious?!"

Meredith removed her pills from her pocket and popped two in her mouth and took the nozzle from the bar and shot seltzer water into her mouth.

But all this was taking far too long for Asshole. The little dog was perplexed. By this point in Mommy's act she would take out the treats, and then he would run onto the stage, and she would give him the treats. So maybe, he decided, he was the one at fault here.

Asshole was a good boy. He was a very good boy. Mommy always told him so.

And so the little dog launched himself up onto the stage.

All twelve pounds of him.

II

Meredith Ladipo did not experience the explosion as an event happening in space and time. Instead, in one instant she was rushing toward the stage, opening her mouth to yell, as Steve Gordon backed away from the little gray drowned-looking dog launching itself at him.

And then in the next instant she was lying on her back over a scattering of tables and chairs with a roaring ring in her ears, like the endless peal of an infinite bell. A bright light filled her vision, then slowly retracted into the hovering singularity of the disco ball hanging from the ceiling, swinging back and forth, back and forth, in violent parabolas.

She became aware of shooting pains in her arms and back from where the metal legs of tables and chairs had slammed into her flesh when she abruptly transitioned from a vertical to a horizontal position. Nevertheless she was able to stretch out her legs — also with considerable pain — and reached to grip the fallen furniture to steady herself as she rose.

When she saw her hands, she started to cry. There was so much blood. That she had any more than a few minutes left to live seemed inconceivable, given the amount of crimson gore speckled across her hands, her arms, her clothes, her feet, splattered across the club floor and walls.

On one of her knuckles she saw a fluff of downy salt-and-pepper fur stuck to a darker red gelatinous bit of something that, until very recently, had been part of something living. She looked to the stage, over which a cloudy haze still lingered, with no sign of Gordo or Asshole anywhere.

She knew then — it was not her blood she was bathed in, but that of a man and a dog who were no longer there.

Her stomach tied itself into searing knots. She wanted to throw up but only tasted blood when she moved her tongue — her mouth must have been open when the blast came.

More overpowering than her nausea was the desire to get out of this charnel house. She slipped and staggered to her feet, pain lancing her left knee. She looked down and saw her own blood for the first time, oozing from a purple-edged gash extending diagonally across her kneecap.

Leave, her mind still burned, *get out of here,* and she turned toward the doorway, where Janet Kahn was standing in her sunglasses and plastic brace and mummy wrappings. Her mouth was moving but she couldn't make herself heard over the still-endless ringing.

Meredith stopped breathing, and her heart stopped beating, and she stepped backward, ankle catching on crisscrossed metal stems lying behind her. She fell over on her side across a fallen metal chair. It caught her badly in the ribs and right arm. And now, officially, every single part of her was in pain.

She had kept on crying since seeing her own *Carrie* impersonation, but now she started moaning as well, from the bruising she just received in the fall and the old pain from the explosion and the past weekend and her whole life up till this point. She cried the way an infant cries, in protest against an entire world constructed in defiance of your own wishes.

Finally, however, she tired of it, once she realized that she was able to hear her own wails, which meant that she could hear anything at all. She stopped, and swallowed, and tried to calm her breathing, wiping the tears and caked blood from her eyes.

Janet Kahn still stood over her.

"Good news, kiddo," she said. "This will all be over soon."

III

"I thought you were dead," Meredith said weakly.

"Yeah, I get that a lot," Janet said. "Do you know I hold the world record for being declared dead by Twitter? Seven times. The last time I started the rumors myself, just to watch the tweeple scurry around like ants."

She reached out her hand so Meredith could take it. "C'mon dear, upsy-daisy."

Meredith slapped Janet's hand away and managed to stand up on her own. The wound on her knee reopened and hobbled her, so she could back away only shufflingly.

"You've had a shock, I get it, but there's no reason we should stick around this abattoir. This plastic brace I'm wearing does not do wonders for my gag reflex, believe you me. Let's get some fresh air. C'mon, step outside."

"You — it was you who killed all those people!"

Janet shrugged. "Ehh, a little from column A, a little from column B. I think it's more a matter of semantics, princess. I mean, sure, I set the traps. But in most of the cases I just gave those people opportunities to kill themselves. No one made TJ Martinez go into that panic room. No one made Ollie attempt the gags in his binder. No one made Gordo get up on that stage. No one made Zoe psychologically incapable of being separated from her dog. No one made Dante drink a wine cellar's worth of booze or Billy the Contractor a tallboy. In the end, they did themselves in."

"Is that a dog whistle around your neck?"

Janet picked up the metal cylinder by its

chain and glanced at it. "Yeah, okay, in Zoe's case I helped her along a bit by guiding her annoying little rat mutt, sure . . ."

Meredith suddenly wagged a finger at her. "Wait! You gave Griffith his tallboy — you did poison him! Right in front of us!"

"Oh, yeah. That was totally me." She held up her hand, which had several rings on it, one of which was a radiant smiling sun. She popped it open and showed a hollow center. "Isn't that neat? Afghan poison ring. I got it from a market in Kabul when I did a USO show, like, ten years ago. Yeah, I popped open the beer and when my back was turned I was able to drop the arsenic in there from the ring, right under your noses."

Janet blinked when she closed the ring again.

"Okay, maybe you're right. Maybe it isn't just semantics and I did kill them all. Oh, well. C'mon, let's go outside."

"Why did you want to kill all those people? What did they ever do to you?"

"Outside," Janet said.

"I'm not going anywhere with you!" Meredith shouted.

Janet sighed. "Typical Millennial."

She produced a revolver from the back of her waistband.

"Sometimes it's not all about you, you

know!" She waved the gun in Meredith's direction. "Do you wanna walk outside or do you wanna be carried outside? 'Cause I'll accommodate you either way."

Meredith threw out her arms. "What is your obsession with me going outside?"

A third person spoke:

"Because he doesn't want to shoot you here, where your DNA would get mixed up with all this other shit. That would mess up his whole plan to get away with this."

Janet turned to the doorway and the source of the voice and said:

"I thought you were dead."

IV

Dante Dupree stepped into the room from outside, holding Meredith's shotgun level at Janet.

Janet did not raise her own weapon, other than to throw up her hands. "You said he fell down the elevator shaft!" she said to Meredith. "That's the only reason I came out! Goddamn it, this screws up the whole thing."

Dante said, "And you're going to — what? You're going to disappear her out in the middle of the ocean, right? Weigh her body down and sink it so it's never found. And if anyone ever finds this, and her fake confession 'speech' on her laptop, they spend all their time looking for her and not for you?"

Janet grinned broadly. "You two clever sons-of-guns. You put one over on me! How'd you do it?"

"You first."

"Never explain a joke. Then it stops being funny. You should know that, Dante."

"True. But I don't mind explaining other people's jokes. Take that shit off first."

"What shit?"

"What shit?" Meredith said. "Why did Janet kill all those people?"

"She didn't," Dante said. "Janet's been dead for at least a week, maybe two. Take the shit off, man."

"Man?"

"Ugh, you're no fun anymore," Janet said, and with her free hand she pulled the plastic collar around her neck and the bandages off her face. Much of the heavy foundation she was wearing came off with it.

"Oh my God," Meredith said.

Janet then pulled off her wig, revealing the graying widow's peak underneath. Next she swapped out the tinted eyeglass frames for a more iconic pair of Coke-bottle glasses.

Oh my God," Meredith said. "Dustin?"

Dustin Walker gestured at his bosom.

370

"Can I keep the tits?"

"Keep the tits, lose the gun," Dante said, shotgun still level.

"Okay, okay, take it easy, man," Walker said. He set the pistol aside on a nearby chair wedged between fallen tables.

"That's better," Dante said. "You got tripped up by Janet's trunk. When you threw it off the dock, it stuck on one of the pylons; it didn't fall in."

Walker made a face. "Aw, shit. Really?"

"So I was able to feel the inside when I tried to pull it back onto the dock, how cold and clammy it was."

Meredith frowned. "And that's . . . significant?"

Dante said, "No, not until Janet's body turned up. When I pulled her out of the pool, I felt how cold she was. But that didn't make any damn sense if she'd just been killed a minute or so before. And her body already had discoloration and rigor mortis way, way, way further along than somebody just a few seconds dead would ever show.

"It wasn't until I found the shotgun trip wire in the bushes that I realized what was going on:

"There *hadn't* been anybody here for a week. Walker started out in L.A., where he killed Janet Kahn and took her place after

371

her surgery. He put the body in this huge trunk that was, what, refrigerated somehow? He temporarily shut down the elevator so we had to leave our bags down by the dock.

"Then, in the couple hours we were getting settled and farting around the house, he got busy. He turned the elevator back on, went down to the dock, and made a mess of the bags. But really he was reclaiming Janet's body. He brought it back up poolside, where he hid it in one of those containers where they keep the extra chair cushions.

"In the process, I'm going to guess he also grabbed Billy the Contractor's photo off the wall — it's the only explanation, that it's the only headshot he grabbed *before* a murder. It was pretty reasonable to think none of us would notice it was gone until after Billy was killed. And since you planned to kill him first, that made it a pretty good bet, am I right?"

Walker smiled and made the "keep going" gesture, rolling a finger.

"He tricked Ruby into separating from the rest of the group — you were with her at the time, so I'm guessing, what, automated text messages set to send at a certain interval from the computer we found in your bedroom? Or some other computer you've got hidden somewhere? You probably have one of those apps that controls your desktop from your phone, so as long as you have it set up right, you can send texts remotely at the press of a button? With Ruby gone, he was able to convince you two to split up," Dante said to Meredith.

"That *was* your idea," she said.

"Duh," Walker said, and he rolled his eyes.

"He goes to the pool patio, takes out Janet's body, sits it in the chair, and shoots her with the shotgun, blowing her face off — which helps hide that even under all that makeup your face and Janet's didn't quite align, particularly with her new Botox job — and knocking her and the chair she's sitting in into the pool. We all come running, and he slips away here, to the club, where he hangs out while knocking us all off. It's the perfect hiding place because it'd already been searched and nobody was found. Although it wouldn't surprise me if he's got another hiding place around here somewhere. Somewhere you can monitor the feed from the cameras — though I bet you got that ability on your phone, too — so you can move freely about the island, always where we're not, setting up traps and removing and replacing photos and whatnot."

"You'd be riiiiiiight," Dustin sing-songed with a grin.

"Because that was Dave's-Not-Here whom Steve and I found hanging at the end of the rope, wasn't it, Dusty? There are a couple personal photos of him in his little hutch you had built for him back there. You two look a lot alike . . . I bet that's why you hired him."

"You two *do* look alike!" Meredith gasped. "Thank God. I thought I was being so racist for thinking that."

"I bet if we went back and looked at the GoPro video real close, we could even see the harness you're wearing under your shirt when you 'hanged' yourself. Then you haul yourself back up with Dave's-Not-Here's help and — surprise! — he takes your place in the clothes you were wearing in the video. Except he doesn't get the benefit of a harness. How am I doing so far?"

"I'm really, really into it," Walker said.

Dante said, "I figured all that out pretty quickly, not long after we found the real Janet's body. But now that you were in the wind, I didn't know how best to lure your ass out into the open. I also wasn't a hundred percent sure you didn't have anyone working with you among the group. So I kept my mouth shut until I decided the only way to get you out would be if all of us, or most of us, were dead.

"So I pulled the same trick as you and faked my death. Damn, son, you think I didn't see your hacky death-by-booze schtick a mile away? I am a trained alcoholic, I can act fake-drunk with the best of 'em, drink enough to fool the cameras while pouring the rest of it down the sink. What was that all about — you were gonna get me so blasted I popped off so one of the others had to kill me, or were you gonna do me in once I was too shit-faced to defend myself?"

Dustin just laughed. "I was adopting a wait-and-see attitude. I had contingencies for everything. Gags all over the island you never found. Fifteen ways to kill each one of you. That's why I came here embedded with you, dressed like Janet. To read the room. Did Zoe bring her dog or not? Did TJ come armed? The first rule of improv is, be prepared."

"Makes two of us, asshole. I wrote a couple notes to Meredith telling her to play along while we were arguing in her room. I made sure I knew where the camera was in her bedroom so TJ couldn't see. The first one said 'THEY'RE WATCHING, PLAY ALONG.' The other was 'GET SHOTGUN

GO TO ELEVATOR.' I knew to play out our little drama just beyond the range of the camera, so wherever you were watching, you could hear but not see when I pointed for Meredith to shoot the shotgun in the air. I hid in the trees until I saw you slink out of the main house heading for the cabana, and here we are."

"That's incredible," Meredith said.

"Thanks, doll," Walker said.

"Not you, you plonk, him. Dante, were you always a black Sherlock Holmes?"

"Girl, please. Grandma could write the pants off that hack Doyle."

"Your grandma?"

"Yeah, Ephesia J. Dupree? She wrote the Miss Maples series of urban mysteries. Her most famous one is *Miss Maples Gets All Up in Your Business.*"

"I've never heard of them, I'm sorry."

"Yeah, you usually had to buy them off dudes with tables on the sidewalk in Brooklyn," Dante said. "But they were best sellers, and Grandma had me proofread every single one."

Walker said, "In his act, Dante made it sound like he grew up in the Gowanus Towers, but really he grew up in the brownstones across the street, with the hedge-fund managers and the corporate shysters."

Dante scowled. "And I never said otherwise! I ran with all those tough kids; they were my damn neighbors! Are you still on about this 'crimes against stand-up' bullshit? Because if you really planned to kill me because you don't think I'm black enough, or TJ for his laugh track or Orange Baby Man for being a phony New Age messiah, or some other vigilante Comedy Batman nonsense, I'm going to blow your head off just on principle alone."

"You made me a punchline," Walker said, the mirth gone from his face.

Dante blinked. "Huh?"

"All of you, in all of your acts, as soon as it became a quick laugh, an obvious laugh, you made me a punchline. I inspired you. You all said so. But as soon as it was convenient you forgot me, you made me into your jokes. You just went for the easy applause line. Dicks, sex, relationships, airlines, farts, Asians, driving. And Dustin Walker. You made me the lowest common denominator. An automatic laugh line. Me. I didn't deserve that. *That* was a crime against comedy."

"Christ, Walker, I don't know what the hell you're talking about. But even if I did — you're gonna tell me you're just like everybody else? You laugh along when it's the other guy being made fun of, but the minute you're on the receiving end of a gag, or your tribe is, then all of a sudden you get offended? Those are just jokes, man. How can you not know that?"

"How can you not know there's no such thing as 'just jokes,' Dante?" Spit flew from Walker's lips. "All jokes are little truths. And your truth is that you think I'm nothing. It's not even worth remembering when you've insulted me or, like Gordo and Ollie, stolen from me. That's how little you think of me, you just said so yourself. Well, what do you think now?"

"I think you're a fucking lunatic now," Dante said. "Is that what you were going for?"

Meredith tried to blink tears from her eyes. "I never . . . I never insulted you, Dustin. Never. How can you say that?"

Walker's eyes flickered at the ground. "I know, baby. But — you know. Collateral damage."

"What?"

"I'm not proud of it or anything."

"Is that supposed to make me feel better?!"

Walker said, "When I met you, at the clinic, before they diagnosed your problems as neurological, I was so flattered that you

378

were starstruck. Someone as young and as beautiful and . . . exotic as you. I really liked you, I did. And I tried to help you. But you're just not funny. I mean, it's bad enough no one understands what you say. But even when they do . . . Some people are funny. Some people are not funny. You, Meredith, are not funny."

Meredith threw up her arms. "You mean I've been sleeping with you this whole time for nothing?"

Walker blinked. "You said . . . you said you loved me."

"No!" Meredith screamed. "I was just using you for my career! I mean, look at you! You are so, so, *so old!*"

Dante raised the shotgun. "This got really sad, really fast. Dusty, you had some exit strategy for getting off this goddamn island, and you're gonna tell me what it is."

Walker made a show of thinking about it.

"No," he said.

"Sorry," Dante said, "let me rephrase that. Either you tell me, or I'm going to shoot you in the motherfucking face."

"No," Walker said.

"Bitch, don't think I have any other reason to keep you alive!"

"Makes two of us," Walker said, and he

lunged for the pistol on the chair next to him.

Dante fired the shotgun. The blast made Meredith's ears ring again.

Walker spun around and fell face-first to the floor.

Dante lowered the weapon, breathing hard.

He looked at Meredith. She looked at him.

"What now?" she said.

"Beats the hell out of me," he said. "If we had Google, we could Google instructions for making a raft. Then we could go drown."

"Bitch!" he yelled at Walker's still form. "Crazy-ass punk-ass bitch. Can't take a joke. Who blows all his money faking his own death and killing whoever made fun of him on stage? What a waste of a cat-movie fortune."

"Did you really make fun of him in your act?"

"Hell should I know? I'm a comedian; I make fun of everybody. That's my damn job."

He looked past Meredith's shoulder.

And pushed her away from him.

He popped open the empty shotgun and fumbled the box of shells out of his jeans pocket.

Meredith turned just in time to see a grinning Dustin Walker, leveling the revolver at Dante.

"You should see the looks on your faces," Walker said.

He shot Dante twice in the chest.

V

Dante kicked convulsively on the gore-spattered floor, drawing grotesque blood angels on the tiles with his spasms. Dustin Walker walked over clutching the revolver, his smile gone, and picked up the small box Dante had dropped at his feet. He spiked it on the dying man's chest like a wide receiver in the end zone.

"*Blanks,* baby! Yeah!" he roared down on his victim. "How dumb you think I am? Why would I give any one of you any advantage for any reason! Now Meredith — I'm sorry, honey, this is all over, but you have one last duty to perform as my assistant. I'm afraid we're going out to the middle of the ocean. You are going to stay there, while I am going to the mainland, where I've got a new identity already set up. You've seen how good a mimic I am. Well, now I'm going to become a completely different person, a comedian with a brand-new act, free of the stink of failure surrounding

Dustin Walker. And with all these talentless hacks no longer clogging up the booking schedule, I'll have much less competition. So come now, what are we waiting for?"

Meredith flailed around for anything resembling a weapon. Her hands closed around the cool metal of the mic stand.

As Dustin turned toward her, she brought it down on his head as hard as she could. It must have already been weakened by the explosion because it snapped in half across Walker's skull.

Still, he staggered and cried out an unintelligible curse. He raised the pistol to her stomach.

Instinctually, she lunged forward with the other half of the mic stand, hoping to push him away.

But her ankle caught on the base of a table lying in her way and she stumbled forward.

The jagged end of the mic stand pushed Walker back with her and he fell on his back, and she on top of him.

The weight of her body pushed the sharp end of the metal pole all the way through his chest.

Walker flailed his arms, gasping like a fish caught on land, and within seconds the light went out of his eyes. His face died before the rest of him did. Meredith saw, horribly, the moment his life extinguished, and, one by one, his other body parts got the message: his feet came to rest, his arms drooped to his sides, his head fell back to the floor, and even his mouth closed.

She tried to get to her feet but her knee said hell no, not after all that, and so she crawled painfully over to Dante, whose chest was still moving. She cradled his head in her arms and said: "How do you feel?"

Dante croaked, "Like I got punched real hard by Superman and he forgot to take his fists out."

"What do you need? What — what can I do?"

"What I could really use," Dante whispered, staring wide-eyed at the ceiling, "is a drink."

VI

Meredith sat with Dante until morning, his breath slow but steady, never slackening below its current nadir. She pressed the discarded pieces of Walker's Janet outfit over his bullet wounds, which finally stopped bleeding.

Not long after dawn, the way she smelled and the stickiness of her skin from the dried blood caking it became unbearable, so she went back to the main house and drew a hot bath in her room and lay in it and soaked.

She fell asleep.

A sound awoke her sometime later, she had no idea how long. She sat up so fast she splashed half the water out of the bath.

She snatched Walker's revolver off the floor and pointed it at the doorway and the window, though nothing moved but the bobbing palms outside.

VII

All her clothes were in her luggage, which had been thrown out to sea. Blood had soaked her outfit through to her underwear, which were spackled reddish-brown. They were her only pair, but she couldn't bear to put them on again.

She pulled on her robe and went into what had been Ruby Ng's room. Ruby had a few clothes in her carry-on but nothing that fit Meredith.

She did not want anything from "Janet Kahn's" room.

She went into Zoe Schwartz's room. The only clothes she found there were a gray T-shirt and a pair of gym shorts lying on the floor. The front of the shirt had a

384

generic man from a washroom sign raising his arms in triumph.

I POOPED TODAY!

She and Zoe were close in size. She put on the shirt and shorts.

VIII

Meredith checked in on Dante, who was still breathing, barely, maybe sleeping, maybe unconscious. She tried to make him drink water from a glass, but after a few sips he just sputtered the remainder down his chin and out the corners of his mouth.

She went outside, into the sun, and looked into the blue sky, whose brightness seemed like a rebuke. The world dared to be beautiful even while her own misery persisted and her demise was imminent.

She paced the grounds, her mind racing:

They had water, but no food. How long could they last? A week or two at best?

What had Dustin told Captain Harry? That it was all an elaborate prank and the boat shouldn't return until he said to?

People would start wondering about TJ, and Zoe, and Dante, and Ollie, and Janet. Agents and assistants would start looking for them when they did not return on Tuesday. There'd be phone calls and emails, but the only contact information they would have was Meredith's, and she had no way of responding.

How long would it be before the celebrities' people took matters into their own hands? Twenty-four hours? Two days? A week? Anyone who investigated would know what times the comics' flights had landed in Saint Martin; they would find the limo company she had hired to take them to Captain Harry's boat. They could find Captain Harry himself.

By one week, at the absolute latest, someone would be here.

She was pretty sure she could survive without food for that long.

But she was equally certain that Dante would not.

And if they found her here, the only living survivor, and with all the evidence that Dustin had painstakingly arrayed against her . . . and the fact that she *had* killed *him,* that much was clear . . .

She knew cops. She knew them well. They would only ever believe the most obvious version of any story.

Not her, not the gold-digging nutter tart. No way, there was not a chance in hell of that.

She had to get Dante to a hospital, not

just because he was Dante Dupree and she wanted him to live, but because he was the only person who could corroborate her utter bollocks story. She needed to get him out alive.

Just as Dustin needed her dead.

He was going to dump her in the ocean, wasn't he, and disappear?

That means he needed a boat. He had a boat. Either one was coming, or one was already there.

But she had searched the island multiple times, all the comics had, and no one had found so much as an inner tube.

Yet, Dustin had an exit strategy. What was it?

IX

Meredith wandered unconsciously past the pink bouncy castle, with its flappy Dustin Walker on top, catching her toe in the metal spike mooring it to the ground. She cut the top of her big toe and tripped and fell onto her knees, exacerbating the laceration she had received in Gordo's explosion. Pain bit into her and it was all she could do to roll around in the grass in a near-fetal position, clutching her thighs, for the better part of two minutes.

She sniffed and screamed curses at the stupid house, the utterly pointless bulbous construct with a half-dozen metal stakes being the only thing that . . .

Wait.

She had loosened the nearest anchor stake when she tripped over it. It was simple enough to wriggle it free of the soil and let it go.

She went into the club and found the empty shotgun. She could use its stock as a lever to pry the second anchor from the ground.

And the third.

When she freed the fourth stake, the other two weren't enough to hold back the wind. The whipping ocean breeze picked up the house and tipped it onto its side, and then with one more gusting push it rolled over again and fell off the edge of the cliff and into the sea.

Revealing a metal hatch beneath.

She threw open the unlocked door and jumped up and down and screamed like a triumphant beast at the uncaring heavens.

Inside lay a jet boat, just over four meters long, resting on casters that could be pulled by a line up a short ramp, out of the bunker and across the island, to the huge elevator on the other side.

While she was jumping in exhilaration, no matter how much it hurt, she thought she noticed something out of the corner of her eye. But it wasn't until she stopped and looked soberly at the horizon that she saw the large boat approaching the island.

X

The boat wasn't Captain Harry's, of that she was sure. It was much smaller, more the size of a pleasure yacht, which perhaps was what it was, white as a baby seal against the blue Caribbean waters.

Fear gripped her chest when she caught sight of it. Her first thought was that these were co-conspirators coming to help Dustin put any final touches to the crime scene, to help carry her body out to sea, where it could be weighted and dropped, transforming her overnight from wannabe nobody to world's most-wanted woman. And once she was never found, into a curious legend, like Amelia Earhart or Jack the Ripper, a mainstay of unsolved mystery programs. That other boat — the one under the bouncy house, it was so small — maybe it was just for backup.

Should she hide? At least until she could determine whether they were rough characters or not?

But the sound of Dante's ragged breathing, as soft as it was in the club room, remained deafening in her ears. And as much as she feared the unknown now nearing the dock, she feared more the certainty of him dying on this green-topped rock and her joining him not long thereafter, if she had miscalculated when rescuers might arrive.

She headed down the stairs, leaning on the banister to keep the weight off her wounded knee, and suddenly realized she didn't have the pistol. Her mind ran frantically over her previous steps before concluding that she must have set it down on Zoe's bed when she put on the dead woman's clothes, walking out of the room without it.

She looked up. She was about halfway down the steep, shuddering, utterly dizzying steps. The elevator was interminably slow and she wanted to make sure she had eyes on the boat and its crew the whole time.

She looked back down at the boat. It was just docking. A sailor in a bright-orange jumpsuit, like a hazmat uniform, appeared on deck and waited until the boat got close enough for him to hop onto the pier with a towrope in one hand.

She looked back up the stairs. She'd have to go back the entire distance, hobble up the house stairs to Zoe's room, then come back down here.

Weariness enveloped her like a lead shroud. She was tired — tired of fighting to stay alive — and if she was going to die because she couldn't be bothered to walk up a bunch of stairs to fetch a pistol with which to defend herself, well, then, bloody hell, that was how she was going to die. She was just sick of it. She couldn't take it anymore.

She wanted to be a comedian, right? She'd just have to read the room. She'd have to charm the pants off these blokes.

She'd have to.

Her life depended on it.

Meredith Ladipo reached the bottom of the stairs just as three people got out of the boat and stood on the dock. They faced each other warily. The three boat people all wore the same orange jumpsuits as the first man Meredith had seen, except they didn't, because they weren't wearing jumpsuits at all. They were black men wearing white diapers, painted from bald head to expertly pedicured toes in bright-orange paint. Only the diapers around their waists were untouched by the hue.

The lead Orange Baby Man said in a thick West Indian accent:

"Is Oliver Rees here, missus? We received his message in Saint Thomas and got here as soon as we could. Is he all right?"

Just then she spotted the logo of Sandals Resorts on the boat's bow.

Meredith Ladipo opened her mouth to reply, but whatever response she was trying to make was overtaken by a snicker.

Then a chuckle.

Which burst open into a guffaw.

And soon she was laughing, heaving, bent over, arms clutching her sides.

She laughed and laughed.

And she just couldn't stop.

LIFE AFTER DEATH (ISLAND)

[As the audience gathers, they see a table and a chair on an otherwise empty stage.]

[A few minutes after the show is supposed to begin, the lights begin to dim and a prerecorded voice is heard:]

Ladies and gentlemen, thank you for coming.

If you could please take the time now to turn your cell phones and, if you are a 1990s drug dealer, your beepers, all the way off, it would be most considerate to the performer and those around you.

That performer is I, Meredith Ladipo.

Due to my unique condition, which I imagine you've read about elsewhere, I'd like to direct your attention to the screens on either side of the stage. If the stage managers discover I have substituted an incorrect word for any correct one in the script, they will flash the correct version on the screen, so keep your eyes peeled.

It's not an ideal situation or a perfect situation, but a wise man once told me never to let the absence of those prevent me from pursuing my dream.

So, I'd like to thank my husband, Dante Dupree, for opening for me. Please give him a hand once more. Wasn't he terrific?

Now sit back and enjoy selections from the acts of the late, great:

Janet Kahn

Zoe Schwartz

Ruby Ng

Billy the Contractor

TJ Martinez

Orange Baby Man

And Steve "Gordo" Gordon.

[The actual Meredith Ladipo walks on stage to thunderous applause. She carries a spiral notebook and a glass of water. She wears eyeglasses, and her hair is in braids.]

Sit back, enjoy, and think of the right answer

to this question:

[She sits at the table.]

Are you ready to laugh?

— Meredith Ladipo
O2 Arena
Greenwich, London
Two years from now

ACKNOWLEDGMENTS

Many thanks to **Aziz Ansari**, **Dave Attell**, Maria Bamford, **Todd Barry**, **W. Kamau Bell**, Mike Birbiglia, *The Carol Burnett Show*, Dave Chapelle, **Louis C.K., Stephen Colbert, Flight of the Conchords**, Stan Freberg, Jim Gaffigan, **Bobcat Goldthwait**, Bill Hicks, Jim Jefferies, Key & Peele, **The Kids in the Hall**, Sam Kinison, Larry the Cable Guy, Bill Maher, Steve Martin, Dan Mintz, **Eugene Mirman**, Monty Python's Flying Circus, Eddie Murphy, Tig Notaro, Chelsea Peretti, Richard Pryor, Joan Rivers, Chris Rock, **Amy Schumer, Michael Showalter**, Sarah Silverman, **Wanda Sykes, Tenacious D**, *Whose Line Is It Anyway?*, Robin Williams, Ali Wong, Steven Wright, *WTF with Marc Maron*, and, most of all, the one who started it all for me, when I was 13 or so, **George Carlin.***

You know, for the laughter.

397

Apologies to the writing staffs of *NewsRadio* and *Spitting Image* for my stealing those two jokes, one from each of you. You know which ones they are. I have no excuse.

Many thanks too to Grady Hendrix for putting me together with Quirk, Jason Rekulak for having the idea in the first place, Tim O'Donnell for that map (that map!), Jason Yarn for superlative agenting, and Crystal Skillman for laughing at more of my jokes than any wife should be required to.

No thanks to those stupid cats of mine, Newt and Zelda. They were no help at all.

* boldfaced = I've seen live

ABOUT THE AUTHOR

Fred Van Lente is the #1 *New York Times* best-selling writer of the comics *Odd Is on Our Side, Archer & Armstrong,* and *Action Philosophers!* He also cowrote the graphic novel *Cowboys and Aliens,* which was made into a film starring Harrison Ford and Daniel Craig.

The employees of Thorndike Press hope you have enjoyed this Large Print book. All our Thorndike, Wheeler, and Kennebec Large Print titles are designed for easy reading, and all our books are made to last. Other Thorndike Press Large Print books are available at your library, through selected bookstores, or directly from us.

For information about titles, please call:
  (800) 223-1244

or visit our website at:
  gale.com/thorndike

To share your comments, please write:
  Publisher
  Thorndike Press
  10 Water St., Suite 310
  Waterville, ME 04901

5082